"There is always one moment in childhood
when the door opens and lets the future in."

—Graham Greene, *The Power and the Glory*

Im memory of my brother Philip

1939–1997

PART

I

1936-1938

1

The Last Man

HE WAS THE last man you thought would lay a hand on a child. His own child, yet? His Danny? You've got to be mistaken.

This was not the kind of man who kicked his little boy like a football just because the kid failed to tuck his shirt tails in. Throw him against the wall in a rage? No way. Danny must have fallen on his face while he was playing outside.

Ask anybody.

■

Was he good to his sisters? Myron Adler was the brother nonpareil.

A friend? The man was a paragon of friendship.

He was the son who always came home for dinner. Even after he was married to Faye, Myron ate dinner at his mother Sophia's house on Friday nights. A bowl of schav, some crusty eggbread, boiled chicken sagging in its bed of fennel. One of his brothers might be there too; usually Herb, until he died from a stroke, with his fidgety wife Birdie tagging along behind him. Sometimes one of the sisters would show up, and sometimes Faye even went along with him, depending on her moods. But there were no moods for Myron when it came to Friday nights at sundown. His week wouldn't be complete if he didn't see his mother's hands circle the sabbath candles, a linen napkin on her head and her eyes shut against the distractions of the outside world.

■

There were always stories about him. Sweet stories. Myron Adler was a man around whom stories assembled on their own. He didn't talk about his own doings, but Myron's actions seemed literally to speak for themselves.

There were customers—Muriel Ritzik always came to people's minds—who couldn't meet their bills, who got grace periods without having to ask, and who paid him back whenever they could. They would insist on paying him interest, though he'd never suggested such a thing. When Muriel Ritzik had her female surgery not three months after her husband was hit by a car, she had a free pullet for dinner every Thursday till she was back on her feet.

There were men like Elmo Stinchner, who'd been exposed to nerve gas during the First World War and needed help getting to visit his mother in the hospital. Myron would leave Gabriel Kozey in charge of the market and drive with Elmo across Brooklyn for the visit, waiting downstairs a half-hour thumbing through magazines. During the Second World War, which Myron couldn't fight because of his eye, he brought freshly killed chickens home for any woman in his apartment building whose husband was in the service. No charge, of course.

There was Si Sabbeth, Myron's friend since third grade. What a pair they made! Si, the great boxer 'Kid Sunday,' was a hulking six foot seven. He'd fought Primo Carnera in 1932 and would have beaten the sorry palooka easily, but he had to throw the fight so Carnera could become heavyweight champ the next year. Took a dive in round four after putting Carnera on the canvas twice. In his corner, there was Myron Adler with a sponge and spit bucket at ringside, almost a foot and a half shorter than Si and barely able to look him in the eye when Si was seated on his stool. You should have seen the two of them doing road work in Prospect Park, wrapped to the gills in their hooded sweat shirts with towels around their necks and weights draped over their shoulders. Four steps by Myron to every two by Si.

When his career was over, who got Si a decent job in the poultry business?

Who put a good word in for him with the right people—the very same people who had promised to take care of Si after the Carnera deal and now looked like they were forgetting all about him? Who got the big guy directly into the wholesale distribution end of things instead of wasting time in the slaughter room? Right you are.

Then there were family stories. In particular, there was the story of how Myron had met his future wife, the costume designer and painter of mannequins, Faye Raskin.

■

The black DeSoto slowed on the gravel driveway. It was a Friday in the spring of '36, two months after German soldiers had violated the Treaty of Versailles by occupying the Rhineland. The spooky goings-on there seemed to jinx the entire vacation season. People from New York City were after something new; they were giving up on New Jersey and going to Lake George instead. Narrow, almost forty miles long, the lake slithered through the forests of upper New York. You should have seen Lake George back in New Deal times. People really knew what a resort was supposed to be then, when times were hard and there was a war coming on.

So it was amazing that there was any room at Scotch Manor for Myron and his companion. Just another sign of Destiny playing a hand in his life.

Myron hopped out while the car, which he'd rammed into Park, was still rocking in place. He darted around the back and opened the passenger door.

From where she sat on the long Scotch Manor lawn, Faye Raskin noticed three things about him at once: That he wore a leather snap-brim cap turned slightly askew; that a long, fat cigar jutted from the corner of his mouth, gripped in place by a dark holder; and that he moved behind the car like a wild boar, head down, his thick legs churning in a kind of tip-toed gait.

But she didn't mention these observations to her friend, Irma Arndt, sitting beside her on the blanket. Irma studied her handiwork in the mirror of an oystershell compact.

"Nice manners," was what Faye said.

"Sure is short, though."

"And what am I, Irma, a colossus?"

"Ahhh, I see." She stubbed her cigarette out on a stone. "You're interested."

"Hardly, dear. The man seems like an animal. But there is a point to be made: as a friend, whenever you meet a man who might be right for me I certainly wouldn't want you to rule him out on the basis of height."

No question about it, the woman who emerged from Myron's DeSoto was ugly. Faye didn't want to be unkind about it, but what could she do, lie? The most gracious word she could manage in describing her was homely.

"My, a gentleman ought to be able to do better than that, don't you think?" she asked Irma.

"The gentleman does."

Faye looked away from the couple long enough to see if Irma was teasing her. "Then I take it you know him?"

"We've met. I thought everybody who lives west of the park knows Myron Adler. Mr. Capon himself. The Prince of Pullets."

"So now you're telling me he's what, a butcher? That figures."

She looked back, watching them stroll up toward the office. Of course, you could see the barbarity in how he moved, rolling his shoulders, kinking his neck as though the effort of being gracious to a woman hurt him inside. Even a homely woman like that one he was with.

"Don't let his being a butcher fool you. That woman he's with? That's his sister Hannah. I worked with her for a while at Minchoffs. Myron Adler is the kind of man who drives his ugly duckling sister all the way to Lake George after working his fourteen hour day so she can meet a man, then turns around in practically the middle of the night and drives back to the city so he can open his market by five-thirty. Doesn't that tell you something about the man's heart? Besides, he's not actually a butcher. He owns his own business."

Faye stood. In her head, she heard the delicate strains of a Chopin nocturne, which swelled her confidence. She dusted imaginary twigs and grass cuttings from her skirt.

"So who kills the chickens, him or the hired help? Owner, shmowner. The man is not of our class."

"Look Faye, you should be so lucky Myron Adler would notice you for a date."

"I thought you knew me better than that. Faye Raskin go out with a butcher?"

Later that evening, Faye was sitting by herself near the dock when who should come up behind her but Myron Adler himself. It was, she felt, a gray-ish, Debussy evening. Couples, sometimes groups of couples, were renting rowboats and disappearing into the darkness of the lake. Not five minutes be-fore, a stunning young man from Utica had invited Irma to go rowing with him. You could never account for a man's taste. Faye watched them climb into their boat, feeling chilled and considering whether to go back inside. She didn't hear Myron coming.

"You look cold," he said from behind and very close to her ear.

"Oh!" Faye jerked her head back and caught him flush on the chin. She struggled to turn while he toppled over backwards. "You startled me."

He sat up, working his jaw. "Chrissakes."

"Are you all right?"

"Yeah, I'm fine." Without even standing up, Myron scuttled closer to her. "Always could take a punch."

Next thing Faye knew, he was sitting on the blanket with her, biting the tip off a new cigar. He spat the piece of tobacco into the night ahead of them, licked the cigar's tip, and worked the holder in place. It was made of plastic, the kind that reminded Faye of a guitar pick.

She looked at him without seeming to, just shifting her eyes in his direc-tion. The profile was very strange. His nose was flat and ridged, as though something sharp had hit him from above. He wore glasses, which he took off whenever he looked directly at her, as though she were pointing a camera at him. His left eye seemed frozen.

He shifted the cigar to his left side. Where his lips met on the right, there was a slick of moisture like a slug's track. But when Myron turned to look at her, his smile was gentle, almost disconnected from the rest of his face. Maybe he was smiling at some memory rather than at Faye. She looked away from him toward the lake, then quickly back.

"Do you suppose they're really going for a row?" she asked.

"There's only one way to find out." He reached for her hand, helped her up, and led her down to the dock. "Let's go."

As she stumbled along with him, Faye kept thinking *I hope he knows how to swim*. She didn't, but this was no time to admit such failings. Surely a man like this, all vigor and strength, would be able to save her, whatever might happen.

Well, he might know how to swim, but he certainly didn't know how to row. They zigzagged toward the middle of the lake, avoiding contact with other boats only, it seemed, through some unfathomable source of luck.

Faye sat behind him, watching his muscles ripple the surface of his shirt as he pulled hard on the oars. He didn't seem to notice the bizarre pattern their wake made. Without looking back at her, he coaxed out the story of her twenty-seven year life, which, oddly enough, seemed to have begun only nine years ago.

"After art school, it was impossible to get work. I mean, you know how it is in the New York theater. Everybody does costumes when they first break in."

"They start you as a seamstress?"

"They would have if I'd let them, but that's not the sort of work Faye Raskin does. To make ends meet, I took a position with this firm that sells mannequins to the theaters. At least I was working in the business, you understand."

"Sure, you make contacts, you learn who's who. I can understand that."

"I liked to leave my mark on them. Anybody could just paint a mannequin, but you'd always know a Raskin mannequin. I spent an extra half hour on the eyes. If you ever see a mannequin with long, curly eyelashes, that's one of mine."

Myron lifted the oars, holding them heavenward while he rested. He listened to the diminishing drip from their blades as the boat drifted for a few minutes.

"In Belgium," Faye continued when he didn't speak, "I met a boy who wanted to marry me on the spot." She looked off to the west, where the lake seemed to melt into the night. "A gorgeous person he was, this Cesar. Very tall and straight like a prince, with a beautiful little moustache. And he had such a gentle soul, really generous despite his family's connections. Oh my, were they connected! His father was a patron of the arts and personally knew Cesar Franck." Myron, deep into his rowing stroke, didn't seem to be listening to her. "Do you know who he is?"

"Who who is? Your old boyfriend?"

"Cesar Franck."

"Brother of Herman, used to catch for Brooklyn?"

She looked to see if he was laughing at her. Myron pulled at the oars.

"Hardly. He happened to have been a great Belgian composer. Do you know his Symphony in D Minor? A true masterpiece."

Myron's position changed slightly, making the boat rock. Faye drew in her breath and shifted her weight. She wondered if he was going to try and kiss her now. He was probably a passionate sort of man. Maybe all the talk of fine arts had gotten to him.

Then she realized that he was trying to turn the boat around.

"Is it time to go back?" she asked.

"Yeah. I gotta get up early. So tell me, why didn't you marry this guy Frank?"

She chuckled and looked beyond Myron's shoulders toward the shore. "Oh dear, it wasn't Cesar *Franck* I knew. My Cesar was named after him, I'm trying to tell you. Cesar Martens." She slowly closed her eyes, let a smile form as if reluctantly on her lips. "We met at Waterloo."

"That's nice." He was sweating heavily, despite the cooling air.

"Have you ever been there?"

"If you mean the Waterloo in upstate New York, yeah I been there. Couple summers ago. They make good sauerkraut. But I bet you're talking a different Waterloo, am I right?"

"It's near Brussels. I take it you haven't been to Europe, yourself?"

"Miss Raskin, I have never been east of Connecticut, much less to France or wherever. Now lemme get you back to the hotel."

Faye didn't kiss him that night, of course. Not that he didn't seem ready to try. A man gives off certain signals. Faye knew what was on his mind, even if he didn't make a single move toward her. When they parted company three hours later, it was with a promise to meet for a game of billiards an hour before breakfast. Faye didn't know how to play billiards and she hadn't gotten up in time for breakfast since 1931. But he seemed like such a sweet man after all.

■

Don't get the impression that Myron Adler was one of those doting men who ran errands whenever his sisters snapped their fingers. True, he'd taken Hannah to Lake George, but not because she demanded it. He practically had to force her to go. Myron could have an inventive kind of sweetness, a flair for kindness. When things were going right, he didn't have to be asked.

For instance, there was the story of how he helped his other sister, little Charlotte, lose forty pounds. As the eldest sister, Hannah was the official storyteller among the Adler's, and she particularly loved to tell this one.

Charlotte was twelve at the time and dreamed of being an equestrienne. Before Myron stepped in, nothing had worked for poor Charlotte, who kept getting bigger. Hannah herself had offered to diet along with her and ended up losing ten pounds while Charlotte gained five. Every evening, each of the boys remembered to ask how her diet was going. Their mother supervised each meal, smacking Charlotte's hand if she reached for a second helping. She made Charlotte flush all the sugar cookies down the toilet and raided her drawers to get rid of the coconut patties.

Finally, Myron offered her a deal. It was a Sunday morning. Before leaving for Prospect Park, where he would spend the morning on the bridle paths, he came to the bedroom Charlotte and Hannah shared.

"Tell you what," Myron sat on Charlotte's bed in his jodhpurs and pulled on his boots. "You like these boots, right?"

"Oh yes, Mashie. They're so fancy."

"Then I'll get you a pair."

Her eyes opened wide. "You will?"

"Sure. All you do is lose the forty pounds. The day you weigh 125, I'll put them on you myself."

It took six months. The key, it turned out, was water. Charlotte would drink three glasses before each meal and then eat as slowly as she could. When he was home, Myron would talk to her while she ate. He would tell her long, slow stories—embellishing every detail—and hold her in his gaze, forcing her to pause between bites of her meal. She carried a bag of carrot sticks and celery in her purse and would drink a glass of water before snacking on the vegetables.

At thirty-five pounds, two problems occurred. First, she'd hit a plateau and couldn't seem to lose any more, no matter what she cut out of her diet. Second, her legs were still fat. The weight seemed to have come off every place except her legs. Charlotte not only looked like a small sled dog, she still couldn't pull on a pair of riding boots.

Eventually, though, she lost the last five pounds. On a Friday evening, just before dinner, Myron came into the dining room carrying a box wrapped in foil. An enormous 40 made out of black electrical tape covered the front.

Charlotte was afraid to open the box. She was afraid she'd have to try the boots on, to be polite, and wouldn't be able to pull them up.

Her eyes met her brother's. He blinked slowly and smiled at her. "Go ahead, open it."

"Oh Mashie. You had them made with laces."

■

It could be said that Myron Adler's generosity was obsessive. Faye said so, over and over through the course of their marriage. He gave comparative strangers more money than he gave his wife to run their household. He'd put her on a budget the year they got married and the only time he agreed to increase it without a fight was when each of the boys was born. But there were lots of stories about his wild largesse with others.

When there was a picnic, Myron was always the one who brought meat. Not just chicken from his market either, but fat porterhouse steaks or spicy sausages bought from Remo Santselmo's market next door, maybe a stack of chops three feet high. Though it was Sunday, the only day he had off, Myron would get up before dawn to go out to buy ice so the meat would remain fresh.

If you went to a restaurant with him, Myron always picked up the check. He liked to slip the *maitre d'* a tip in order to get the best table. If he took you to a Dodgers game, you sat in box seats on the third base side, seats he'd already paid for, and you never bought the peanuts or the hot dogs. He brought along the cushions, he brought the flask of rye, the pen for you to keep score with, an extra hat in case you forgot yours. And he knew his baseball, cold. Why did the Dodgers lose the pennant this year? Two simple words: third base. After all, who would you rather have, Cox or Hoak? You had the feeling Myron knew these things not because he cared much about them but in order to make your time at the ballpark more enjoyable.

Hannah Adler Stenn, talking about Myron later in her life, attributed these qualities in her brother to his eye. She thought the eye had given him a complex.

The eye happened when Myron was eight. One evening, he was running relay races in the street. Two manholes out and two manholes back. In the last race, he'd come from five steps behind after being handed the broomstick-wand by his brother Herb, and won by three steps. Jogging back to shake the hand of the boy he'd beaten, Myron looked up just as the stone the boy threw reached him.

This was 1916. The doctors gave up on saving his left eye almost at once, and worked desperately to save the uninjured right. Sympathetic blindness. Years later, when Danny nearly lost an eye himself because Myron knocked him into a sink, was the only time Faye had seen her husband cry.

After he lost his eye, Myron missed a year of school. Everybody knows kids can be cruel. Hannah said that when he got back to school, most of his friends were ahead of him and his new classmates were abusive. The glass eye looked strange.

"He made up for it," Hannah would say, "by being driven to excel."

He joined the track team and won the Public School hundred yard dash. He also did the broad jump. Since he had no girl friends, either Hannah or Charlotte would come to watch his meets.

"Even if you didn't know him, you could tell which one he was," Hannah liked to remember. "He had this funny stride, almost a gallop. Every couple of steps he'd be in the air and you could see his head bobbing up. His coach said he'd be the fastest man in the world if he learned to stay near the ground when he ran. And he'd do anything to win. If the race was close, he'd throw out an elbow or wobble close to the next lane. Because his style was so awkward, it always seemed like an accident. His only loss was in his last meet, the City Championships, when he fell. Said he was tripped, but I think he just couldn't see the edge of the track because of his eye."

After school, to keep him busy since he had no friends except that lunk Si Sabbeth, his mother sent him for violin lessons.

"He wasn't Jascha Heifetz," Hannah said.

■

Myron Adler. Stocky little guy with one eye, one friend, one year behind in school, screeching away at his violin while his sisters made dinner with their mother. He couldn't even help Si sell papers because his parents didn't want the two of them hanging around together. His career was clearly going to be in chickens.

Myron's older brother Joseph was already in business with their father.

He'd been at the family market ever since leaving high school. Herb, the younger brother, was a wizard at science; fourteen and he's all set to become a doctor.

Perhaps it was no surprise, then, when Myron decided to open his own market. He didn't like working with Joe and his father, who were content to do business the old way. Myron wanted to branch out, to serve other customers, wholesale and retail both. He wanted to be in the Battery section, not the old neighborhood.

But raise a hand against his own child? Sure, the pressure was on. It was costing more to protect the market and the supermarkets were on their way. But people knew Myron Adler. He was no child abuser.

2

The Game

SHE WAS THE last woman you thought would lay a hand on a child. Hell, Faye Raskin Adler was the last woman you thought would *have* a child.

But if she did, if indeed she found a man worthy of marrying and a nanny suitable for raising her child, Faye Adler would no more strike such a child than she'd strike a sour note. And you know she'd never strike a sour note. Not the Voice of the Air, not the woman whose soprano would bring audiences to their feet if only she'd gotten a few breaks here and there. Why, Faye would as soon choke the precious voice out of her own throat as choke the voice out of her son. Everyone knew she was incapable of violence. It took too much effort.

This was the kind of woman who appreciated the glory of a Dvorak serenade. The delicate, paper-thin petals of a poppy made her flush with joy and race for her watercolors. She adored certain de Maupassant stories read out loud from the depths of a plump love seat, the niceties of a lilac sunset over the city with the scent of summer on the breeze, zabaglione if it was not too thick. Hardly a woman to stalk her son through the apartment hallway, to laugh as she trapped him within the open door's vee and watched him sink to his knees.

Ask anybody.

■

Sure it was difficult to be the daughter of Jules and Ava Raskin. But Faye never gave them a moment of trouble. And by herself she practically raised that brother of hers, Frederick, who became a well-known diamond merchant Senators and Ambassadors fondly called Red. A loyal, devoted girl. Men were always after her but she would turn them down till Red was 18 and could take care of himself. This was a woman with values.

Of course, the parents were always at work. He made the rings and the necklaces, Jules and his jewels, and his tiny wife Ava waited on customers, calling Jules out from the back of the shop whenever somebody came in with a lot of money to spend. So there wasn't time to lavish much attention on a child, especially on a girl like Faye, who was more interested in painting and singing and playing the piano than she was in cooking or cleaning. Taking care of her little brother ought to teach her some of those skills. Jules and Ava had no intention of housing a spinster.

There were stories about Faye Raskin, though. Stories that let you know she got out a little, she was a woman of the world. You heard that she sang at charitable functions, that she designed centerpieces for her friends' weddings, entertained neighborhood children by the elegant folding of linen napkins into animal shapes. She knew the names of all the avant garde artists in every medium, the finest professional men and where they had their country homes, the best clubs.

It's a wonder she had the time, but that's how Faye Raskin was. A woman of destiny, you just knew it. She didn't believe in reincarnation, of course, but if she had, it wouldn't be out of the question to see herself as royalty in some past life.

■

Someone was pounding on the apartment door. It was just past noon on a Sunday in late July, 1936. Wrapped in his shredding terrycloth robe with coffee stains on the belt, Red Raskin stumbled across the foyer and yanked open the door.

He could not believe his eyes. Maybe he was hallucinating. Maybe he shouldn't have kept on with the gin last night.

Because look at this. Standing at the door with a white panama in his hand was the famous film actor Jackie Palisade. Red would know that face anywhere. Palisade had probably been knocking on the door with that chin of his. How could anybody run so fast with ears so big? It was Jackie Palisade, all right. Maybe drinking gin, Red thought, was the way to go.

Once, Jackie Palisade was supposed to be the next Jim Thorpe. He had played football at Columbia in the autumns. Then there was a famous picture of him in the new *Life Magazine* shooting a basketball with both feet off the ground, a jump shot when the only shots people took were set shots. In the springs, he played baseball and ran track—just think how good he could have been at either sport if he'd just had time to practice it.

Everybody knew he was a better all-round athlete than that Finn who'd won the decathlon in Amsterdam. Palisade would surely have gone to Los Angeles in '32, representing America in the Olympics there in sunny California, but then there was a knee injury. Dancing, of all things! Lickety-split, there was Jackie Palisade waltzing opposite Adele Astaire for an entire number. There he was spinning Ginger Rogers. The man was a wizard.

And now here he was standing in front of Red Raskin asking if his sister Faye was home.

What's Red going to do, say "Sure, but I'll have to wake her up. After all, it's only noon"?

"I'll get her," he said.

"Tell her to hurry, pal. We're running late."

"She's almost ready."

"Oughta be. I called at nine."

He led Jackie Palisade into the living room and asked him to sit down. He fetched a cup of coffee.

"I'll be right back."

Faye was fast asleep. She was doing her double-snore, with deep noises on both the inhale and exhale. Red closed the door, sat on his sister's bed and shook her shoulders.

It was almost impossible to wake Faye by conventional means. He was afraid he'd have to go downstairs and phone, letting it ring beside the bed until the jangling got through to her. That had worked a couple of times. Might be hard to explain to Palisade, though.

"Get up, Phase. He's here."

Nothing.

"Phase!" He shook her shoulder. "He's here."

"Who's here?"

"Jackie Palisade, that's who. Why didn't you tell me you knew him?"

Faye sat bolt upright. She could only hold one eye open, but that one riveted her brother. "Don't kid around with me, Frederick."

"He says he called at nine."

The second eye cranked open. "I thought that was a joke." She looked at the phone as if it had been a party to the prank.

Red took her hand and pulled her out of bed. He nudged her toward the bathroom. "He says you're already late. How'd you meet Jackie Palisade?"

"I've got to think," she called out in a strained whisper. "Hand me that dress I wore to the Botanical Gardens Wednesday. It'll have to do."

"You don't remember how you met him?"

"It was at Uncle Maxie's party last year, the one at the Astor. Maxie invited me so I could meet some big shots. Your Mr. Palisade was just one among many."

"That was a long time ago."

"Yeah. That's why I thought it was a joke this morning when some guy called and said he was Jackie Palisade."

"Look, I should go out and sit with him. Hurry up."

"I'm hurrying. But I'm not even awake yet."

"I'll tell him five minutes."

Palisade was standing by the window in the living room, looking down onto West 72nd Street. He held the coffee cup with two fingers and his thumb pinching the lip.

"You can see Central Park from here if you stand in the corner," Red said.

"The only park I care about is my chauffeur DOUBLE-PARKED down there in front. He better not get a ticket while I'm waiting on that sister of yours."

Palisade reached into his jacket pocket and drew out a matchbook. He held it up, turning it over as though trying to read the fine print.

"Need a light?" Red asked.

"Nah, I'm just looking to see can I figure out where I met the broad. Found her name on this matchbook when I put my jacket on this morning. Must've been a long time since I wore the damn thing. Can't remember for the life of me who she is."

Red sat in the chair nearest the hall so he could look back and see if Faye was coming. The guys were not going to believe this.

Faye always talked about the famous men who asked her out, men she met in the theater world where she worked, men she turned down without batting an eyelash. After all, she was a well-brought-up girl and these star types always wanted something. Especially the film stars. At least actors from the legitimate theater, she would say, had a modicum of manners. She'd just wait for the right man to come along, however long that took.

Every once in a while, he seemed to. Faye was not immune to being knocked off her feet. Hell, just a month ago she'd met some butcher from Brooklyn while she was up at Lake George. To Red, this one sounded like an amalgam of the very qualities Faye always said she hated in a man. But she was hoping he'd call soon. She was talking about him over dinner, looking out the apartment window as though conjuring up his spirit.

Red didn't quite understand how the phenomenon worked. He loved Faye, but wouldn't call her pretty. For one thing, she carried a little extra avoirdupois, as his pals called it. Of course, some men liked their women fleshier and soft, he understood that. But it was more than weight; she was also very short, so that in some dresses she looked encased rather than clothed, like a sausage. And there was also Faye's schnozz, which looked like a lever with a boulder on its end. With her bulging forehead and short chin, the effect was one of collapse, as though her face might be caving in under the weight of her head. Still, she carried herself regally and had a certain charisma, there was no denying that, especially when she lapsed into a slightly Hungarian accent which Red thought she must have inherited from a second cousin on their Polish mother's side.

Nonetheless, Faye seemed to be in demand. Her tastes ran to performers —to actors, athletes, and musicians, which is why the butcher was so confusing—and Red couldn't argue with her success. At least with her reports of success. Whatever she had, it worked.

But he didn't like to hear that Jackie Palisade couldn't remember her. That didn't sound right. What was the last picture this fella was in, anyway? Something about hobos, if Red remembered right. Maybe the guy's career was on the skids. Certainly seemed like a jerk. Red would have to think more about Faye's taste in men.

"My sister's a costume designer. Maybe you've worked with her professionally."

Palisade turned from the window and looked around. He found Red, then smiled.

"I doubt it. Tell me, is she a baseball fan?"

Red shrugged his shoulders.

"Well, let's hope so. I got two tickets to the Yankee game and that's where we're going if she ever gets ready. Ruffing pitches against that big fella from Texas. Jack What's-his-name."

"Knott."

Palisade opened his mouth without speaking, as though he'd forgotten his lines. He winked at Red. "Yeah, Knott. Jack Knott. Worthless bastard, ain't he?"

"Hard to show much when you pitch for a team like the Browns."

Palisade turned back to the window and looked down. "I give her maybe two more minutes."

"I'm a Giants fan, myself," Red said.

■

Faye looked good. Given that she'd had maybe five minutes to get ready, Red thought she actually looked terrific. Might even be losing a little weight, she was always on a diet. That calico sundress was lovely and the wide-brimmed hat matched. Also covered her sleep-squashed hair.

He stood by the window to watch them leave. Jackie Palisade whisked her out past the gaping neighbors and gave a couple of coins to the doorman, who actually bowed. Palisade jerked open the black Packard's door, climbed in ahead of Faye, and had to reach across her to shut the door. Through the open windows, Red could hear Palisade's voice from four stories up. Well, at least the bastard could project.

"Move it, Henry."

Henry stopped tapping the wheel. He turned around to look at Faye, then at his boss. Palisade winked. Henry screeched away from the curb and headed uptown.

Palisade sat back, looking toward the park, and ignored Faye. She would have liked a quick cup of coffee, maybe a sweet roll. Something to help her wake up.

She couldn't remember where he'd said they were going. The 9:00 conversation was simply gone.

"It's a lovely day," she said.

"Little windy, though. Gonna be coming in hard from right field."

Oh, yeah. A baseball game. Just what she wanted. A movie would've been better. She could stand to see *The Great Ziegfried* again.

"Who's playing?"

"Yanks, Browns. Gehrig's having a great year, could even hit fifty homers. I used to play with him."

"You boys from the same neighborhood?"

He looked at her to see if she was teasing him. "At Columbia, doll. We went there the same time."

"I didn't know you had an Ivy League education. That's very nice."

"Education?" he laughed. "I didn't have time for no education. All I did was play ball and, uh, maybe rest a little between seasons."

"I'm sure you'll get your degree some day, though. It would be a shame to waste that opportunity."

Palisade chuckled. From the front seat, Henry answered with a chuckle of his own.

Faye shifted her weight. "I don't think it's right that women aren't allowed to study at those Ivy schools, do you?"

"You serious, lady?" He leaned forward and tapped Henry on the shoulder. "Hear that, pal? Sounds like what's-her-name, that broad wanted me to do the film about a dying suffragette."

"Mimi Harrison."

"Right. Old Hairy Mims."

"Mimi Harrison is a wonderful actress," Faye said. "Has a funny nose, though."

"Listen, Miss Raskin," Palisade said, turning to face her. "You like this car?"

"It's very nice, Mr. Palisade. A Cadillac, if I'm not mistaken."

"Well, why don't you take it this afternoon? I'm serious. Drive it around wherever you want. See, me and Henry are gonna go watch the ball game, you could maybe pick us up afterwards. Say 5:00."

Faye sat up straight. She folded her hands in her lap. "That's not very funny."

"I mean it, doll." Henry turned into the parking lot. "Take the car. I don't think you'd like the game anyway."

■

Red heard her come in. He was still listening to the game in the living room, so he knew something was seriously wrong. It was only bottom of the seventh. Knott was shutting the Yankees out.

"You're back early."

She nodded, but didn't speak. She sat on the sofa next to her brother.

"Hungry?" Red asked.

She shook her head. "Went around the corner to Nudleman's, had some brisket." She took a deep breath, looking down at her chest as it rose. "Thanks anyhow."

"What happened?"

"Nothing. Nothing whatsoever. I guess Mr. Jackie Palisade didn't like what he saw. He wouldn't even let me go to the game with him. Took his driver instead."

"That slimy son of a bitch!" Red reached over for Faye's hand. "I didn't like the looks of him close up. I tell you, the movies, they're all fake. He isn't even that good looking in person."

"It's all right. I don't like baseball anyway." She picked at some imaginary lint on her dress. "Besides, I showed him what Faye Raskin is made of; I wouldn't let him pay for my cab."

Red shut off the radio. "You know what we should do? We should tip off the papers about the famous Jackie Palisade, what kind of jerk he is. Invites a woman to a ball game and drops her for his chauffeur. Hedda Hopper would have fun with that, I bet."

Faye smiled at him. She freed her hands and patted Red's arm.

"At least he was honest. I mean, a lot of men I've been with would have pretended they liked me. Hoping I'd be nice to them later, you know? I'd say he's a real gentleman."

"I'd say he's an ass."

An ass, Faye thought. Brother, let me tell you about a man who makes your

Jackie Palisade look like a true gentleman. Like a *Mensch*, he is, by compari-
son with Herschel Idstein. Yes, THE Herschel Idstein, the now-world-famous
composer who, when I knew him, was nothing but a pusher of other people's
songs for some third rate music publishing concern. Worked right around the
corner from me. I'd run into him at every party on the upper east side, he'd always be there in the living room playing somebody's piano, playing those
songs of his, or snatches from his fancy 'compositions,' those Preludes and
Rhapsodies he was always so proud of. And oh, God, when he decided he'd
write a symphony, the whole of New York society was plunged into chaos. Nobody could even talk at those parties, the piano drowning out every word unless you hollered at the person standing beside you. That song of Idstein's,
"Hey, May!"? That song is really about me, you know. Originally, he wanted
to call it "Hey, Faye!" but I made him change the title, I didn't want the world
to know I'd ever had anything to do with that man. Because he certainly
didn't know how to treat a woman, a well-brought-up woman who wasn't immediately ready to crawl into bed with him the first time she saw his bald head
bent over a piano or heard his croaky voice crooning. Famous for those magic
hands of his, well I could tell you all about Herschel Idstein's magic hands
that he could never keep to himself. I don't know why I went out with him for
those two years, he was such a cheapskate and a grabber, such a lower-class
sort of man despite his pretensions to higher things. Absolutely reeked of cigars and his teeth were stained the color of chestnuts. His fingers too, on those
magic hands, stained beyond cleansing. So one day Herschel Idstein waltzes
right into my office at lunchtime, all the girls couldn't get over it because of
course they knew at once who he was, and he invites me out to a concert for
that evening. The nerve! Well, I'm not busy that particular night, it so happens, and I agree to go with him. He should know how rare it is that I've got a
night free like that. We walk there from downtown after work, it costs him
nothing to get in because everyone knows Herschel Idstein. Come right in
Heschie, who's the little lady. He didn't introduce me by name to anyone, like
he was ashamed or like maybe I wasn't important enough. *Say hello to Mr.
Charles Hambitzer, the great teacher. Say hello to Maurice Ravel*, but never
I'd like you to meet Faye Raskin, Mr. Kern. What am I, one of his dancehall
dames? Some kind of chorus-line floozy? What's worse, I have to sit through
this program that's 94% noises from the gutter, 3% sounds remotely recogniz-

able as music and 3% silence, blessed silence. And then it's time maybe to eat, you might think. Oh, no. Mr. Idstein isn't hungry, let's go back to my place. Only he hasn't got enough money for two trolley fares! Do you believe this man? Of course, I did the only thing a self-respecting woman could do: I took his money, rode the trolley home myself, and told him he could walk sixty blocks through the rain if he wanted to see me again that night. He never showed up and I never went out with him again. Which is something I should have done two years earlier.

Or Dr. Norbert Ritter, the well-known heart man. A doctor of such standing, patients could die while waiting to see him and not be upset because at least they'd made his appointment calendar. A pioneer in his field, with the special diets and the pills. But me, his little Fay-Fay, I'm embarrassed to say I could see him any time I wanted, not even call ahead. Always with the smooth line, always talking about hearts. He used to wink and say he was going to look after my heart, he was going to take care of my heart, he knew about hearts. Pumps, he knew; about women's hearts, he was an ass. One day I walk into the office, he's 'not available;' you don't need to be Albert Einstein (who I also dated a couple times, he had a child-like heart but there was no romance in his soul so I let him go) to figure out there's a nurse in the picture somewhere. That's it, I don't care who the man is, no one plays that way with Faye Raskin twice. Not even that gorgeous Count Emil Shopsky, a direct descendent of Frederic Chopin and a wonderful dancer, who made me wait an hour on the corner of 72nd and Central Park West while he, if I were to believe him, tried to select the finest roses for me. Not scientists working on things that were so secret they weren't even permitted to dream about them, not fancy designers of haute couture dresses, not breeders of thoroughbreds, none of them if they didn't know how to treat a woman. So don't tell me about gentleman, Frederick Raskin. Your sister knows what men are, all right.

■

Faye was glad when Red left for the evening. She put a capon in the oven to roast and sat down with a double shot of rye.

Red was right, of course, she was in demand. She had dates. But she didn't have suitors, and it was a suitor—someone to court her—that Faye was after.

A man who followed her, who came to call. She wanted a man who would sit courteously in the living room and listen to her father, charm her mother, humbly beseech them for their daughter's hand.

All right, so maybe it was hard to picture this guy she met at Lake George, this Myron Adler the butcher, sitting there listening to Jules Raskin rant about inferior gems or charming Ava Raskin, to say nothing of humbly beseeching them for Faye's hand. It was hard enough to picture him sitting in their living room at all. But he could be a suitor anyway, she thought. He could perhaps try to gain her affections. On the weekends, anyway.

There's a big difference between that and dates, which Red was probably too young to understand. Dates, she had. It was just that she didn't have a very good eye for men. Her father had been telling her that for years. Jules Raskin also believed that all the men she saw were unworthy. It wasn't that he thought Faye was so special, just that the men were consistently inappropriate for a daughter of the renowned jeweler J. Raskin. But at the same time, he wasn't really surprised. From the beginning, he'd said Faye had no taste. No taste in friends while she was in school, no taste in clothes, no taste in accessories. So why should he suppose she'd have taste in men either?

Faye remembered the night a year earlier when she had danced with Jackie Palisade, the night of her uncle Maxie's party. She'd danced with several well-known men that night at the Astor, in fact, and it was hard to keep them all straight. There was the architect Irwin Chanin, who designed several Broadway theaters; that cartoonist from the *Brooklyn Eagle*, what's-his-name Macauley; and the nephew of Treasury Secretary Henry Morgenthau, who was doing very well on Wall Street, thank you. So Mister Jackie Palisade was lucky she even recalled who he was.

As she was dressing for the party, her father had come to stand in her doorway. He folded his arms and leaned against the jamb with his shoulder.

"You make sure to thank your mother's brother for inviting you."

"I already did, Poppa."

"Do it again anyway. It's very nice of him to let you come, you know. There are always a lot of wonderful people at Max Raskin's parties. He has no reason to invite you except he loves his sister so much, so you thank him for sure."

"Yes, Poppa."

"What's that you're putting on your neck?"

"A topaz. You know it's my birthstone."

"This I know. What I don't know is where you got that particular stone. The five and dime?"

"Poppa, this is a very nice lavaliere. It was a gift from a friend."

"What's the matter, you can't wear J. Raskin jewelry when you go out?"

"It goes with this dress."

"In your eyes, yes; in my eyes, no. These are things I know about, young lady. That dress doesn't want anything around the throat. Like this you look cheap."

Faye reached behind her neck and unclasped the lavaliere. She put it in her jewelry box.

"What should I wear, Poppa?"

"First, that thing should go in the garbage, not back in the beautiful teak box your mother bought for you. Second, I think you should wear the ruby earrings I made special for your trip to Belgium. Third, if you must wear a ring, then wear the one that I reset, the little diamond you got from the tax attorney who wanted to marry you. I told you twenty times, that was a man you should have said yes to."

"Oh Poppa, I couldn't wear his ring."

"Forget sentiment. It's a beautiful setting." He straightened up and spun quickly from the doorway, leaving Faye to watch his retreat without further comment.

Later, as she draped a fox stole around her shoulders, Jules Raskin had reappeared to open the apartment door. Faye's mother trailed them into the foyer a few seconds later. She came up to her husband's elbows.

"Have a good time, dear, " Ava Raskin called. "You look very elegant."

"Tidy, perhaps," Jules Raskin said, "but I wouldn't say elegant. She's too short for elegant."

Faye rode the elevator down trying not to cry. At least he'd advised her this time. Last time she went to an important party, he wouldn't look at her. That had made her so upset, even her mother spoke up.

"Jules, look at Faye's outfit."

"You look at her outfit. I never wanted a daughter and I don't have anything to say about how this one dresses up to find a man."

Faye checked herself out in the lobby mirror. She knew her eyes would clear by the time she reached the party. It was a good thing she'd had enough control to stop the tears from overflowing. At least she wouldn't have to go back upstairs to redo her makeup.

Later that evening, when Jackie Palisade asked her to dance, Faye looked at him for a full thirty seconds before extending her hand. Never did say yes. It was important to create the proper first impression.

Now she went in to baste the capon. It was surrounded by new potatoes and onion quarters, all browning nicely, all wanting just a little more paprika. It used to take her three days to finish eating one of these; now Red would be lucky if he found a drumstick to nibble on when he got home. She promised herself to leave at least half a bird for him this time.

3

The Fights

WHAT A FALL, what a winter. First Roosevelt got reelected, trouncing Landon by eleven million votes. This was the best the Republicans could do, the Governor of Kansas? Then sit-down strikes spread like influenza out of Flint and soon half a million people were striking auto plants across the country. Plus the Germans were still up to no good, building the Siegfried Line, and you had a rebellion in Spain, and all of a sudden there was war between China and Japan. The world was a mess. January of '37, it was forty-five below zero someplace in California, fifty below in Nevada! Even a subway World Series between the Giants and Yanks had done nothing to ease Myron Adler's nerves.

Which were shot anyway, after Sally O'Day.

He was not a particularly nervous man and he was not at all accustomed to following world news. But his time with Sally O'Day had changed Myron. She could fill an entire evening with talk about a guy named Gandy teaching people to farm in India or about American troops pulling out of Haiti, which Myron never knew there were troops in. Starting when Sally slid into the car beside him, she'd carry on while they drove through the boroughs, sat in some night club for a few drinks, walked through a park or Coney Island, ate a dozen cherrystones. Sally couldn't believe Myron did not know where Ireland was exactly, or what her beef was with England. He'd felt proud of himself one night when, having accidently listened to the news on the market's radio that afternoon, he mentioned that King George V had died. Sally flushed in an instant and began a string of curses against the king's soul that took Myron's breath away. It was like sticking your hand in a coop without paying attention. Soon he began to read more than the sports section of the morning newspaper. He felt like he was back in school again.

Myron met Sally O'Day at the fights in Rahway, January of 1934. God, was it really three years ago already? He wanted to marry her by Valentine's Day, and had even considered proposing in late September. But first he would have to bring her home to meet his parents and Myron hadn't quite figured out how to walk into the apartment in Brooklyn and announce to Emanuel and Sophia Adler that this blonde Irish girl was his intended. He could just see his mother, whose rhomboid face had yet to be cracked by any lines of habitual smiling, poised with utensils in mid-air, staring at his father, the would-be rabbi, the son of three generations of rabbis, who puts his knife and fork down with a careful clatter against the flowered *Shabbos* china, who looks up at them from under unruly brows—the only disorderly things in his life—closes his eyes, and with perhaps the hint of a smile says "I don't believe so."

Myron would never forget that first night at the fights, when Sally's face floated up over her brother's shoulder like the moon. Si Sabbeth was still boxing then, though his loss to Carnera had ended any dreams they might have had of a championship bout. Of course Myron was in his corner. It was snowing lightly; they'd already accepted the fact that there would be fewer than fifty people in the gym. Si, as Kid Sunday, was scheduled for ten rounds against a guy from Queens called Matthew Monday. *Come to Rahway and See Sunday fight Monday on Tuesday the 21st!*

That evening at 5:00, Si came to Myron's market dressed in his fight-night leopard skin coat that reached to his ankles. He loved to say the coat took a leap of leopards. Despite his size, Si moved with the true grace of a great cat, especially when he wore the long coat. He'd walked through the doors without a sound and suddenly loomed over Florence Teitelbaum, who was waiting for her Tuesday pullets. She shrieked, leaping aside and losing her balance. She banged into the coops lining the market wall and was so upset that Myron gave her the birds for free.

Modulating his bass voice still lower, so that he seemed to be growling instead of speaking, Si apologized. "I'll pay you back out of the winnings tonight, Mashie."

Myron closed the market an hour early, throwing his bloody apron onto a pile in the back room, by the plucking machines whose odor he no longer smelled. "What the hell," he said, "you'll scare off all my customers anyway."

"You mean the weather will."

"Shaddup. Cold nights, people need their poultry even more."

As they drove out to Queens, the snow began. Myron flicked on the windshield wipers.

"It's a sign," Si murmured.

"Yeah, right. A sign we're gonna make about twelve bucks tonight."

"Wish I could have another shot at Carnera."

"He's fighting Loughran down in Miami in a couple months. Which it shoulda been you, a rematch. We could swing over to Havana after, have a nice little time, get some fresh cigars."

"What have I got, another couple years as a fighter, the most? I'm about old enough to be Matthew Monday's father, for Christ's sake. When boxing's over I'm not even sure I could be in the poultry business. I'm through with blood."

"Look: A, you're gonna be in the wholesale end, not retail. So B, you don't have to put your hands on a bird if you don't want to because C, you're gonna be an owner just like they agreed when you made that Carnera deal in the first place. So stop worrying. You fight this kid tonight and be ready to rock him back to sunny Ireland or wherever the hell they got him from."

"We'll see about this *owner* business. Those boys we dealt with, sometimes they have very short memories."

"I don't," Myron said. He took out a long Havana cigar and began to unwrap it with one hand. "There's a guy comes into the market every month or so; I mention it to him from time to time."

If there was a part of being in Si's corner that Myron hated, it was when they first entered the ring. He didn't mind sitting in the dressing room trying to keep Si's spirits up, taping his enormous hands, rubbing down his shoulders. He didn't mind tromping down the aisle to the ring and hearing the loudmouths blather. But once they were there, with his short arms Myron could barely hold the ropes apart far enough for Si to squeeze through, and then they had to stand together for the introductions. Like a clown act, with Myron maybe coming up to just past Si's solar plexus. He was much happier once the referee had told everybody the rules and sent them back to their corners. He got Si seated on the stool, spun out to straddle the post, and put his chin on Si's shoulder so they could both look across the ring at Matthew Monday and glower.

That's when he saw her. Sally's head of pale curls just rose into view, shrouded in smoke, as she stood to cheer her brother on. She was the most beautiful woman Myron had ever seen, despite a nose that looked as though it had been broken more often than her brother's and a thick scar that crossed her face—now crimson with excitement—running from the corner of her left eye to the center of her chin.

During the fight, Sally O'Day made Myron sloppy with his sponges and water. He conked Si's jaw with the spit bucket between rounds four and five. Drenched by a spray of sweat and spit and blood and water, forgetting to holler either encouragement or advice in Si's ear, smiling incongruously as the two fighters traded blows about six inches from his face, Myron was as dazed as Matthew ("Come on, Matty") Monday by the time Si put the kid down for good in the eighth.

"Great fight," he managed to say over the ringing of the bell.

"You were there?" Si answered. He leaned back against the ropes in his corner, waiting for the formal announcement of his victory, trying to get his breath back to normal.

"Come on, it was me that kept you together after the third round, which he almost had you with that uppercut."

While Myron untied the gloves, Si said, "In case you couldn't tell, that girl over there's no Jew. And your name's Myron, not Seamus."

"Ayyy, what makes you think I was looking at some girl? Everything I was looking at was between the ropes, which we had a fight going on."

Si snorted. "Mashie, I've known you since the third grade. Only thing is, she's not as bosomy as you like."

After the referee had held Si's hand up and the gym began to clear, Myron dallied in the corner, taking a long time to gather up their things. He watched

Sally comforting her brother, helping him down from the ring, gazing after him as he made his way to the dressing room.

"Fought a nice fight, your brother."

She turned slowly, not seeing him at first, tracking the voice like a wary animal. "How big's your friend there, three-fifty, four hundred pounds? Fucking mismatch."

■

Sally liked Marx Brothers' movies and Charlie Chaplin. She enjoyed film biographies—Pasteur, Emile Zola. They went to see *Captains Courageous* and she swore he looked exactly like Spencer Tracy. In the first six months with her, Myron saw more films than he'd seen before in his whole life. She'd slouch beside him in the theater, legs over the seat in front of her, an arm around his shoulders, and munch on shelled peanuts smuggled in her purse. They'd pass a flask of whiskey back and forth. She was so slender, Myron couldn't account for her huge presence beside him. Her longshoreman's laugh filled the loge, as did her sobs, and she seemed to envelop him.

She loved to ride horses with him in Prospect Park. Sunday mornings, they'd meet at a diner in her neighborhood, Kinsella's, wolfing down their eggs-over-easy and fried potatoes so they could be at the stables early. Once, Myron reached across the table to dab at some yolk that was congealing in the scar near Sally's chin. She slapped his hand away hard, making him knock over her glass of grapefruit juice.

Before he could think—it had all happened so fast and the mood at their table had mutated so suddenly—Myron's hand had formed a fist and he was about to launch a right cross at her. He froze. They stared at one another, hands still in the air, and didn't speak.

Finally, Sally looked down and said, "It was an accident, see. My father, you'll meet him someday, he was drunk. We went over the side of this road up near Tarrytown. There was a lot of glass. He wasn't scratched."

"Look, you know?" He gazed down at his hand as if it belonged to the table rather than to him. "I wouldn't really hit you. I mean, I don't know."

"It's all right." In a moment, she looked back up at him. "At least you didn't follow through."

Sally wanted to ride a different horse each week. Myron, who always rode the same thick palomino named Zev, after the '23 Derby winner, thought Sally lacked discipline on a horse. But he liked to watch her gallop and to see the smile it brought to her face, the only time smiling actually transversed her scar to include the entire face.

One spring morning while they were cantering, she shot away from him. She was on a flashy bay named Burnt Sienna, who was known around the stables as headstrong. Myron, still sluggish from breakfast, was slow to react and Zev was confused beneath him. It was five or six seconds before they took off after her. He could see that Sally was almost out of control, maybe because of the wind, maybe because she was distracted by how far ahead she'd gotten. Although it was invisible from where she was, he knew she was nearing where the path would plunge downhill and suddenly cross a street heavy with church-going traffic. This was no place to be galloping. There were signs, but she wasn't likely to read them and it was useless to call to her. He began to catch up. Then Myron saw that the wind was toying with her hat. She straightened in her saddle and Burnt Sienna slowed slightly. Myron urged Zev on and was close enough behind her that, when the hat blew off, he leaned down and snatched it out of the air.

"My hero," Sally said, laughing as they came to a stop.

Myron put her hat on his head, where it just managed to cover his bald spot like a yarmulke. Their horses were edgy, wanting to run again. Sally reached down to stroke Burnt Sienna's neck. Myron was sure she'd be bucked off in an instant, but he'd learned by now not to try controlling her horse. He kept his hands to himself.

"I like you better without the hat," he said.

"Myron Adler, what a bold thing to say to a lass. And on a Sunday, no less."

They began to walk along the trail again, headed down toward the street. "I think you'd better stay with me," Myron said.

"And why should I do that?"

"I know these paths. And besides, you're a little wild."

They reached the street, holding up traffic while they clopped across. Then she turned to fix him with a smile. "Exactly, my brilliant. And wild is why you'll keep chasing me."

She took off again. Myron laughed out loud. Before he went after her, he tucked Sally's hat into his belt.

∎

A little over a year later, Si had a bout scheduled for April 12, a true Friday night fight, the best card he'd been on since Carnera. They'd have to drive to Philly and stay overnight, but it would be worth doing. Si was actually smiling again, at least once in a while, and talking about putting enough money aside to buy a little place near Sheepshead Bay.

Training was the worst time for Myron because he had to squeeze road-work in before he opened the market at 5:30 in the morning. Now that he was seeing Sally in the evenings, Myron was always exhausted when he met Si at 4:30 in the park.

Si's voice rumbled out of the depths of his toweled, hooded head. "You don't look so good."

"And you look like a peccadillo in that getup, so don't give me any crap."

Myron handed Si two socks filled with weights. They began to jog along the same bridle paths Myron had ridden with Sally. Every quarter mile or so, Si would throw a few punches at the air, turn to dance a few steps backwards, then spin forward again, still jabbing away. Myron would run loops around him during those interludes, chanting *keep it up keep it up*.

"So what's new with you and Our Lady of the Mondays?" Si said.

"Let's talk strategy, ok?"

"You're not supposed to have strategies in love."

"I'm talking about your fight, Simon. You know, the reason we're out here in the middle of the night, which I should be asleep right now."

Si was moving backwards again, with Myron circling him and feinting punches of his own. "I mean it, Mashie. What's going on with you two? It's been what, sixteen months? I haven't met her yet."

"*Keep it up keep it up*. Jesus, nothing's going on. We just keep to ourselves. I haven't met none of her friends and none of her family, myself."

"That's not technically true. If I recall, there was her brother, young 'Look Out Matty,' around that first night. Hey, maybe that's it. He probably doesn't like the friends you keep. She neither. Is that why I haven't had the honor?"

"What're you talking about? Come on, let's do the miles, I gotta get to the market."

Si reached out to grab Myron's arm and they stopped jogging. "What is going on! Why don't I meet her? Why don't your parents? Why don't you meet her people? And why the hell did you just call me Simon? I've known you since we were nine and that's the first time you ever called me Simon. What did you do, knock her up?"

"Shaddup." Myron turned away, hunched his shoulders, jogged in place. "Its just, well, I . . . . Jesus, *Si*, we got some roadwork to do."

The night before the fight, April the 11th, Myron closed the market early again. He scrubbed up in the back room, but there wasn't any soap left and he couldn't get all the dried blood out from under his fingernails. He knew he smelled like gizzards. Good thing he wasn't going to see Sally tonight. And tomorrow he didn't want to think about. Which there was no choice, he had to leave it up to Gabriel Kozey to run the place tomorrow while they were in Philly, to open it on time, to keep it open all day. And it was Friday, no less! *Shabbos*, when all his best customers would come in for their sabbath chickens.

He walked up the street without seeing anything, all his concentration focused inward on the horror of what would probably happen tomorrow in the market. The floor would be filthy, Gabe would forget to put down fresh sawdust during the day and there would be clots of blood everywhere, he'd be rude to women who weren't pretty enough, and the birds would not be properly drained. So when he reached the car, sunk in a morbid despair, Myron was astonished to find Sally leaning against the driver's door.

"What's this?" he said.

"This is a valise."

"That's not what I mean. What're you doing here?"

Sally's eyes narrowed. "Don't be ridiculous, all right? Just open the door, I don't want to stand here like this."

"Look, we're going to Philly, you know that. Si's got a fight, which we sleep in some cheap joint afterwards and then come home."

"I know all that. Jeez, I thought you'd be happy I was coming with you."

"It's no place for a girl."

She put her elbows on the hood of the car and stared at him. Myron held her stare.

"I grew up around fights, Myron. Maybe you remember where we first met? And I'm not only coming to Philly, I'm coming to that holy chicken market of yours when we get back. I want to see you in the real world."

Myron was shaking his head as he unwrapped a cigar and bit off the end. He wouldn't look at her.

"Besides," he said.

"Besides, nothing. It's time I got to know Si as somebody other than a gorilla who tore my Matty apart."

He walked around the car, unlocked the passenger door and waited for Sally to get in. Then he squatted down and leaned in next to her. "Si and me, we do a certain way before he fights. Which we haven't done it any different for maybe ten years."

"Like what?"

"Ok, just tell me this. Where you gonna sleep?"

"Why, Si usually sleeps in the bed with you?"

When they stopped in front of Si's apartment, he was just locking the door. His enormous, leopard-skinned back filled the doorway. He turned, grinning, with two cigars stuck in his mouth and pointing skyward. When he saw Sally next to Myron in the car, both cigars dove toward the ground.

He tried to climb into the backseat and couldn't make it, so he stepped out, turned around and tried to back in. That didn't work either. "I'm terribly sorry, but either you have to grease me or Miss O'Day sits in the back."

For the first fifty or sixty miles, they couldn't get a conversation to last for more than a minute at a time unless it was about directions and route numbers. Finally, Si squirmed halfway around in his seat, trying to look at Sally with both eyes, but could only manage to turn far enough to see her with one.

"Miss O'Day, I have to ask you something. I tried asking Mashie over here, but that's like talking to a radish when something like this comes up. Ok?"

"On one condition, Mr. Sabbeth. From here on, you call me Sally and I call you Si. Unless you'd prefer Kid."

Si smiled. "Tell me, Sally, where do your parents think you are every night you go out with Mashie?"

"Jesus Christ," Myron said. He looked quickly at Si, then back out at the road ahead. "I mean, Jesus Christ."

"No, that's a fair question, Myron." Sally said. "They think I'm at political rallies, Si, sometimes at discussion groups, that sort of thing. Sinn Fein."

"You're kidding me," Myron said. "They don't know about me at all?"

"I don't believe this," Sally said. "And where does your family think you are?"

Suddenly, Myron had to change lanes, which took an extraordinary amount of concentration. He took a quick peek at Si, who was still torqued around in his seat and looked as though he might never be able to straighten out again.

"I mean it, Myron," Sally said. "Where?"

"All right, all right. I get the point."

"Where!"

"They think I'm with Si a lot, which we're looking for a place to open a market together. Or I'm playing poker a couple times a week. Work on the books."

"Boy," Sally said. "You too."

"Take a left here," Si said. The rest of the way, they talked about the Baer-Braddock fight, which was coming up in a couple months; they talked about the sorry Brooklyn Dodgers, who looked about as bad as last year except thank God for Van Lingle Mungo and Watty Clark; they listened to Sally talk about *Mutiny on the Bounty* and some discussion program she liked to listen to on the radio. They got a good twenty minutes out of the Delaware River.

From the moment they entered the arena, nothing went right. The dressing room didn't have anything big enough for Si to lie down on except the floor, there wasn't enough tape, and the fight before Si's ended with a first round knockout so they had to hurry to get ready.

Myron knew Si was in trouble as soon as the opening bell rang. He wasn't moving right, as though he still had the weighted socks around his shoulders, and he was a half-second slow. The guy was nailing him with jabs. What was it, had they overtrained? Si was actually five pounds light, they thought he could use the extra sharpness. Maybe they'd done too much roadwork. Si missed a roundhouse right and almost flipped out of the ring.

Between the fourth and fifth rounds, Myron finally said, "What's wrong, Si? Just make him come to you and nail him with a left hook, he's wide open."

"There's nothing there, Mashie. Maybe I should sit on him."

Myron had never seen Si get knocked down before. Except for the Carnera fight, and all that knocked him down then was a promise. When Si hit the canvas on his back, arms flopping over his head, tears rushed into Myron's eyes, which astonished him even more than the sight of his friend prone and being counted out.

They ate dinner in a small cafe near the hotel—soup all around, since Si didn't feel like chewing and Myron and Sally weren't hungry. They sopped up the last bits with soft white bread, looking into their bowls, not speaking much.

Myron took care of room arrangements while Sally held Si by the elbow on the front stairs. Si stayed in a room down the hall from them. He bid them goodnight and walked slowly away, a hand up to wave, without really looking back.

Inside the room, Myron went directly over to the window and looked down at the street. Sally sat on the bed. He was still except for the clenching and unclenching of his hands.

"He'll be fine, Myron. Time alone's good for him tonight."

"Maybe. But did you see him there? I mean," he turned back to her, "Si on the floor, you know?"

"I know. Come here."

As he began to sit beside her, Sally turned toward Myron and wrapped her arms around him, throwing his back onto the bed while his legs dangled over the edge. She straddled him. She took off his glasses and leaned over his head to put them on the bedside table, her breasts moving across his face.

Myron reached up for her. Sally gripped his wrists, lowered his hands to the bed and spread them wide.

"Be still," she whispered.

"I"

"Be still, Myron."

He woke up at about four and Sally was staring at him, her breast against his, her fingers tangled in his chest hair. They were still on top of the blanket, still naked.

"What?" he asked.

Sally closed her eyes. Gently, she shook her head and put it down against his shoulder.

"This was different," Myron said. "This was very different."

"Yes."

■

One Sunday in early April of 1936, Myron drove Sally to the south shore of Long Island for an afternoon at the beach. He had been to this small resort town of Long Beach before and jogged along its boardwalk a few times with

Si when they wanted someplace different for Sunday roadwork. Afterwards, they'd eat a couple dozen clams and drink beers on the bay side of town.

Today, though, was not about training or eating clams. In the evening, they would go to Myron's home and finally have dinner with his family. Emanuel and Sophia didn't seem surprised when Myron said he wanted to bring a girl home to meet them. Apparently, Myron's sisters had long suspected he was seeing someone; it had been a topic of their dinnertime conversation for quite a while.

He took Sally's hand and led them east on the boardwalk. It was windy and cool for May. Sally's face was bright red before they'd walked two blocks.

"You wanna go into the Jackson there and have some coffee?" Myron asked. "Maybe this wasn't such a bright idea I had."

"I'm fine. Only let's get down onto the sand."

He led her down the ramp at the next corner and turned back to pass underneath the boardwalk. The sand there was dark gray and cold when they took off their shoes and socks. Once out from under the planks, though, the sand seemed much warmer than the air. They headed east again, moving slowly through the softness.

"The water looks unbearable," Sally said.

"Not if you don't go into it."

"Myron, you have to use your imagination."

"I left it in the glove compartment. Look, Sally, I got a question for you."

She pulled him closer and put her arm around his waist. "And I have the answer: chopped liver. It's probably the only thing I refuse to eat and it's exactly what I think they're going to serve."

He stopped. "Which I been thinking about this for a long time, all right? I mean, would you wanna marry me?"

Myron could actually see the redness fade from her skin, as though he'd thrown bleach in her face instead of asked her to marry him. But wait, it wasn't that. What was happening was all the red from her face was seeping into her eyes.

"Mother of God, Myron."

"Hey, I don't speak Irish, remember? Does that mean yes or no?"

"Shouldn't we wait to see what your parents think? Or mine?"

"It won't matter."

Sally took a step to the side, still holding his hand. She looked away, watching a wave die out in foam. "Yes."

"You will?"

"No. I mean yes, I will. But I was saying yes, it will matter. To me, anyway."

For the rest of the afternoon in Long Beach, they were shy together. It wasn't how Myron thought it would be, after you asked a girl to marry you. They drove back into Brooklyn early, got dressed early, and arrived at the Adler's apartment forty minutes ahead of schedule. From the hallway they could smell the roasting chickens. No liver, he was sure of it.

As though they knew he'd be early, Emanuel and Sophia were fully dressed and standing together in the foyer when Myron opened the door and led Sally in. Emanuel had on his best cardigan, a deep piney green one, and Sophia wore the ruffly blue dress with millions of buttons that Myron always loved. He was deeply touched.

After the introductions, they went into the living room where Myron's sisters were waiting for them—Hannah, Charlotte, and even Bella, who was married and lived in Trenton. Of course, his brothers Herb and Joseph were not there, that would have been too much. A wedding, yes, or a funeral, but this was just to meet a girl they didn't know he'd been seeing for over two years. Of course, Myron hadn't brought home many girls at all.

"So tell me, dear," Sophia said when they had all been introduced and served their crackers. "Where did you two meet?"

"In New Jersey, Mrs. Adler. I was at a function there with my brother."

Oh, very good, Myron thought. There's plenty of time to talk boxing.

The evening went splendidly. Bella knew about the issues of Irish unification and British colonialism. Charlotte had read *Gone With the Wind.* Hannah was the same size as Sally and also loved to sew. Myron stole glances at his parents, who were smiling as though he'd brought home someone named Rose Goldberg.

Emanuel was waiting for him when Myron returned after driving Sally home. It was 2:00 a.m.

"Pop, you waited up."

Emanuel nodded. "Your mother and I wanted you to know how pleased we are that you brought Miss O'Day home to meet us. And she's a lovely young lady, I can see why you're attracted to her."

"It's more than that, you know. We've been seeing a lot of each other."

"I thought as much."

Myron walked past his father into the dining room and sat at his usual dinnertime place. "It's. I'm. We're pretty serious." He looked down the table as though wondering where the succotash had gone. "I want to marry her, Pop."

"You do." Emanuel sat at the table's head and folded his hands where his plate should be. "I can certainly understand why, too, seeing her and listening to her. Very sharp, she is. But you know it would be impossible."

Myron looked at him. "It's is 1936, Pop. Brooklyn, not Crackow."

"This I know. But in our family, Myron, you cannot do what you're thinking of doing." He spread his hands on the table. "Cannot."

"I'm 28 years old. I own a business."

"In a building that I own, Myron."

Emanuel was watching the kitchen door as though expecting Sophia to emerge with a platter of flanken. Myron was looking across the table, to where his sister Charlotte used to sit and gorge herself with food while talking about losing weight.

"What are you saying, Pop?"

"Only what you heard, Myron. Nothing more or less."

"Which it's if I don't listen to you I'm outa business, right?"

Emanuel's brows jerked, but otherwise he was still. "You know, your mother and I, we feel there should be no confusion over how our grandchildren will be brought up when we're gone. We feel that it's best for everyone that we stay together, the family. That's what I'm saying."

●

Something went out of Myron after that. It was not, he thought, a quick extinguishing as of a flame that had burned hot the last 28 months. He felt it was a slower and more gruesome process than that, like plucking a chicken by hand while it was still alive. Or maybe it was something else entirely, something like a door creaking behind him and finally clicking shut.

When he told Sally, it was as though she were expecting to hear what he had to say, knew it before Myron spoke. She kissed him passionately and ran her fingers along his cheek, roughly where her own scar would be if it were on his face.

"It matters. I always knew it matters."

But what do you do? You carry on, that's what, Myron thought. You take Hannah up to Lake George in the spring so she can meet a guy, you get Si set up in the wholesale poultry business so he doesn't have to have any more blood on his hands, you start seeing someone new after a while—maybe someone like that Faye Raskin he'd taken rowing. Seemed like a nice enough sort, after you cut through the bullshit about princes and actors and Belgium and whatnot. A little on the portly side, but who was he to niggle, with his bald head and glass eye and razed nose? Yeah, he'd give her a call sometime. Not quite yet, though. Not yet.

4

War of the Worlds

MYRON COULD NOT understand why Faye had to choose the night before Halloween for him to tell her parents. A Sunday, yet. She knew he had to be back home in Brooklyn by nine-thirty at the latest, since he had to open his market at dawn on Monday.

And of course October 30, 1938, was turning out to be a bitterly cold night, with threatening skies and a harsh wind straight out of Greenland. Like a scythe, the quarter-moon pierced a thick tuft of cloud and was gone for the night. Leaves skittered along the gutters and occasionally blew across the hood of his car. Myron had meant to buy a new winter coat all month. Now he was going to show up at the Raskins' apartment wearing his drab, woolen overcoat with the expanding oblong hole under one arm, the missing belt loops, the bottom and collar all frayed. Being with the Raskins on the upper west side was still like being in another world for him, a little further from the sun than the world in which Myron had grown up. It was always cooler and darker out there, and difficult to breathe, as though the Manhattan atmosphere had too much heliogen in it or something. Plus when they were all in the same room, the Raskins seemed to speak two languages simultaneously. For guests, they spoke an English spiced by some kind of Polish-Hungarian powder, like cooks trying to conceal spoiled chicken, while for each other they used a visual language of gestures and glances which actually carried the essence of what they wanted to say. Maybe in twenty years Myron would be able to fathom it all. So the Raskins' apartment was never his favorite place to go, to say nothing of a Sunday, which he had to work the next morning.

Agreeing to come tonight had been a moment of weakness on Myron's part. The lipsticked impression of Faye's lips on the brandy Alexander glass followed by her batting those inch-long eyelashes at him. A couple of promising kisses in the front seat of his Buick, one of her soft embraces that enfolded him so that he lost track of time, then a whisper near his ear.

"I'm ready," she had said.

Myron had bolted upright, knocking his elbow against the car door. "You're ready for what?" He reached quickly into his back pocket.

"The Hotel St. Regis, I think."

"Not here?"

"Or the Waldorf Astoria."

"I'm lost." He plopped his hand onto the steering wheel.

Faye nestled against him. "We should set a date, Myron. It's time we got married." She patted his chest. "Right after New Year's, hmmm? Perhaps the Sherry Netherland."

"Netherlands? Let's at least keep it in America so my family can come."

So tonight they were going to have an early dinner. Myron was going to inform her parents that he and Faye would be getting married in nine weeks. Jules would wonder why the sudden rush. But he wouldn't dare ask because then he might get an answer that he didn't want to hear. If Myron was feeling generous, he might ease the old man's mind, depends on how the evening goes. Then they would drink some schnapps and Myron would drive home through the Sunday traffic, which it would be terrible at that hour. Plus throw in a few early trick-or-treaters on the street to look out for. What was he doing here?

As usual it took him three loops along 72nd to Columbus, then up and down to 67th and back along Central Park West before he could find a place to park the car. What the hell, it was cold but he'd carry the damn coat over his arm rather than wear it. He stalked along the sidewalk, trying to lose the song that had been in his head all day, *Flat foot floogie with a floy floy*. He'd have to tell Gabriel Kozey, his assistant at the market, to knock off playing the radio back there by the plucking machines. All they ever spun on the station Gabe listened to was silly songs like that and maybe "A Tisket, A Tasket," which was even worse. What's the world coming to? Europe filled with Nazis and Fascists and Communists and he's got to listen to "Jeepers Creepers" while he's slicing a pullet's neck.

The doorman made Myron stamp his feet for an extra few seconds before letting him in. What's he think, I'm in costume here? Trick or treat.

"Good evening, Mr Adler."

"Hiya doin', Jerome?"

"I'm well, thank you, sir." Jerome seemed to be scenting Myron's coat like a beagle. "The Raskins are expecting you."

Myron could smell Ava Raskin's noodle kugel as soon as he stepped off the elevator. There must be a quart of cinnamon in the thing. And what was that behind it, stuffed cabbage? Nah, borscht. Myron didn't know what was wrong with a roast capon on Sunday night, throw a little tsimmes on the side, but he'd eat borscht again if he had to. Might be better if she cooked the beef a day or two less, but the stuff was hearty, he'd give her that much. The Raskins were nice enough people, especially Ava, whose sweetness had given Myron hope about how her daughter might mellow over time. But Jules wasn't going to like having a wedding date firmly set. As long as the engagement remained open-ended, he could pretend there wouldn't be an actual wedding to pay for. Especially a wedding to a butcher, which it's not exactly a diamond merchant or a furrier he was investing in.

Myron and Faye had been seeing each other for a year and a half now. Plenty of time for everybody to get used to it. Hell, Myron had gotten used to it, hadn't he? Used to her cockamamie stories, the litany of rich and famous men she could have married, her size, her temper. Well, Myron had a temper too, they'd had one or two little events in the eighteen months. And it turned out she'd been right, he *could* enjoy an evening in the theater once in a while. "Our Town" wasn't bad and "Babes in Arms" had a couple good songs. There was nothing wrong with the occasional museum either, even if Faye made it seem as though she was visiting old friends every time she stood in front of a wall of paintings. At least she'd go with him sometimes to the fights or a ball-game, and she was a sport about all the Adler family get-togethers, remembering all his brothers' and sisters' names. The woman even made some cute centerpieces for his mother's birthday party out of empty toilet paper rolls. She played the piano and sang "Happy Birthday" in her soprano voice that was plunging toward contralto with all those Chesterfields she smoked. Okay, okay, so he smoked a couple Havanas every day. They were made for each other.

Myron cranked the Raskin's door bell. As the sound faded, he could hear Jules marching down the foyer toward him. The hallway outside their apartment was so narrow Myron's shoulders barely fit and it was close enough to the neighbor's door that he felt caged while waiting there.

Jules opened the door, then backed away as though the effort had knocked him off balance. "Nu?" he said over his shoulder, heading back to the living room. "She'll be ready in a few minutes. Come sit."

Ava put a cracker laden with chopped herring in Myron's hand almost before the sleeve of his jacket had cleared it. Then she disappeared into her kitchen, where Myron had never been allowed. Back by the windows, surrounded by an array of liquor bottles with silver pourers and blue seltzer bottles with spray tops, Jules carefully measured out a scotch and soda.

Myron finally cornered Jules against the bar. He reached to shake his future father-in-law's hand and came away with an icy glass. Jules clapped Myron's shoulder.

"I know," he said. "I know. My daughter told me ten minutes ago, January two. So?" He raised his glass. "L'Chayim."

"L'Chayim, Jules."

"So what's the rush?"

That was quick. Myron took a deep sip of his drink. "I think it's Faye just turned twenty-eight, which she didn't want to start another year single. Plus I'm thirty. She thinks it's time."

Jules paused, absorbing this information. "I see."

"We been seeing each other a long time."

"You know what you're doing, Myron?"

Just then, Faye flowed from the bedroom in a swirl of gray and olive taffeta, like a wave on the beach at Coney Island. Myron turned and took an unexpected step toward her, so Faye crashed into him, almost knocking him into the radiator. Backpedalling and twisting, Myron guided them onto the sofa instead. Jules continued working at the bar with his back to them, as though such gymnastics were an everyday event in the apartment.

"You told them?" Myron whispered.

"Poppa wondered why you were coming over on a Sunday night. He was very suspicious. I just couldn't make up a story, could I, Myron?"

"But the whole reason I drove into Manhattan, which I have to wake up in about fifteen minutes to go to work, was because you couldn't tell him yourself."

"Don't start with me." She stood, smoothing her dress, and moved toward the kitchen. "Let's have a peaceful dinner to celebrate the good news, all right?"

She was out of the room before Myron could respond. As he turned his head toward Jules, he found himself nodding like a marionette. So was Jules.

■

"Now tell me where you're going for the honeymoon," Ava said over sponge cake and coffee. "In all the excitement, I forgot to ask."

"Cuba, Momma."

"*Gottenyu!*," Jules said. "You want to go to such a place? Why not go to Harlem and save the fare? Better yet, do it right and take a honeymoon in Nazi Germany, surrounded by thugs and brutes."

"Cuba's all right," Myron said. He slowed himself down by taking a cigar out of his breast pocket and unwrapping it. "There's this place in Havana I heard about from my friend Si Sabbeth. He just got back with his wife Gloria, they got married last month."

"And what is this place called?"

"Casino de la Playa, I think."

"*Oy Gevalt.*" Jules reached over to the bar for a bottle of plum brandy and poured a double shot into his coffee cup. He replaced the bottle without offering any to Myron.

Myron lit his cigar and sat back before saying anything. Keep calm, look at the man's face, which he has two eyes, a nose, mouth, some scraggy gray hair, he's a human being even though he sounds a little like a capon.

"Maybe I got it wrong. Maybe that Casino de la Playa's the place Si told me about for dinner. I think he said they stayed at the Sans Souci."

"Myron, there are some very seedy places in that country. Filthy, and everybody and his brother-in-law is a criminal. Why, it's almost like Brooklyn. I would like to know exactly where you plan to stay."

"Look, Jules, if you want I can call Si right now and ask him. Would that be all right?"

Myron left the table before Jules could answer. Jeez, there was no such thing as idle conversation around these people, was there? *Flat foot floogie with a floy floy.* He was marrying Faye, not Jules, all right? And he did decide —all on his own—that she was the one to marry. So don't push me too far, old man. As Myron picked up the phone in the bedroom, he looked outside the window and saw a crowd gathering in front of the apartment building across the street. While he watched, it moved across the street and was met halfway by a similar crowd from the Raskins' building, pooling in the middle of the street. The honking of horns and chatter floated up, nothing Myron could make out. He turned away and dialed Si's number, but the line was busy.

He had left the piece of paper with notes about Cuba on his dresser at home. He could call his mother and get her to look for him. Line was busy, too, which was not at all like Sophia Adler on a Sunday night, which she was usually in front of the radio listening to Edgar Bergen and his smart-mouthed dummy. He tried Si again with no luck.

"I can't get through to anybody," Myron said when he returned to the table. "And it's time I was getting home already, so let me call you tomorrow with all the details."

Myron realized that none of the Raskins was looking at him. Or at one another. They'd stopped talking and moving when he came in; Jules was studying the space between his wife and daughter, Ava was fixed on the space between Jules and Faye, Faye had her eyes closed and her head tilted back. They were perfectly still. It was as though Myron had accidentally kicked the plug out of the family socket on his way to the table. No, wait a minute, he could see at least Faye was breathing.

He wondered if they could hear the racket from the street. It was beginning to sound like Myron's chicken market at peak time. Perhaps the Raskins thought the noise was something they imagined, say chaos among the angels brought on by the shock of their daughter's impending marriage to this butcher, which he was about to take her to Cuba for a honeymoon.

It was a cruise, that's right, Myron had forgotten. Stops at Nassau and Haiti too. Voodoo, Jules. I get her out of Havana safe, we could still lose her in Porter Prince.

Faye walked Myron to the elevator. She held onto his arm with both hands and squeezed. "I think it went well, don't you?"

When he got outside, Myron was accosted by several people at once. He turned east and noticed a woman on her knees, praying at the entrance to Central Park. People had formed a circle around her and several had their hands raised toward heaven.

"What's the latest?" a man asked, grabbing Myron's arm.

"They don't approve of Cuba," Myron muttered. "Let go of me."

"I mean about the Martians. Haven't you heard? It's been on the radio."

Myron shook himself free and turned south toward the car. Martians, huh? Bad enough I gotta deal with Raskins. There were crowds in front of every apartment building. People carried loads of possessions on their backs or squatted against walls, trembling with fear. He saw a couple bent over a trash can, throwing up in synchronized heaves. At the corner of 70th, a man wearing a woman's mink coat over his pajamas stood drinking from a bottle of champagne, his face covered in tears.

"It's happening too fast," he said as Myron passed. "You'll never make it, young man."

Oh, this is wonderful, Myron thought. I forgot to figure in the Halloween crazies when I thought about driving home tonight. Might as well go straight to the market, sleep in back on a sack of sawdust.

His car was surrounded. Several women were crying and one had thrown herself across the hood of Myron's Buick. She was still sobbing, but her eyes were wide open and focused on the stars.

"What the hell's going on here?" Myron said in the general direction of his car.

"Martians have landed over in Grovers Mill, New Jersey. Where have you been, buddy? Big as skyscrapers, huge metal hands, and they're attacking everything with these heat rays of theirs. Jersey's gone. Nothing can stop them."

"Yeah? Well, I gotta get to work in the morning, which I need all of you to get off my car."

"They're coming this way," said a man who emerged from the building behind them. "Like express trains, the radio said." He had a wet handkerchief over his face. "And there's a poisonous black smoke from the marshes they set on fire, one breath will kill you."

Another woman emerged from the building, carrying a cage in which a canary was wildly chirping and flapping. She looked at Myron as though checking to see if he might be a Martian, then hurried up the block, a thick quilt wrapped around her shoulders and her bedroom slippers flapping against the sidewalk.

"Why tonight?" Myron said.

He drove downtown. Not only were the streets filled with people, now cars were pouring onto the Westside Highway. Nobody seemed to care about knocking into other cars. Myron saw four wrecks occur within the space of one block. The cars simply untangled and continued on their way. It was worse than he'd feared. Half the people in the city were out, probably more, as many trying to get to Brooklyn as to Yonkers and upstate. Great, escape to Brooklyn; the Martians wouldn't dare come after you there.

Near the mouth of the Battery Tunnel, Myron came to a complete stop. He rolled down the window and leaned out to see how far ahead the jam reached. The night air was thick with exhaust. Horns blared and so many voices were raised it sounded like Ebbets Field during a ninth-inning rally.

"I hear they're wading across the Hudson right now," shouted the driver of the car next to him. "I bet no one wants to go through the tunnel in case the Martians break through."

"Are you nuts?" Myron said.

"I'd rather drown than face them, I'll tell you that."

Myron opened the glove compartment and drew out his flask of scotch. He unscrewed the lid, took a belt, then held the flask out toward the driver.

"You look like you could use some of this."

"Maybe we should abandon ship," the man said. "We could run toward the East River and try to escape that way."

Myron took back the flask and rolled up the window. Hopeless. He finally turned on the radio and heard nothing about any Martians landing till he picked up the tail end of *The Mercury Theatre of the Air*. What the hell, it was just what's-his-name, the guy with that incredible deep voice. Must be one of those plays of his. Myron recognized him from some of the dramas Faye liked to listen to. Some kind of Halloween prank, right? Martians crossing Fifth Avenue. Things couldn't be that bad on Mars.

He got out of the car to scan in every direction for a way out. But there was no place for Myron to go. He could do nothing except stay where he was for an hour, sit in the car turning the engine on and off to run the heater for a few minutes until traffic started moving through the tunnel again, wondering if maybe there was a message here he ought to be paying attention to.

PART
II

1939-1962

5

The Sacrifice

RICHARD NORMAN ADLER was born in September of 1939, nine months and three days after his parents were married. This was the same week the old country of his grandparents fell to the Nazis, which, it turned out, was not his fault. Neither was the splitting of the atom, nor the A-Bomb that came of it. The closing of the World's Fair for the season before his parents got to see it, nylon hose replacing silk stockings, the death of Sigmund Freud, frozen peas, Pope Pius XII—none of this was actually Richard's fault.

But something was, something very significant. Richard entered the world, and particularly the world of Myron and Faye Adler, knowing that something was seriously wrong and it was probably because of him. The weight Faye gained during her pregnancy clearly was Richard's fault. So was the complete and total end of her art career—painting, singing, costumes, the whole works. And there was the increase in protection money Myron had to pay at his market! Foul odors permeated the apartment, they hadn't been outside New York City since who knew when, the Goddam piano was permanently out of tune, and now lookit: eight years later there was a baby brother named Daniel.

Whom Richard was, apparently, not holding correctly.

"He's not a tray of cold cuts, Richie," Faye said. "Hold him against your body before you drop him."

Richard looked down at his five-day-old brother and felt sad. He'd heard that in three more days they would be cutting Daniel's penis off. Worse, they were going to make Richard watch. Some sort of religious ceremony, every boy has it done, but Richard knew for sure he still had a penis and he'd be damned if he was going to mention anything about it right now. They'd probably go ahead and chop his off at the same time.

It was a good thing his mother had never changed his diapers, leaving that to the nanny, Sugar Adams. This was another thing he was to blame for—a nanny who, his father had said, pounding the dinner table with his fist, they could not afford and should not have.

"I *will* have help Myron," Faye had said, laying knife and fork across one another on her plate. "That's all there is to it. You'll simply have to find the money."

Myron had calmly cut another piece of meat and put it in his mouth. "Just tell me one thing, all right? What is it you do all day which you need a Goddamn servant?"

Faye's eyes widened dramatically. She pointed her finger at Myron. "Don't you start with me."

Then Richard watched his parents glare at one another for what seemed like a half hour. Myron chewed his porterhouse; Faye showed no movement at all except for the slow pursing and relaxing of her lips, what Richard always thought of as her air-kiss. Richard could feel coldness descending onto the food. He didn't think he was to blame for such arguments, but felt responsible for the wasted food on his mother's plate that was their result. He would linger after his parents had left the table to eat what remained because our people who lived through the Hollercoaster had all been so hungry.

He carefully shifted his brother in his arms. "That's right, Richie. Now support his head and you can lay him against your shoulder."

"Maybe you better take him back, Ma."

"Not now, I'm resting. Sugar will be here at 9:00. Surely you can hold your baby brother for fifteen minutes and let me relax like the doctor said. You know I just got back yesterday from the hospital."

What about me? Richard wanted to say. Remember I'm supposed to be resting too? In fact, my eye still hurts sometimes and it gets worse when I have to stand for a while. My whole head starts to grow bigger, then it shrinks real fast and grows even bigger. Suppose I get dizzy? Suppose I drop the baby because I get dizzy because you made me hold him for fifteen minutes because you got so tired being the mother of *two* kids now?

"I have to go to the bathroom, Ma." Which reminded Richard, he'd have to be sure and lock the door whenever he went to the bathroom from now on. His mother wouldn't like that at all, but it might help him save his penis.

"Just sit down."

Richard hadn't thought of that. You could just sit down. He sat on the sofa, which normally he was forbidden to do because he might make it dirty or leave it wrinkled. He didn't risk leaning back. His mother closed her eyes.

It was eleven months ago that Richard almost lost his left eye. He had been sitting beside his parents watching a dumb movie called A *Tree Grows in Brooklyn*, wearing his new eyeglasses and eating Black Crows that he'd snuck into the theater in his pockets. The candies were covered in lint, but Richard didn't care. The point was, he'd gotten them in without his parents or the ticket taker or the ushers knowing about it. His mother always hogged the popcorn and his father, who was diabetic, couldn't eat candy and couldn't be around anybody who did. Well, as far as Richard was concerned, he wasn't next to his father, he was two seats away, which was far enough to eat candy. The problem was, Black Crows were noisy to chew, especially soft ones like these that stuck to your teeth. He tried to time his chewing to blend with his mother's popcorn crunching, but Black Crows could be so good he'd sometimes be unable to wait. Suddenly, from across his mother's torso, the back of his father's hand smacked into Richard's face. The wedding ring caught his left lens in a way that shattered it. Two slivers pierced Richard's eye.

Most of what he could remember about the next few weeks was the darkness beneath the bandages, the sound of whispering voices and whispering shoes, and how you could hurt in places you couldn't reach. He also remembered how hard it was to feed yourself when you couldn't see, especially corn. There were several operations and he was groggy a lot of the time. But it wasn't all bad. For instance, he remembered waking in the middle of the night feeling convinced, absolutely and with great excitement, that this would mean his parents wouldn't dare hit him again. At least not in the face. One day, just after the bandages had come off and he could see a little again—especially out of the right eye—his Uncle Red Raskin showed up with a huge smile on his face and a stranger somewhere in the haze behind his right shoulder.

"Got someone here wants to meet you, Richie boy. He heard what happened and just had to come up to see you."

"Hello, Richie," the stranger drawled. "My name's Pee Wee Reese."

Holy Toledo! Richard struggled to sit up. He might not be able to see the guy, but he certainly recognized his voice. Only the best shortstop in major league baseball! Only Richard's favorite Brooklyn Dodgers player ever! Richie had learned to play marbles because that's how Pee Wee got his nickname. He understood that it was all right not to hit a lot of home runs.

"Stay there, son," Pee Wee said. "There's plenty of room for me." And he sat down on the bed! He touched Richard's hand and put something into it. "Know what these are?"

Richard brought them close to his face. "No, sir. Some kind of cards?"

"Tickets, Richie. Your Uncle Red tells me you'll be out of here in bout ten days. Well, we got this homestand startin in three weeks, you should be up and attem by then. You're comin to Ebbets Field, see us play St. Louie, eat some dogs and goobers. Sound all right?"

Richard nodded. He was trying hard not to cry.

"I think it's gonna be us and them Cards for the pennant, so this should be the best games of the season. Have your Uncle bring you round to the clubhouse fore the game, hear?"

Then he stood up. Uncle Red bent down and put his hand on Richard's head, or rather on the bandages over Richard's head, and he could smell the familiar Sen-Sen breath.

"I'll be back to see you Saturday," Uncle Red said.

And of all things, he was. He actually showed up Saturday, just like he said. This was one of the things Richard remembered most vividly as he sat holding his baby brother and watching his mother doze. Uncle Red had always been his favorite relative, but Richard never thought much about things like promises adults made because nothing ever seemed to come of them.

■

The apartment was more crowded than Richard had ever seen it. Faye was frantic in the living room, where the sacrifice would take place, worrying that people would leave crumbs from the cake or slosh their drinks, they would smudge the walls with sweaty fingers. Richard himself was concerned about the gushing blood, which he knew would hopelessly stain the beige carpet, and was relieved to see a sheet spread under the altar or whatever that table was.

Myron was in an incredibly jovial mood, considering what was about to happen to little Daniel. It made Richard nervous to watch his father. He was behaving like this was one of their costume parties, though he was dressed up as himself. Richard thought of the story of Abraham and Isaac, which he'd just covered in Hebrew school. Myron jingled coins in his pocket whenever one of his friends came over to shake hands and smiled constantly, although the smile had a strange edge to it, like a stick of margarine melting down at both ends. Richard was concerned about the snippet of toilet paper stuck to Myron's jaw where he'd cut himself shaving; he wanted to remind his father to remove it, but couldn't get close enough to say anything.

Just then, Si Sabbeth walked in, towering over everyone, his voice booming. "Mashie, you rascal. Another boy!" The old fighter strode through the crowd, consumed Myron's hand in his own vast hand, and nonchalantly plucked the toilet paper from his friend's jaw.

Soon a rabbi walked in, though he wasn't dressed like a rabbi, and everyone began clustering in the living room. Richard couldn't get close to the front; he could barely see what was going on. He heard Si in a deep whisper explain to someone that the rabbi was actually a mole, which probably explained why he didn't mind cutting off little boys' penises.

Faye handed a pile of blankets over to Myron in which little Daniel was wrapped like a plucked chicken. Myron looked down, opening the top of the package to be sure, Richard supposed, that Daniel was rightside-up. Then he handed his son over to the rabbi.

Richard wanted to see exactly what happened but could not bring himself to watch. Besides, he was too far away to catch the details. But he certainly heard his brother's sudden scream, despite the whiskey they dropped in his mouth to drug him, and his vehement crying. Poor kid. All of a sudden, Richard had to pee. In fact, he had to pee so badly he wasn't certain he'd make it to the bathroom.

Trailed by his brother's wailing, Richard worked his way back through the crowd and made it to the bathroom just in time. As he peed, he looked down at himself in wonder, feeling intensely grateful to be still intact. He marked the water with an X, trying to be careful not to get any on the rim, when the bathroom door burst open. He jumped, spraying wildly, and turned to see his mother staring at him, her eyes red with tears, her mouth grimly shut, one hand atop her bosom.

"What are you doing!" she growled.

Richard couldn't answer. Moving like a robot, he zipped his pants, tore off a piece of toilet paper to wipe the rim and the few other spots he could see in his haste, flushed, shut the lid, washed his hands and marched out past his mother toward his room. Astonishingly enough, she let him pass without comment and without cuffing his ear for whatever wrong he may have done that she'd missed.

Distracted, that's what she must have been. Maybe she hadn't seen his penis. But Richard knew he couldn't count on that. It was even possible that as soon as she finished in the bathroom she would go into the living room and inform Myron so that they wouldn't have to pay to bring the mole back another time. He had to get out of there. Now.

Because they'd do it, he knew they would. His mother had tried to pull his ear off twice that he could remember, including once when he could not think of anything he'd done wrong, and just three weeks ago his father had thrown him clear across their bedroom into the door of the armoire when he'd asked how old he'd have to be to start smoking cigars. There was that time, when his mother wasn't feeling well because the baby was kicking her insides, and Richard wouldn't eat his cauliflower, which they knew he hated anyway, that they both kicked him under the dinner table at the same time, as though they'd choreographed it. When he brought home his last report card from school, or when the Hebrew school teacher had called to say Richard wasn't behaving in class, they'd slapped him in the face and knocked his glasses off without even hearing his side of things. He'd been terrified the glasses would explode in his face again.

So of course they'd do it, if he gave them the chance. Richard had been too distracted to lock the bathroom door, but now he was careful to close his bedroom door. He knew he'd need some underwear, socks, shirts and pants; he thought a game would be useful, maybe Parcheesi, but it was too big to carry, and he didn't feel like reading. Money would help, but he didn't have any of his own. He wrapped his clothes in a sweater that he spread on the bed, then opened his door to check the hallway. People were still milling around in the living room and dining room. He dashed into his parents' bedroom, found his mother's handbag on her dresser, and took out her beaded little change purse. His hands were trembling. If they discovered him now, they'd cut off more than his penis, he knew that. Closing his eyes, he snapped open the change purse, dumped everything into his hands, snapped it shut, stashed it and took off.

Since the apartment door was open, and all the adults were busy eating or drinking, Richard got out without anyone noticing. He stormed down the stairs two at a time instead of waiting for the elevator, and was on Lenox Road before he'd even run out of breath. It could be three hours before they missed him, he thought, and if they drank enough during the party it could be overnight before they realized he was gone. He could be in Cuba by then and set up a coconut business, or maybe Nova Scotia where he could fish for lox all day.

Then he had a brilliant idea. He would do exactly what they had told him to do at school if he ever got in trouble. Go to the police. He'd go right to headquarters and tell them that his parents had just cut off his baby brother's penis and were going to cut off his next. He'd tell them about his ears and eye and, oh, he forgot, he'd tell them about the time his mother had bitten him on the hand—when he'd had to run away from home that first time so she wouldn't go ahead and eat him alive—or he'd tell them about when his father tripped over him while Richard was playing with his toy soldiers in the hallway and his mother hollered that Richard was always doing the same thing to her and his father picked him up by the belt as though he would toss him out the window.

But he'd waited too long. The front door of the apartment building opened and a mob of his parents' friends came out. They saw him right away. All he could do was toss his bundle into the courtyard so no one would guess what he was up to, wave back at them, and head past them into his home. That was probably where the police would make him go anyway.

■

Richard couldn't sleep. The apartment was filled with adult smells, though everyone had gone home. There was something he recognized as dark drinks and there was meat. There was smoke, that odd mingling of cigarette and cigar smoke he was used to from his parents, but more intense and complicated than usual, and some men had been smoking pipes. And through it all there was that body smell adults had, probably sweat, it was July and terribly hot. But it wasn't the smells that woke him.

There was a strange sound from somewhere in the apartment. He could hear it again. At first he thought it might be his brother Daniel crying, but now he could tell that wasn't it. Not that he'd blame the kid, but the noise was fainter and coming from the wrong direction. And it wasn't steady, like Daniel's cries.

Richard got out of bed and walked to his window, which looked down into the apartment building's backyard where he would play punchball and stickball with his friends. The only thing he could see were lights on in two apartments across the way—Mrs. Sussman, whose husband was about eleven feet tall and worked all night, and Mrs. Aragon, who was his friend Bruce's mother and liked to stay up late thinking about her husband who burned up on a ship in the war. Richard couldn't figure out why the ocean water didn't put out the fire, but he didn't think he could ask Mrs. Aragon about it and Bruce didn't know.

Whatever it was, the noise wasn't coming from the out there.

Richard went into the hallway and stood still. He heard it again, from the direction of the living room. Tiptoeing he wondered if it could be maybe some kind of angel come to collect Daniel's penis. Richard had forgotten to search for its whereabouts when he returned. Or maybe it was a robber and Richard would get to save his parents' and his brother's lives. That might make them happy with him.

The window to the fire escape was open. That was strange. Usually, his mother shut the windows at night, even in the summer and even up here on the fourth story, to keep out dirt and of course intruders. Richard stopped in the middle of the living room and peered outside, not daring to get any closer. Someone was out there, all right.

It was his father. Myron sat with his legs dangling over the edge, arms through the metal lower railing, with a bottle of Scotch in one hand. He was looking up toward the sky.

Richard could hear the occasional sound of a car passing below and see moving lights. His father took a swig from the bottle and his lips continued to move after he swallowed, as though he were enjoying a lingering taste. Then Richard realized that his father was talking.

He came closer. No one was out there with him, so he must be talking to himself, which scared Richard about as much as his father's sudden silences always did. With sagging shoulders and, in profile, his grim face, Myron did not look happy.

"New car. A fall wardrobe for the new figure. Doctors of course. Probably need two servants now; hell why not three." He took another swig. "Communists all over the place, and where there's no Communists I got the Mafia down my throat, and these damn Chink restaurants starting to shop around for better deals on their birds. Pretty soon I'm gonna have to sell the thing, which it's the only thing I got left of my own."

Suddenly Myron's upper half spun around and he was staring back in the window, right at Richard, who was frozen in place. Myron put the bottle down on the floor of the fire escape, untangled his legs and began to crawl on all fours toward the window. Could he see Richard? Was he coming to get him?

Richard backed up, hoping to make his way into the hallway, but he was slightly off-center and ended up stumbling into his father's easy chair. It seemed to embrace him and he sank into the cushions.

Myron came through the window and Richard could see something was wrong. Glasses! His father didn't have his glasses on. Oh God, what if he wanted to sit in his easy chair? Richard held his breath. His father turned back to the window, reached through for his bottle and stumbled toward him. But he kept on going, not seeing Richard at all, leaving the bottle on the dining room credenza and then sitting at his usual place at the head of the table. He put his head in his arms and fell asleep instantly, his snores filling the hallway as Richard tiptoed past.

6

They Love You Very Much

DANNY WATCHED his parents through the bars of his crib. They moved in and out of the evening light and the light was fading as though each time they passed they drew a little more of it off.

When it got too dark to see themselves in their mirrors, Faye switched on the bedside lamps. First she took care of the lamp beside Myron's bed, squeezing past his body as though loath to brush against him where he bent toward his image in the glass. Then she squeezed by him again and walked to her own bed, switching on the lamp and exhaling a lungful of cigarette smoke. Danny watched the smoke rise and spread itself thin, inching closer till he had to look away again.

New Year's Eve, 1949, was very cold. Zero and falling, and they had the radiators cranked all the way up. The Adlers were dressing for a party that would take place in Mr. and Mrs. Sussman's apartment downstairs, and as usual they were not talking. Faye strung pearls around her neck, took them off, tried on her old topaz lavaliere, frowned. She could just hear her father's voice from somewhere over her shoulder. *That thing should go in the garbage.* She glanced back there, just to be sure, and all she saw was Danny sitting up in his crib, staring at her.

"Go to sleep," she barked.

Turning back to the mirror, she put on the ruby earrings and matching necklace her father had made for her trip to Belgium in 1928. Belgium seemed like eighty years ago. Beautiful people, the Flemish. Faye remembered that sweet young man, Cesar Martens, a veritable prince, who so badly wanted to marry her. What a fool she had been. She could be living now in Brussels or Antwerp, or even Charleroi, what a gorgeous sounding place that was. I'm Faye Martens of Charleroi and this is my husband Cesar. He's in glassware. Oh no, instead I'm Faye Adler of Brooklyn and this is my husband Myron. He's in slaughter. The chicken butcher whom they affectionately refer to as Mashie.

Myron kept knotting and reknotting his tie. He leaned so close to the mirror, it seemed as though he would poke his thick cigar smack into the face that glowered back. Wonderful, he thought. Just what I need. A night of schmaltz herring and overboiled chicken which they did not buy it from me, cheap red wine and if we're lucky maybe a toast of Chivas at midnight and kiss the lovely wife. He suddenly stopped moving his hands. He was looking at Danny in the mirror.

"Do what your mother tells you! Go to sleep."

Danny flung himself back away from the bars of the crib as though they were molten. He rolled over to face the blank wall.

■

Sunday mornings it was Danny's job to wake his father without waking his mother. Sundays were the one day Myron Adler did not set his alarm clock. He was always awake by the time Danny got up and slunk into the bedroom; hell, he was awake at four as usual, but he lay there pretending to be asleep because it was nice when his son came into the bed for him. Myron missed the little guy's presence in their room ever since Danny had outgrown the crib and been moved into Richard's room.

Faye slept on her side, facing away from Myron in her own bed, separated from his by a walnut end table draped with lace doilies. Her head was cocked at an odd angle on the double set of pillows, but she seemed to be sleeping soundly. Sometimes, looking at her asleep way over there, Myron held his breath and tried to stop imagining life without her. She had almost died twice in the last eight years. After both abortions. Look, he simply would not hear about having another child after Richard, which it was Faye's own fault if she got herself pregnant again. Hard enough living with her alone; throw in Richard and it nearly drove Myron crazy. A second child was unthinkable. She'd cried and screamed and threatened, but both times he had prevailed. Myron knew some people. It had cost more than having a baby would have cost, and it put her in more danger with the hemorrhages and the rest of her women's business, which it wasn't something he cared to know about, and she would barely talk to him for months afterwards—he certainly didn't mind that—but there had never been any question for him about letting her have the baby. This last time, though, he'd relented. She'd actually gone to his mother and told Sophia she was pregnant before telling Myron. She'd called her parents and her brother Red, whom Myron loved at least as much as he loved his own two brothers. Red had shown up at the market with a bottle of champagne, something neither of them liked as much as good old Scotch, and that was how Myron learned he would be a father again. Son of a bitch. Sure, she could have "miscarried" again, but she swore she would tell the truth. What the hell, he'd put a little money aside, they could afford the kid and maybe this time it'd change her or something. All Myron knew was that the night Danny was born he felt more alone than he ever had before.

Now as he watched his wife sleep and waited for Danny to sneak into the room, he kept thinking of the whole apartment building going up in smoke. God damn it. Which it's not something he really wanted to happen, you know? Faye didn't like it that he'd volunteered to be an air-raid warden now that the country was at war in Korea. But Myron again could not serve in the military because of his missing eye and he was not about to go through another war feeling like a eunuch. After Inchon, Myron was proud to put on the helmet and lead his neighbors down into the basement once a month or so.

"Bad enough you go putting on your silly little helmet and your armband in the middle of the night," Faye had said. "But marching me and the children down four flights to sit in a dingy little storage closet for an hour, that's criminal."

Myron heard Danny get out of bed. The boy had learned to be very quiet in his movements around the house, but Myron could sense him drawing nearer. Danny stopped at the foot of the bed to stare at his father as though taking aim. The huge belly moved the bedsheets up and down in a way that fascinated him.

This morning would be a right-side attack. Sometimes Danny crept onto the bed from its foot, sometimes he jumped on from the left, but coming from the right was his favorite. It gave him more room to operate in and put him further from his mother's bed, reducing the risk of disturbing her. Danny heaved himself up and across his father, mounting his belly like a cowboy mounting his horse on television. He rocked back and forth, kicking his feet, slapping his father's face gently, and whispered "up and at 'em, cowboy."

Myron whisper-roared with laughter, grabbing Danny by the shoulders and pulling his son down beside him on the bed. Danny was beaming. He'd done it right.

■

Unlike getting dressed for dinner last week. Danny had been looking forward to Sunday dinner at his Grandmother Sophia's apartment since Wednesday, when his mother had taken him shopping for new clothes. He'd gotten a new pair of shoes, which he had no trouble tying because they slipped right on his feet. They were brown and had a place in them to hide a penny. He'd gotten a new pair of pants the color of chocolate licorice, which Sugar Adams had shortened and even put cuffs on. Best of all, he'd gotten a striped boat-neck shirt with tails that meant he wasn't supposed to tuck the shirt into his pants.

Such clothes were a terribly exciting and sophisticated development. Twice since Wednesday, he'd modeled the outfit in the dining room, where his mother was sitting to talk with Sugar and sip her afternoon Savarin. They smiled and nodded at him. The tails hanging over his belt made Daniel feel chic, or whatever it was that his mother felt as she dressed for an evening of theater, and he couldn't wait to wear his outfit in public.

Sunday after breakfast at Kinsella's Diner, Danny and Richard had gone with Myron to visit their Grandfather Emanuel's grave. Danny always liked the drive out to Long Island. His father would listen to the radio, often to a comedy show with a lot of routines in Yiddish. While Danny never under-

stood the jokes, they made his father laugh so hard he had to take his cigar out
of his mouth. Such laughter was so astounding to witness coming from Myron
that it made both Danny and Richard laugh too.

They drove through the cemetery's ornate gates, past an office that squatted like a shrine on the left, and went slowly along a very narrow road to the
end of the grounds, their tires scrunching on gravel for the final hundred
yards. They piled out of the car and walked through the high marble posts
that bore the family name.

Grandfather Emanuel's was the only headstone in the plot, which seemed
large as a garden to Danny. It was neatly kept, but pocked here and there with
bare patches that made Myron curse. He put three pebbles at the base of his
father's headstone, then sat on a marble slab perched obliquely on its base and
began staring at the ground between his feet. Danny walked over to Richard.

"Why's there so much extra space, Ricky?"

Pointing, his brother said, "Because that's where Grandma Sophia goes
when she dies, and that's where Dad goes, and mom, Uncle Herb and Aunt
Birdie, Uncle Joseph."

"Shaddup," Myron said.

Richard shrugged. "I was just answering his question."

Myron didn't speak again. He just glared at them till Richard turned away
and approached the headstone. What he did next practically made Danny's
heart stop. He vaulted over the headstone like a gymnast!

And Myron didn't do anything! He just sat there.

Richard vaulted back over, then walked to Danny and took his hand. "It's
all right. He told me I could do it a long time ago. Come on."

After the cemetery, it was too late to go horseback riding so they stopped for
an hour at Coney Island. Richard and Danny got to drive bumper cars and
ride the Tornado, but they didn't have time for the Steeplechase. They had to
get home and wake Faye.

Danny dressed for dinner an hour before anyone, but stayed in his room
looking through his baseball cards so that they wouldn't see him. His Clem
Labine had a crease right through the face from the time Danny had accidentally sat on it; he would have to get another one. If it wasn't a Dodgers
player, he wouldn't bother. At three o'clock, as his parents were in their bed-

room just starting to dress, Danny walked in with an enormous grin on his face, his new clothes hanging perfectly—no wrinkles, no dirt—and even with his hair parted true as the flight of a bullet.

Faye saw him in her mirror and smiled. As she turned to welcome him, Myron also turned from his side of the room and saw Danny standing by the bed.

"What the hell is that?" he took his cigar out of his mouth and pointed at Danny's chest with it.

Danny, still smiling, said, "My new shirt. It's a boat-neck."

"Boat-neck, shmoat-neck. What's it doing hanging out?"

Danny looked over at his mother. Faye had turned back to the mirror and was putting on her lipstick. She didn't speak.

"This is how you wear it, Dad." He lifted out the tails to show his father that they were split to fall neatly over the belt.

"No it isn't. Tuck it in."

"Mom bought it for me."

"I don't care if the Pope bought it for you. Tuck it in or take it off." Myron turned back to his dresser. Faye was still working on her makeup and was silent.

Danny went back into his room and sat on his bed. Richard was in the living room watching television, but even if he was there Danny knew he would not help. A week ago, Richard had suddenly turned around and smacked Danny on top of the head because Danny was making too much noise with his baseball cards. So he had to be careful now around Richard too.

It didn't make any sense. He was wearing his brand new clothes exactly the way he was supposed to. If he tucked the shirt in, it would be wrong. If he didn't wear it, after his mother had gone to all the trouble of buying it for him, that might make her as angry as wearing the shirt right had made his father.

Then Danny had a brainstorm. It was such a brilliant idea, he had to smile at himself for thinking of it. He undid his belt, dropped his pants to his knees, and tucked only the front of his shirt in. The back tail he left hanging out. He went to the mirror behind his door and liked what he saw.

But Myron didn't. Before Danny had even stopped walking into the room, Myron kicked him like a football. Danny landed on his mother's bed and bounced off, hitting the back of his head on the end table. His first thought was, Thank God I didn't knock off the doilies! Then, still too stunned to cry, he got up and darted out of the room.

■

A week later, the black Buick crawled through Sunday afternoon traffic. August heat stewed them, but they couldn't open the windows because the breeze might muss Faye's hair. Her cigarette smoke mixed with Myron's cigar smoke to turn the seething interior into a sapphire caldron. Danny tried to open his window a crack, just to let out some of the smoke, but his mother caught him.

"Daniel Adler, shut that window this instant," she said without even looking around.

He rolled it up fast. That was The Tone. Danny knew it meant his mother was furious. Maybe not entirely about the window, but about something, and there was no point in setting her off. Danny looked over at his brother to see if Richard thought whatever was wrong might be something *he'd* done, but Richard was staring at the back of their father's head with no expression on his face.

Danny noiselessly slid off his seat onto the floor of the car. The air down there was a little clearer. He coiled into the small nook between his seat and his mother's, and just got settled when Richard kicked him. He sat back up.

Danny had last heard The Tone a few days ago. Faye had walked into his bedroom and found lots of toys scattered on the floor around him as he dug into his toy chest. He was looking for Mr. Potato Head, which he was certain had been on the top layer of toys. Now it was gone, there was not even an ear to be found.

"I told you before, one toy at a time!"

Danny hadn't heard her coming. He struggled to get his upper body out of the toy chest and turn around to face her, but he was off balance and banged his chin against the rim.

"I'll clean it up," he said. He did not touch the sore place on his chin.

Her tone changed, each word getting crisper. Her nostrils flared and he could see her hands begin to shake. Oh boy, was she mad. "Every speck. And please tell me, how many toys does a little *pisher* like you need to play with at once?"

"I was looking for Mr. Potato Head."

She bent down and grabbed his ear, straightening him to look at her face. "Don't you talk back to me."

"I didn't mean to."

"Answer my question. One, that's how many."

"It's gone."

"You know why you lose things? You lose things because you keep your toy chest so messy."

She tightened her grip on his ear. He was trying not to cry.

"Put them away," she said, releasing him with a final squeeze. He fell back against the toy chest.

Quickly, he began to gather things up—soldiers and a fort, a fire truck, some loose Lincoln logs and tinker toys. In his haste, a few soldiers slipped out. That was when his mother screamed and grabbed him by the belt, lifting him off the ground. She stuffed him into the toy chest, flung the remaining cars and soldiers in after him, shut the lid and sat on it.

He'd landed with the roof of the fort poking into his face and something thick, maybe his dump truck, against the small of his back. But he couldn't move and he knew better than to knock on the lid. He kept his eyes shut, though it was so dark he wouldn't see anything if he opened them.

Now with the window closed and his brother on the river side of the car, with traffic hardly moving and his parents beginning to quarrel again, Danny decided to close his eyes and ears completely, as he'd done when he was inside the toy chest. He went around the Dodgers' defense, position by position, naming the names to himself, imagining the faces, seeing the players crouched with their gloves poised to field the ball when it came their way: Campanella, Hodges, Gilliam, Reese, Cox, Robinson, Snider, Furillo, Erskine.

Westside Highway was always jammed on Sunday afternoon, which is the reason Myron had wanted to leave earlier. But oh no, Her Royal Highness couldn't possibly be ready before two o'clock. He'd already gotten up with the kids and taken them to breakfast at the diner, gone horseback riding in Prospect Park and for a quick visit to his mother. When they returned to the apartment, Faye was still in her bathrobe with her hair in curlers, sitting at the dining room table with a half-finished cup of Savarin.

"What are you doing?" Myron had said.

"Reciting Keats' "Ode to Autumn."

"Yeah, well it's August."

"I take it you don't know that poem, my dear?"

Myron sat in his easy chair and unfolded the Sunday paper. "We're supposed to be at your parents in two hours."

"Don't you start with me."

"We leave at two o'clock, which then we won't get there till four, I don't want to hear a word about being late outta you while we sit in traffic."

Faye turned away from him, gazing in Danny's general direction, and looked amused. She stuck the tip of her tongue out and picked off a fleck of tobacco. "Wash up, Danny. You're filthy. Him and his fancy horseback riding, as if he were a man of breeding. Lord Capon himself."

As they waited among the honking, restless cars, Danny would have loved to look at the piers. Occasionally he could glimpse ships docked at the piers and people walking around on them. It was fun to imagine sailing away to the Congo or maybe Florida. His biggest mistake so far this afternoon had been to mention the ships as the family was getting in the car, because immediately his brother Richard sat on the left side to block Danny's view.

He finished reciting names of the Dodgers players and began on the Giants. Westrum, Lockman, Williams, Dark. But the Giants weren't as much fun. He opened his eyes and, imitating his brother, stared at the back of his mother's head.

Danny remembered sitting next to her on the piano bench a couple of days ago. It was late afternoon, before Richard got home from playing with his friends, before his father got home from work, and Danny was playing penny-baseball in his room. Sugar had gone home for the weekend. Faye was in a wonderful mood. She'd sat down at the piano and played a few of her favorite songs—"Give My Regards to Broadway," "Can't Help Lovin' That Man of Mine," and the one that was written just for her by a famous man, "Hey, May by Herschel Idstein." Danny liked to hear her. The music stopped for a moment and then she was standing in the doorway of Danny's room.

"What?" he'd asked, sitting on the floor among his baseball cards. "I didn't do anything."

"Would you like to come in and sit with me, Danny? Help me sing a song?"

He quickly began stacking his cards. "Ok."

"Just leave them there, sweetheart," she said softly. A smile made her cigarette jiggle between her lips. "You can come back and play in a few minutes."

He always welcomed the chance to watch her play. Faye was so short, she had to sit perched on the edge of the bench in order to reach the pedals and she had to stand altogether to reach the ends of the keyboard. Her trademark was a grand finish to each song in which she rose and ran her hands from one end of the keyboard to the other. This was Danny's cue to applaud and one of those moments when his laughter was acceptable.

"What shall we sing?" she asked when they'd sat together.

"Old Man River?"

"How about "Hey May!" She played a few chords.

"Hey May be my gal," Danny sang. "Hey May you're a pal."

It was 4:00 when the traffic eased and 4:30 when they finally arrived at Jules and Ava Raskin's apartment just off Central Park West. Everyone was hot and tired. Ava had cooked borscht, brisket, sweet potatoes, and green beans in her tiny kitchen, filling the two-room apartment with added heat as the late afternoon sun poured though the windows.

The dinner table was set and the food was ready when they arrived, so they immediately sat down for dinner. The six of them could barely fit around the loaded table. Jules turned the sound down on the television, but kept the picture on since he had no intention of missing the evening news just because his snooty daughter had to be late everywhere she went.

Danny loved to watch the news on the sofa beside his grandfather Jules. The old man would echo the last words of the broadcaster's sentences, accompanied by a vigorous nod of his head. Danny ate quickly and kept sneaking looks at the screen during dinner to gauge the time. Later, they might even play a few hands of gin rummy. His grandfather would do the same thing during the game that he did during the news, narrating each discard with an emphatic nod. Danny would laugh and the nodding would get wilder. At some point, he would even get to hear his grandmother Ava's laugh, the best of all, a wheezy, body-shaking giggle that was worth almost any amount of sitting in a hot smoky car.

Dinner finished in time because everyone ate quickly and there was hardly any talk. Danny climbed onto the sofa and leaned against his grandfather. Richard went into the bedroom to play solitaire on his grandparents' bed. Faye helped her mother clear the dishes and was shooed out of the kitchen. She sat back at the dinner table with Myron and they began to talk softly.

"You know what the big one did?" Faye said.

Myron poured a shot into his coffee and leaned forward. "What did he do, Faye, knock off Brink's? Sell secrets to the Commies?"

"Oh, that's fine, Myron. You're not with them all day. It's fine for you to make a joke of everything."

"And you, you're with them? I thought that's why I'm paying Sugar all that money, which you're spared having to raise your own children."

Danny could hear them, despite his grandfather's duet with the newscaster. He tried not to listen.

"Police suspect homicide," the newsman said.

"Homicide," said Grandfather Jules.

"So he hits Reuben Aragon, little Bruce's brother that plays with Danny, he hits Reuben over the head with his cap pistol. Not once, Myron. Twice. He bled like one of your chickens, she had to take him to the doctor. Three stitches."

"Whaddya want me to do, hah?"

"Cloudy and hot tomorrow, with a chance of thunderstorms in the afternoon."

"In the afternoon."

"And the little one, he's too smart for his own good. Will not, absolutely will not eat his vegetables."

"That he gets from me, Faye. I don't eat 'em either."

"He should do what he's told," she hissed.

"The Dodgers won 3-0 on another shutout by Billy Loes."

"Loes."

At the commercial, Danny excused himself and went into the bedroom.

He walked past Richard, who didn't look up from the his game. "Don't forget to lock the door," he said as Danny went into the bathroom.

When he came out, Myron was standing next to the bed, looking down at Richard. The solitaire game was all scrambled up and Richard was looking up at his father. Both were pale and completely still.

"Wash your hands," Myron said to Danny without taking his eyes off Richard.

"I did."

Danny didn't even see the blow coming. His father's hand caught him on the side of the face. He stumbled backwards and his feet caught the edge of the small step leading to the bathroom. He turned, spinning halfway around, trying to catch himself, and his face hit hard against the bathroom sink.

The next thing Danny remembered was being held in his grandmother's arms. There was ice against his eye. His parents were in the other room and he was alone with his grandmother.

"What happened?" he asked.

"Shhh."

"She squeezed me in the door again? Grandma, did you see her? I tried to run out of the apartment and she grabbed the open door and she knocked me back in the corner, right? She had me trapped, I remember. Like last time."

"They love you, Danny," his grandmother was saying. "Your mother and father, they love you very much."

7

The Royal Family

SOME SATURDAY MORNINGS smelled like meat. When Myron woke Danny in the dark, an odor of raw pork was already on his hands.

One hand was spread across Danny's brow, the thumb and pinky squeezing his temples in a steady massage. Danny's eyes fluttered open. It never occurred to him that his father was a small man. Everything about Myron Adler seemed large. He spoke in salvos and his whisper was like the eye of a hurricane. Danny could hear him breathing anywhere in the apartment. Myron had corded, hairy arms and fingers that were so thick he had trouble buttoning shirts. His nose, smashed twice by falling chicken coops, sheered his shadowed face toward the jutting jaw and seemed stretched to a point by its own weight. His huge belly didn't jiggle when he walked. He would make Danny punch him there as hard as he could and would never flinch.

Even when his father stood near Si Sabbeth, Danny didn't think of him as small. It just seemed that Si was a giant. Si had bought Danny a fishing rod for his birthday and brought it to the house covered in an acre of wrapping paper. Both men laughed when Si told Danny his father would teach him how to fish. Maybe Si would show up at the market today.

Myron was dressed for work, wearing black corduroys and a maroon flannel shirt that didn't show blood. His socks sagged into boots he wouldn't tie until leaving the apartment. Their lace tips clicked on the linoleum when he walked.

"C'mon, pal, it's past time to get up. Now tell me the slogan."

"Kill or be killed," Danny mumbled.

"Right you are. And don't forget: Mr. Alfred J. Honts, which he used to be my friend Alf, will gladly take every one of my customers if I'm not careful."

"Except the Chink restaurants."

"Except the Chinks, right. That's another thing to remember. Your uncle Joseph wanted no part of the Chink trade, which explains why he's gonna be selling hats someday. Makes me laugh."

Danny turned his head away and gazed at the map hung on his wall. A huge red oval seemed to glow down at him. Ask him to find any volcano in the Ring of Fire and Danny would jab a finger right to it on the map. From Chile up to Alaska and down from Siberia to New Zealand, he could place more than six hundred of the world's most furious mountains. Someday, he promised himself, he would walk within the Valley of Ten Thousand Smokes. He would visit Burney and Barren Island, Tarawera and Ulawun, Purace, Mt. St. Helens. He loved just saying their names.

"Uncle Joe's going to be a hatdasher, right?"

"Haberdasher." Myron rolled Danny's head back away from the wall. "Now let's get moving, we open at five."

■

Danny's clothes were in a tall chest that was backed into his closet. He found a pair of dungarees with their cuffs still rolled properly. His father got furious when cuffs were too high or uneven, when they sagged against his sneakers, when they had fade marks. Danny's mother always made Sugar Adams unroll the cuffs when she did the wash. He wished Sugar would leave them alone, since it was always so hard to get the cuffs right again, but he didn't have the nerve to tell his mother. She would get enraged if he asked questions about housekeeping and would scream *just like your father!*.

Danny slipped on a sweatshirt the same shade of dark blue as his dungarees. He thought his father might appreciate the match. He wished he had a pale blue bandanna to go with them, like the cowboy he'd seen in the circus last month. Even without that, if his father liked the outfit this could be his market-uniform from now on. Then his father might take him along for more Saturdays, the way he used to take Ricky. Danny hoped he had finally figured out the right thing to do.

Before leaving the room, Danny checked to be sure he hadn't disturbed his brother. Ricky slept on his back with his bad eye half open, so it was difficult to be sure. On Saturdays, Ricky had to meet all morning with his tutor. He hadn't been allowed to go to the market since failing Algebra and History.

Ricky's bad eye had been bad since before Danny was born, so it couldn't be Danny's fault. Something about a broken lens, glass in Ricky's eye, one entire summer of surgeries. Danny dreamed about it sometimes. In the dreams, he always saw their father's fist, with its black hairs standing sharp and tall as spikes, that made his brother's glasses explode in his face.

Ricky was asleep. Danny could tell by checking whether the bad eye moved. He could remember to call him Rick when his brother was awake, but Danny still thought of him as Ricky. It had only been a few weeks since Ricky demanded the name change. Every time Danny forgot, his brother would punch him on the arm. There was a big bruise now on his biceps, but Danny hadn't told his mother the truth about how he'd gotten it. Rick said that if he did, it would cost him his leg. Danny had trouble keeping up with his brother's names. A year or so ago, he had a long struggle replacing Richie with Ricky. Now he had to remember Rick.

Danny checked himself out in the mirror behind their door. Everything looked neat enough, but you could never be sure. He wiped the residue of a sleepstring from the corner of his eye.

Danny had finally understood that when he dressed for Sunday dinner, no matter where they were going and no matter what Danny had put on, his father would make him go back to his room to change shirts. It was like when he washed his hands before a meal and showed them to his mother. He might as well march back into the bathroom without holding them up for inspection. For market-going on Saturdays, shirt selection was the first real crisis. No matter which one he chose, Danny's first selection would be wrong and the whole day could end right there.

He kept hoping Saturday mornings would be different. As he checked his shirt one more time for cleanliness and color, he thought he might be getting the knack of dressing right. How could a boy look any better?

■

Myron Adler flung open the furrowed gray doors of his poultry market. They rumbled in their tracks like subway train cars and disappeared.

"Wake up and fly right!"

Adler's Live Poultry flapped wildly in the coops that lined one wall. As they screamed back at him, their cries ricocheted through the air.

"Help! Help!"

Danny stared at the faces of three scales, which threw dawn light onto him. The market's floors were covered with fresh sawdust spread last night by his father's assistant, a grizzled old man named Gabe.

Soon, Danny knew, the floors would be patched with clots of feathers and blood. He would feel their lumps under his soles all day. There would also be more meat smell. It would remind him of breakfast and make him want to skip lunch. But he couldn't refuse to eat Saturday lunch with his father. That got him madder than anything.

Besides, his father said he would get used to the smell. He said Danny would get used to the racket from the coops, too. But it hadn't happened yet.

He stood on the tracks listening to the birds go crazy. His father hurried to the plucking room for aprons. Danny watched him move, the massive shoulders rolling through the air as though he were swimming.

Suddenly, out of the darkness behind him, two hands folded themselves around Danny's face. He was yanked backwards, feet off the ground like a fryer being snatched from its coop, and his head struck something solid. He sank into a heavy stench of offal.

"Ayyyyy, little Myron! Guess who?"

Danny squirmed in the iron grip of his father's assistant. Gabriel Kozey once told Danny that his hands were so strong because he'd been plucking feathers out of freshly killed birds for forty years, before there were any machines to do the job. He'd illustrated the comment by putting his thumb and forefinger together on Danny's nose and tugging hard.

"You think they wanna come outta there, the plumages?" Gabe had laughed. "It's like pulling off this schnozz of yours, or better yet, jerking out a lady's eyelashes, you know what I mean?"

Danny hated to have Gabe's hands on him. The hands were mottled with blank patches, scaly sections paler than the rest and hairless. Probably from all the blood and featherjuice, which Danny could imagine staining like acid.

He thought Gabe must never wash his hands right, the way Myron had taught Danny. He'd bet Gabe didn't flush toilets with his feet, either. He smelled even worse than liver.

No wonder Gabe never got invited home for dinner. Danny liked to imagine his mother sending Gabe away from the table to wash better, and checking to make sure Gabe had cleaned the sink after himself. She would probably throw the napkin he used into the incinerator when Gabe left.

Before letting him go, Gabe rolled Danny's head a few times across his belt buckle. Then he nudged him toward the coops and headed back to the plucking room to find Myron.

Danny approached the coops. The chickens crowded into the far corner.

"It's just me. I won't hurt you."

They kept backing up, bunching together and beginning to cry out. Danny stuck a finger in to attract them.

"Here girls."

"Help!" they squawked.

"GET INNA THE OFFICE!" Myron yelled from behind him. Danny hadn't heard him coming. "How many times I gotta tell you keep your hands to yourself? Here, home, everywhere. The hell am I gonna do with you, anyway?"

He threw an apron over Danny's head. Despite the fresh soap, he could still smell old blood on it.

"Now don't touch anything." He drew a knife from some place beneath his apron. "You wanna lose a finger, here, I'll chop it off for you."

Danny put his hands in his pants pockets. "I'm sorry."

The office was small and warm. The squat cash register filled most of the table. Above it was a shelf that held the old radio. Danny didn't like hearing it talk about the new H-Bomb, so he climbed onto the table and turned the dial until he found a song he knew. *Hey there, you with the stars in your eyes.* His mother could play that one on the piano. He climbed back down. There was a chair on wheels with a flattened cushion sheathed in old aprons. Danny sat in the chair, wheeled it over to the damp window, and wiped a circle clear to watch his father getting the market ready.

First, Myron reached back to slide his hand under the apron and draw out a small plaid flask. He took a deep drink, replaced the flask, and rubbed his arms hard to warm up. Next, he tested the scales. He swept the entryway and put out a fresh roll of brown paper to wrap the dead chickens in. Finally, he lit a cigar, first biting off its tip and screwing on the brown plastic holder that was the same color as the floor of the market.

■

The last time Danny had been here, it was mid-morning when things started going wrong. He remembered his father glaring at him from in front of the coops. The knife he used to cut the chickens' necks gleamed in his hand.

By noon, Myron had called Faye to come down on the bus and get Danny out of there. When his mother arrived, Danny had burst into tears and his father had thrown a rag at him covered in blood and featherjuice.

Now, Danny wanted to stay out of trouble. He just wished he knew what he'd done wrong last time.

That sort of thing kept happening. Two or three market visits ago—it was so long now that Danny wasn't sure when it happened, but he remembered the weather was very cold because their breath was all vapory in the pre-dawn Saturday air—Danny had done something wrong before they'd even had breakfast. They were in the kitchen. Danny hadn't realized his father could find anything there, or knew what to do with it if he did, but he sat at the table and watched his father bring the place settings and food over. Danny almost fell back to sleep, mesmerized by his father's tidy, hushed activities. Then he joined Danny at the table and began his preparations. With one hand Myron cracked two eggshells on a jam jar's lip and with a quick dip let the yolks slip through his hand whole. Next he shook a drop of hot pepper sauce into the heart of each yolk and pierced it with a fork. The yellow ooze had nowhere to flow in the glass, so it rose as though breathing and then pooled. When he poured on a fist of salt, Danny saw the same smile Myron wore at the market. It was almost as though his father had slit the egg's throat with his gleaming knife instead of piercing the yolk with a table fork. Before Danny knew what had happened, Myron looked up and caught him staring. There must have been some sign of distaste on Danny's face, or some shuddering at the thought of having to drink down a raw egg, because Myron's smile faded. He reached across the space between them and pressed the jar to Danny's lips.

Now with his face pressed close to the cleared circle of the office window, Danny watched his father yank open the door to a coop. He watched him snatch a capon's feet and sweep him face down through the gate.

Wrists snapping, arms flapping faster than wings, he wrapped the legs above the spurs with wire and dangled the capon from the scale's hook.

"Four pounds six," he called over his shoulder.

The old woman, who looked like Danny's Grandmother Sophia, shrugged her shoulders. She looked over toward the office, where Danny peered back at her wondering if she was thinking about having him weighed too.

"Why not?" she said.

Myron cut the capon's neck. He took it back to Gabe and then came back to talk to the woman.

Danny came out of the office to watch Gabe thrust the bird, squawking blood, legs kicking air, slit neck down into a can to die. Gabe turned to the plucking machine. He removed a pullet he'd been cleaning for someone who said she'd pick it up at ten.

He addressed Danny without looking at him, as though they'd been chatting all morning. "So, you gonna be a lawyer when you grow up?"

"I don't know." Danny couldn't stop watching the capon's legs. "Maybe."

"A doctor?"

The bird let out a weird rattle and was still. "I don't think so."

"Right, too much school." Gabe put the capon into the plucker and turned the machine on. Danny stood on his toes to watch the feathers fly. "You like school?"

"Can I take him out to my dad?"

"This is an it, not a him." He lifted the carcass and brushed it vigorously. "But sure, do it."

He ripped paper from the fat roll and wrapped the capon quickly. Danny carried the spotted package, taped shut, back to the office. Myron came in to ring the sale.

"Nice job," he said, patting Danny on the head. When Myron left to hand the package over to the old woman, Danny ran a hand through his hair to check for featherjuice.

■

Danny didn't see anything special about the man. It was just before noon when he sauntered in, hands in his jacket pockets, and smiled an aardvark's jagged smile.

Myron jerked a thumb over his shoulder like an umpire signaling an out. The man, dressed in a gray overcoat and a hat with one long gray feather, nodded and walked back toward the plucking room.

Gabe burst out of the room as though ejected. He wiped his hands on a towel strung through his apron string, then hurried to the front. He whispered something to Myron, who shook his head and then spit something onto the sawdust.

Danny watched his father come toward the office. Myron's face was suddenly drawn tight, as it had looked just before he'd lifted the glass of raw egg to Danny's lips. Danny took a few steps back from the office door until he reached the wall, wondering what he'd done wrong. He hadn't been letting his nose touch the glass, he hadn't handled anything, hadn't spoken. Except the radio! Oh God, Myron would hear the music!

Myron stuck his head into the office, but didn't enter. "Stay put," he hissed. "I'm going out back for a while."

Danny was so relieved he wasn't the cause of his father's anger that he couldn't ask any questions. Myron went to where the stranger was waiting, brushed by him without a word, and disappeared.

Danny didn't know Gabe was allowed to wait on customers. He worried that people wouldn't want to buy anything from a man who looked so gory. If somebody came, Danny thought he'd better go out and keep an eye on things. His father probably meant for him to do that, but he'd been too preoccupied to mention it. He left the office and moved closer to the scales.

No one came into the market, though. Gabe stood outside in the morning sun, eyes shut and head tilted skyward. Soon Remo Santselmo, the man who owned the meat market next door, appeared beside Gabe, who accepted the proffered flask and drank as deeply as Myron had earlier. Danny thought Mr. Santselmo looked like a messed-up copy of Yogi Berra. He was a little too short and a little too chunky, his skin was just a bit more pock-marked than Yogi's and his chin was slightly too pointed, but it was close enough that when Danny first saw him he'd almost asked for an autograph. For a Yankee, Yogi was all right.

It was still cool, despite the growing brightness. Danny watched as Gabe offered Mr. Santselmo a Lucky Strike. He hung back in the shadows of the coops, watching the men pass time. Mr. Santselmo, who traded Italian sausage for chickens with Myron on Friday nights, seemed angry.

"*Criminale*," he muttered. "Let's talk about something else, hah? We don't gotta talk about those bastards."

"Sure, sure. Sons of bitches are gonna ruin the whole Battery no one stops them. What about the Series? You ever see anything like that catch?"

"Willie Mays, you know he's gonna do good for you, it's no surprise the catch. That Dusty Rhodes, he's the guy wins you a Series, surprises your ass right off your back."

"The pitching. Indians give us 21 runs in four games. You and me coulda won it, we don't need no Willie Mays."

"Ahhh, the hell with it. I like Brooklyn next year anyways." Mr. Santselmo threw his cigarette down and stomped on it. "How much longer's Myron gonna put up with this? Makes me embarrassed I'm Italian, even. Goddam."

"Myron's tough."

"That don't make no difference, we're all tough. Your tough, I'm tough. I been tough since Brooklyn was still a city. Hell, now you can't make no money at all, you gotta keep giving to these people more all the time."

A woman entering Mr. Santselmo's market brought the conversation to a stop. Gabe watched him leave, then turned around and saw Danny standing there. He looked over the boy's shoulder and frowned. Danny understood. He went back into the office and stood as far from the door as he could.

■

Later that evening, Danny watched from the floor of their room as his parents got dressed for a costume party. It was his mother's annual Raskin Cousins'

Club meeting, a tradition on Halloween weekend. Danny stayed out of their way, but listened to everything they said. The air was filled with the scent of Old Spice and Scotch.

"Sixteen years ago tonight," Myron told Danny, "Martians landed in New Jersey. They helped me tell your grandparents that me and your mother were getting married."

"Myron," Faye giggled. "Don't scare him."

Danny loved to see them like this. Nothing they said or did would scare him, as long as he kept quiet.

"So what's Red going as this year?" Myron asked. It was his father's mild voice, the one Danny hadn't heard since first thing in the morning.

"Oh, you know Red. My brother wouldn't tell me the truth if I begged him."

"Probably doesn't even know, himself. I bet you his Commie wife plans their whole life."

"Sasha's no Communist. What's wrong with you? She's simply a nice rich girl from Scarsdale, as you know perfectly well."

"Got a name like a Cossack is all I know. Plus she whispers all the time, like she's got something to hide."

Last year, Danny remembered, they'd dressed as gangsters. Myron had worn an overcoat and hat like the man who'd come to the market. He carried a bottle of liquor under his arm. Danny had thought they'd decided not to wear costumes, but Faye explained that his father was pretending to be Al Capone and she, with a fox stole around her neck and rolling pin in her hand, was pretending to be his moll.

This year, Danny thought the costumes were much better. His father had a moustache painted on and wore a gold satiny cape that matched his crown. He looked like some movie star king. Faye had made a Queen costume for herself out of sky blue material seasoned with sequins.

"We're The Royal Family," she said.

"Right," Myron grumbled. "King Tut and his wife Nut."

All day, she'd been practicing her Queen Dance. She showed Danny the routine, putting her hands together above her head, shutting her eyes, and bobbing like a turtle going in and out of its shell. Her eyes were encased in black triangles that matched her thickened lips.

"You're doing your head wrong," Myron said.

"What do you know about it?"

"I know that your head should go side to side, not front to back."

"Mr. King of Egypt, the dance expert."

"I've seen it done right, if that's what you mean. Seen it lots of times."

Faye turned away from Myron and spoke to Danny. "Your father, whose idea of world travel is a weekend at Lake George, is going to tell *me* about foreign culture. This is a man who thinks Picasso is some kind of flower."

"Drop it," Myron said. "What do I care if your damn cousins think you're a turtle."

"Don't start with me."

Danny kept playing with his baseball cards on the floor. He had them spread into a field between his parents' beds. Using a pencil for bat and penny for ball, he conducted a full nine inning game, announcing each at-bat to himself in Red Barber's Mississippi accent.

He needed to be near his parents as they prepared to go out, even if they argued. He had to fight back tears when the gray-haired babysitter would arrive from the sixth floor and make him go out into the living room.

"Who's better, Dad? Johnny Antonelli or Johnny Podres?"

"Podres, which there is no doubt about it. I mean, Antonelli's Italian."

"Mr. Santselmo thinks Antonelli won the pennant for the Giants last year. I heard him tell Gabe."

"Well, Remo Santselmo doesn't know anything about anything. Not baseball, not business, and certainly not life. Don't expect a Santselmo to say anything bad about an Antonelli. Which Remo's as bad as Alf Honts, but at least he sells sausages instead of poultry."

"Who was that man who came in today, when you had to leave? I didn't like him."

Myron looked over at Faye, who was watching them in the mirror. He spoke to her, not Danny, when he said "Guy who used to be my friend."

"Now what is he?"

"He told me today he's the future. Now go answer the door, pal. Mrs. Auer's here."

8

The Mad Bomber

WHEN THE POLICE caught The Mad Bomber they didn't put him in jail. They put him in King's County Hospital under heavy security, across the street from the Adlers' apartment building. Danny wanted to move away immediately.

For as long as Danny could remember, The Mad Bomber had been terrifying all of Brooklyn, planting his bombs in public places, in telephone booths and bathrooms and subways, maiming and crippling innocent people. A moment before, they had no idea they were about to be torn apart by one of his blasts. It seemed that The Mad Bomber would never get caught, but piece by piece all of Brooklyn would blow up and then he could move on maybe to the Bronx. No place was safe. He might hit the carousel in Coney Island next! Danny wanted to tell his father they should stop going there, but was more concerned with his father's reaction to such a suggestion than with being blown sky high while reaching for the golden ring.

Some days, Danny's mother would talk about The Mad Bomber on the phone with her friends. Martha Sussman had once called Faye from a phone booth kitty-corner from one that had been blown up by The Mad Bomber two years later. Mrs. Aragon knew a woman whose husband worked with a man whose sister-in-law had been hurt by flying glass in one of the explosions. She was on her way to the Botanic Gardens and BOOM!

Some nights, Danny would have nightmares about The Mad Bomber sending one of his explosive packages up through their radiator pipes, or leaving it in the elevator to tear everyone to shreds between the second and third floors. He would cry out in the night and his father would come into the room—nothing short of an actual bomb would wake his mother—and try to comfort him. Finally his parents agreed to remove the ticking clock from Danny's bedside. Richard complained at dinner that Danny was driving him crazy. It was Danny's fault that Richard was too tired to behave properly at school. And he was giving Richard nightmares too, bad ones full of torpedoes in the bathtub and hand grenades in the closet.

Danny didn't want to tell his parents about this and worry them unduly, but he could see The Mad Bomber peeking through the hospital's barred window every morning while he walked to school. Danny had to look carefully and not let The Mad Bomber see him looking, but the man was there, squeezed into the far corner of his cell, hands gripping the bars and long crooked nose poking out for air. His name was George Metesky, which sounded just like a lot of people who lived in the Adlers' building. Sometimes Danny could see The Mad Bomber's eyes, which were such a bright and wild blue that they must have captured all the fire from those explosions of his. His hair was fiery red and stood straight out through the bars when he leaned forward, which he seemed to do whenever Danny passed by. And if Danny looked just right, he could see that the fingers had been misshapen by flames. It was terrible.

Faye explained that the police would never let The Mad Bomber out of the hospital. They brought him there all the way from Waterbury, Connecticut, where they'd arrested him. But if they did happen to let him out someday, it would only be to go straight to prison or to the courthouse for a trial. He would be guarded. There was nothing to worry about.

"But suppose he explodes the guards on the way out? Suppose he blasts his handcuffs off and runs away?"

"Don't start with me," his mother said. "They watch him all the time, so he can't get hold of that stuff he uses to make bombs with."

"Suppose he still has some hidden on him? Suppose someone sneaks it in to him?"

"If you don't stop nagging me, I'm going to blow you up myself."

Danny knew that The Mad Bomber was probably a very nice man most of the time. There was a regular family back home, Danny was sure. Mrs. Metesky cooked dinner for him and the two children every night. And unlike at Danny's house, she got up extra early to fix a couple of sandwiches with maybe a ripe pear and some cookies, and she would pack it all with a bunch of napkins in one of those metal lunch boxes that The Mad Bomber would carry to work. She didn't know that he would eat the meal she'd prepared and then use the lunch box for his next bomb. He told her every month or so that people kept stealing his lunch box, and she knew how the guys at work were. It was all in fun, she didn't think much about it. The children didn't even know that their father was The Mad Bomber till the police caught him. He would play catch with them, sometimes he read them stories or took them to Coney Island on Sundays. Most of the time he was a very good father. George. But then something would set him off.

■

Sometimes at night, Danny would lie in bed across the room from his brother and they would listen to the radio. When Richard was feeling especially friendly, they might even push their beds closer together and put the radio on the table between them. If they kept the volume on low, their parents never heard the radio and left them alone.

Danny always wanted to listen to a ball game. He remembered when he heard Jackie Robinson steal home and had to leap out of bed yelling SAFE, it was so exciting. That had brought both Myron and Faye running into the room, and led to the radio being incarcerated in the top of Myron's closet for a month. Richard had been furious with Danny. He said it would cost Danny one baseball card for every night the radio was gone. Before going to bed, Danny had to hold up his stack of cards, let Richard select one without looking, and watch while Richard tore it to shreds. When Richard picked out Reno Bertoia, a card that had taken months to get, Danny simply could not watch it being torn. Closed eyes had cost Danny a punch high on the thigh, in a spot where his parents probably wouldn't see the bruise.

Richard liked to listen to rock n' roll, especially the patter of the deejays. He would imitate them under his breath the same way Danny imitated Red

Barber calling a ball game. Since it was Richard's radio, they mostly listened to rock n' roll.

One night in March, when there wasn't a ball game to listen to, they had on an all-request show and Danny could concentrate without worrying about how the Dodgers or Yankees were doing. People called the station, asking the deejay to play a song dedicated to someone they knew—a girlfriend or boyfriend, *that special someone under the el tracks,* a buddy who was gone. There was something wild in the deejay's voice, something that made Danny edgy. *This one goes out to Bobby and Rosie; Sal and Rita; Joyce, June, Janice and Jocelyn—hi Joss from Ripper; this is for Bonnie, hugs n' kisses Carol from Boo.* His voice kept getting higher and the words came faster till it seemed to Danny the deejay was about to burst. *From Mickey to Charlotte, The Bomber to Flo, from Hank with love, from Norm thinking of you Nita.*

Danny sat bolt upright. "Did you hear that?"

"Shhh," Richard hissed.

Tina, I'm yours, Roy Boy. To Maggie, to Sue, to Delilah.

"Ricky, didn't you hear him?"

"Who's Ricky? I told you not to call me that anymore."

"The Mad Bomber called in!"

"What the hell are you talking about?"

"He said it. He said from The Mad Bomber to Flow. Didn't you hear him?" Danny had pulled the covers around his shoulders and was staring past his brother to the window.

"What are you doing? You're crying, for Christ's sake. I'm trying to listen to this, Danny. C'mon, it's gonna be The Dell Vikings."

"But we're going to Grandma's on Sunday."

"What are you talking about?"

"We're going to Grandma's. We have to go through the tunnel. I told Dad what if The Mad Bomber blows up the tunnel while we're in it, we'd all drown. The Mad Bomber said he's going to make it Flow, Rick. He just said so!"

"If you don't shut up, Danny, it's gonna be your blood that starts flowing. Here, listen. 'Dom dom dom dom dom, dom be dubey dom, wha wha wha wha-ah.'"

■

It was late afternoon and the light in the apartment was drab, like a slip-cover his mother would have replaced months ago. She was sitting at her desk off the foyer, talking on the phone and doodling on a pad. She always started with grand strokes, big hoops that she'd make smaller and smaller until the center of her doodle was solid blue.

Danny had his baseball cards spread out on the living room floor near her, reorganizing them. They'd been in number order for a week. Now it was time to arrange them team-by-team, though he'd need sixteen rubber bands and wasn't sure his mother would give them to him. She didn't sound happy.

Faye and Myron were going out to dinner with Si Sabbeth and his wife Gloria that evening. This was something they had done every other Thursday night since 1945—when Si got back from overseas—with rare exceptions such as the Thursday night in 1947 when Danny had been born. Usually, Faye looked forward to these nights out, but this time something was wrong. Danny tried to listen without being too obvious about it. Eddie Mathews, Braves; Gus Triandos, Orioles.

"They talk about boxing," Faye said, stubbing out her cigarette, "or they talk about chickens. I'm tired of listening to them."

She nodded as though agreeing with what her old friend Irma was saying at the other end of the line. Faye and Irma had been friends almost as long as Myron and Si, but oh no, the Adlers never had dinner with Irma and her husband Gil because Myron couldn't stand Gil, the stock broker. Well, Faye wasn't so crazy about Si either. Si knew too much about her husband that Faye didn't know, and he would exchange looks with Myron that she didn't like at all. Plus Si seemed amused by her in a way that she found extremely irritating. The big oaf. If he's so smart, how come he had to be a prizefighter half his life? Got hit in the head one too many times when he was the famous Kid Sunday.

"So how's Gil?" Faye asked. She nodded some more. "Nu? My Myron too. For his mother, there's time. For taking the boys horseback riding, for fishing with Si, for cards there's time."

When Faye hung up, she stared at the floor without saying anything. Danny could see that her eyes were working their way systematically along the hallway toward where he had the cards spread. If she was upset by the phone call, it might not be good when she saw them, but now it was too late to get them picked up.

But when she saw him, Faye smiled. "Come over here," she said.

Danny started to pick up his baseball cards, but his mother said, "Now, sweetheart." He dropped them and walked to her; even though she'd said it nicely, he knew what 'Now' meant. Sure it was a risk to leave the cards spread out, but that was a longer range risk than ignoring a 'Now.'

Faye opened her arms and he came close for a hug. She kissed him, then held him at arms length and asked, "Why don't you go outside and play in the lot? You haven't been out after school for days. What's the matter?"

"Nothing." He didn't want to say he thought it was too dangerous. From his window, The Mad Bomber could see the lot where he and his friends played stickball.

"Well, something's wrong." She stroked Danny's back. "I was coming home yesterday and all your friends were playing in the lot. Bruce even asked me if you were being punished. So what is it?"

"I don't know."

Danny could feel his mother stiffen. She didn't like to hear 'I don't know' but he couldn't think of anything else to say without telling a serious lie, which was far more dangerous than 'I don't know.'

"Daniel Adler, now you tell me what's going on."

Without knowing he would, Danny began to cry. Faye put her forefinger under his chin and lifted his face.

"Do you have to go out tonight?" he asked.

"Of course. We go out with Si and Gloria every other Thursday night, you know that. Mrs. Auer will be here to stay with you."

Danny's crying became more intense. He tried to hide his face in Faye's bosom.

"Now stop that." She shoved him back and looked in his eyes. "Oh my God, this is more of that Mad Bomber nonsense, isn't it?" Danny was lost in his tears, almost hysterical now. "Isn't it?"

He nodded his head.

"What am I going to do with you?" Danny tried to pull away from her. "Stop it this minute!" she said.

She turned in her seat and picked up the phone. Holding onto his arm with her left hand, she tucked the phone under her jaw and dialed with her right. When she was through dialing, she let him go and put her left forefinger across the cradle to disconnect the call, but Danny didn't see her do that.

"Hello?" she said. "Is this King's County Hospital? Good. Please connect me with the psychiatric ward. Thank you." She was not looking at Danny any more. He had backed away from her and was leaning against the hallway wall.

"Yes, this is Faye Adler of Lenox Road. I have a boy here who simply cannot behave himself. That's right. Crying all the time, makes a mess of his room, will not ever obey his parents. Oh, that's wonderful, you have room for him. Right next to The Mad Bomber? I see. Just a moment."

She held her right hand over the receiver and found Danny with her eyes. He was sitting with his back to the wall, watching her, his nose and chin a mass of mucous and tears. She raised her brows.

"Well?" she whispered. "Are you ready to control yourself?"

Danny nodded. He was afraid to move a muscle, afraid even to wipe his face though he knew his mother hated the way he must look. Faye slowly closed her eyes as though thinking her decision over carefully. If she didn't take him now, there might not be room next time. She removed her hand from the receiver.

"All right, will you hold that room for him for the next few days? His name is Daniel Adler. Yes, I'll call you back if we need it, thank you."

She hung up and folded her arms across her chest, watching him. Danny reached toward his nose but stopped, knowing he had no place to wipe his hands. He sniffled once and swallowed, getting himself under control. Faye continued to watch him in silence.

When he had calmed down, Danny got to his feet and made his way to the bathroom for some kleenex. He washed his face, dried, and went to his bedroom.

"Why don't you go outside to play now?" Faye called.

"Ok," Danny said.

9

Practice

MYRON HAD TWO box seats behind the Dodgers dugout, about fifteen rows back, for Sunday's game against the Giants. The game wouldn't mean much to the Giants; they were almost twenty games out and had no chance for the pennant. But the Dodgers needed every win to hold off the Braves. It would be Craig for the Bums against Al Worthington. Not exactly the pitching duel of the decade, but Myron was excited. It would be great to be out in the September sun, to be over in Pigtown again, to stand in that incredible Ebbets Field rotunda underneath the chandelier with its baseball bat arms and baseball globes.

Myron hadn't spoken to Faye about the game. She hated baseball. Never wanted to go to the ballpark and wouldn't have gotten up in time anyway. He also hadn't said anything about the game to the boys, since he only had two tickets and they would both want to come. Couldn't a guy take a Sunday to himself once in a while? Couldn't a guy, which he works six days a week, twelve/thirteen hours a day, never takes a vacation, couldn't he have an afternoon to himself? Besides, Myron wanted to spend a couple hours with Si Sabbeth. They were seeing less and less of each other, especially now that Faye had gotten it into her head that Si didn't care for her. Well, he didn't, that was true enough; but Myron hadn't noticed that Si was rude or acting any differently toward her. He wasn't crazy about Si's wife either, but that didn't stop them from eating dinner together.

So of course first thing Sunday morning Si called, ignoring the dreadful risk of waking Faye up, and canceled out on Myron. Si's father-in-law had had a stroke during the night, it was touch and go, Si had to be with Gloria. All right, Myron could understand that, something comes up with the family. He'd send flowers in the morning.

Myron hung up and tiptoed into the living room instead of going back to bed, hoping the boys hadn't been awakened by the phone or by his hurtling past their door to answer it. He sat in his easy chair. This called for a pipe, not a cigar. The meerschaum that his sister Charlotte brought back from somewhere for him, it drew pretty well. He stuffed Mixture No. 79 into the bowl, tamped it all down, lit the pipe and nearly flipped out of the chair when Richard materialized next to it and said, "Can I come?"

"Jesus Christ, Rick. Don't ambush me like that. What the hell are you, an Indian scout or something?"

"Sorry. I heard you on the phone."

"How? I mean, I said maybe two words and both of those I whispered."

"I've been really good, Dad, haven't I? No trouble at school or anything. Besides, the Giants are playing and I'm the one who thinks Willie Mays is great, Danny likes Mickey Mantle better. I think you should take *me* to the game."

Myron sucked on his pipe and looked at Richard, their faces reflected in each other's eyeglasses. "I don't get it. How did you know I even had tickets to the game?"

Richard looked over at the drapes, then at the sofa with its upholstery that matched the drapes. "Also, Danny's so little, he'll just want you to buy him peanuts and hot dogs all day and you won't get to watch any of the game."

"I thought maybe I'd ask Uncle Red."

"He's in Italy."

"What're you talking about?"

"With Aunt Sasha. I heard Ma mention it last week on the phone. And that place where Sasha went to school, The Sore Bone, they're going there too."

"Italy, huh? Did you know that's where the marble comes from, which it's in the rotunda there at Ebbets Field?"

"Yeah, of course I knew that. That's another reason I want to come, to see the rotunda. So can I, what do you say?"

"Danny'll be very upset, I take you and not him. Maybe I oughta just go alone."

Richard was trying not to whine. He knew his father didn't like it and anyway, whining seemed inappropriate for a teenager. Still, there was a ballgame at stake.

"He gets to do all the special things," Richard said, trying to sound monotonous and calm, like the lawyer who'd visited them twice the last month to talk about the chicken market.

"I'll think about it. Meanwhile, get your brother up. Quietly, right? And get dressed, the two of you. We'll go to the diner for breakfast, maybe drop by see your grandma Sophia for an hour, which she hasn't seen you boys in a month."

■

Around noon, as Myron and Richard were heading toward the door, Faye sat bolt upright in bed, staring down the hall at them, and said, "Oh, no: You're not leaving me with him all afternoon. No sir, not on a Sunday while you two go off to a ballgame."

They froze in their tracks. Myron could not understand how everybody seemed to know what he was planning to do when he hadn't told a soul.

He turned to look back at his wife sitting among her pillows and wrapped in her blankets. He'd never understand how she could sleep with all that hardware in her hair.

Richard refused to budge. He continued standing where he'd stopped, facing the door and simply not acknowledging the conversation that was taking place behind him. However, through the closed door of the bedroom he shared with Danny, Richard could hear his brother crying. He could make a lot of noise for such a little kid.

"We'll be back in plenty time for dinner," Myron said. "We'll go out to Lundy's, have the Shore Dinner, a couple brandy Alexanders, all right? Hell, go back to sleep, Faye, you'll just be getting dressed by the time we get home."

"One: do not tell me when to sleep and when to get up, thank you very much Mr. Big Shot Butcher. Two: do not leave me with a crying little *pisher* on a Sunday while you go gallivanting around Brooklyn like a child yourself. And three: if anyone's going to the baseball match with you, I am."

"Game."

"What?"

"It's a baseball game, not a match, and you don't wanna go."

"Richard, take off your jacket and hang it up. Go to your room and play with Danny, you've made him very upset."

Richard didn't move. She couldn't see him because Myron was in the way, so she didn't know if he was weakening or trembling with anger or making faces at her.

"Did you hear me, young man?"

He still didn't move. Myron put a hand behind him to hold Richard in place.

"We gotta leave," Myron said.

"No you don't!"

"The game starts in an hour. We gotta find a place to park and Rick wants to see the warmups, the Knot-Hole Gang, get a hot dog." He turned away, nudging Richard toward the door. "We'll be back after."

Faye flung the blankets aside and struggled to get out of bed. But the mattress was too soft for her to make quick progress. She stopped, regained her balance, and said, "I said No. You. Don't."

"Bye."

"Bye, Ma."

■

Top of the fourth, still no score. It was a good game. The Dodgers couldn't hit Worthington at all, five strike outs already. Craig was wild but he was getting himself out of trouble every inning, even though Mueller had come too close to the Schaefer Beer sign with his double. The crowd had stayed noisy since the first pitch, they showed no sign of quieting down and the Dodger Sym-Phoney was in great form.

Myron took a miniature bottle of Dewar's out of his jacket pocket while the Dodgers infielders threw the ball around. He worked at the cork with his pocket knife. Richard opened a second bag of peanuts. He loved to suck on the salty shells till they were soft and work them open with his teeth. His feet were already buried in a mound of soggy shells.

Foster Castleman stepped up to hit, digging himself into the batter's box as though he were a big time slugger instead of a .226 hitter. Castleman lifted off his hat and scratched the top of his crew cut head hard. If Faye were sitting there, she'd tell Richard that Castleman probably had lice in his hair because he didn't shampoo after every game. As Myron lifted the little bottle to his lips, Richard lifted his scorecard, folded into a funnel, and booed Castleman.

"I could hit better than this guy," he said to his father.

"Holy shit!"

Richard looked over at Myron. His father might be coarse and rough, but Richard didn't often hear him curse. And lookit: the old man wasn't even watching the ball game, he was staring over Richard's shoulder at the aisle. Richard turned to see his mother leading Danny by the hand down toward the dugout. About six rows from the field, they began moving sideways toward two empty seats in the middle of the row. People had to stand to let them pass, leaning this way and that so as not to miss the next pitch.

They were not only at the game, they had better seats.

"I'll be God damned," Myron said.

Richard was too stunned to speak. He popped two peanuts in his mouth and watched Castleman hit a grounder to Reese at short. Pee Wee, whom Richard felt was a good family friend, fielded it cleanly and threw on to Hodges for the out. Richard didn't even mark the play in his scorecard.

At the end of the inning, Myron and Richard watched Danny stand up on his seat to cheer. Faye's head was turned toward the Dodgers dugout as though she thought her friend Irma might be in there with the players and would walk out in a moment. She seemed hypnotized. But when Danny started to turn on his seat to see if he could find his father and brother, her hand shot out and grabbed him like a line drive.

■

When Danny got home from school on Monday, his mother was talking on the telephone. She blew a silent kiss in his direction, raised her forefinger to her lips warning him that she didn't want to hear any noise, then pointed with it down the hall toward the bedrooms.

That was where Danny wanted to be anyhow. He put his books away and got his bat out of the closet. It felt light in his hands, as though having seen the Dodgers play yesterday had given him new strength. He took the bat into his parents' bedroom, where there was a full-length mirror behind the door that he shut quietly.

It had come to him clearly yesterday at Ebbets Field. If he truly wanted to play center field for the Dodgers after Duke Snider retired, he'd have to become a switch hitter. It wasn't enough to be a good right handed hitter; he'd have to hit lefty too, so they would never want to take him out of a game, no matter who was pitching.

He took his normal stance in front of the mirror, waggled the bat a few times and swung. Perfect. He knew his right handed swing was absolutely level because he'd practiced it every day for two years till he got it smooth and balanced. His head stayed still and his eyes never left the ball, which he could see more clearly than if it had truly been there. He swung again. Perfect.

After ten swings, including two that were designed to smack the ball behind a runner into right field, he took a deep breath and switched around. For a while, Danny just stood there with the bat resting on his left shoulder, delighted by the reversed image of himself. The bat was black from the handle to halfway up the meat, where it was the color of pale wood. He thought he looked as good as Mickey Mantle, the great switch hitting centerfielder whose exploits Danny intended to eclipse, probably by 1974.

He pumped the bat a few times, then did one slow-motion swing just to see what it looked and felt like. He thought he'd better choke up a little to give himself more control instead of holding the bat down by the handle, as he did right handed. But it didn't look very sharp to choke up, like he wasn't strong enough to swing hard.

Going into a crouch, Danny focused on his own form crouching in front of him, then slowly imagined beyond himself, looking past his neck and head, until he could see the pitcher deep within the glass. At first he thought it was Sal Maglie glaring down at him, the infamous 'Barber' who starred for the Giants and liked to shave batters close with a fastball. Yeah, well that didn't scare Daniel Adler one bit. Danny took in the stubbled visage, the glower, and just waggled his bat in response. But wait, it couldn't be Maglie. Maglie was with the Dodgers now and so was Danny. For an instant, he realized that the jaw and glare were those of his father waiting to deliver the pitch, probably a sizzling curve that looked as though it would hit Danny in the head and, when he ducked away, would jump over the plate for a strike.

Danny stepped into the pitch and swung. The bat flew out of his hands and shattered the faces looking back at him.

10

Twilight Time

THE ADLERS MOVED from Brooklyn the year the Dodgers moved from Brooklyn. The small barrier island where they settled off the southern end of Long Island wasn't California, but it might as well have been. It was even named Long Beach. What did the Adlers know about living in a house? What did they know about tides and island life? There were gutters and downspouts, laurel hedges, leaves on window sills, pruning shears hung on a hook by the door. What did they know about living with no one above them and no one below?

But the world was changing fast in 1957. You could make telephone calls to Europe, you could fly in a jet, you could get rid of your ice box and clothes line because there were machines for everything. Soon there were satellites in orbit. Foreigners won the Little League World Series. Supermarkets were coming, tossing aside the small markets like timber in a volcano's blow down zone.

And Myron Adler was going to sell women's clothes.

■

"Sit, sit," Sophia Adler said to her son. Her eyes were closed as if in prayer.

She was completely gray now. From cloud to ash to iron—her hair and eyes, her teeth, her skin and fingernails, certainly all her clothing—with the exception of black ankle-high shoes and, on the sabbath, a fuchsia scarf her late husband had given her.

Myron hung up his jacket and went to his customary dinnertime seat opposite his sister Charlotte's empty place. Sophia was at the table's head, where her husband would have sat if he were still alive. She looked off toward the window as though waiting for Emanuel's spirit to arrive. Her hands were folded where a soup bowl would normally be steaming.

"Where's Joe?" Myron asked.

"He called. The guy who drives a truck for him, that Willie, he had a wreck over by Avenue X, a bad one. Two cars, he hit. The way that man drinks, I told Joseph a thousand times already, it's a miracle he hasn't had a wreck before and killed ten innocent people already."

Myron nodded. "He all right?"

"He's upset. Nu? The truck's a total loss. It was Willie's entire fault and the insurance is going to be a nightmare."

"I meant Willie."

"Who knows from Willie? I only pray your brother gets rid of the man. That's what your father would have done, may he rest in peace."

Myron nodded again and looked away. He didn't smell any food cooking and that confused him. His mother hadn't mentioned dinner when she asked him to stop by after work, but it was dinnertime and Myron had assumed she'd be feeding him. He'd called Faye, who wasn't happy to hear she would be eating with Danny and Richard by herself. "Sugar made a tongue, special for you," she had said. "The kids don't like tongue."

Now Myron looked back at his mother to find her staring at him. "What, Mama?"

"Business. You're not listening to me. I said How is the business these days?"

"You know. Things are tight. I got the Italians asking for more money over there, they're gonna protect me from trouble; I got the big markets coming over here, they charge two-thirds what I charge and never mind the birds have been dead for a week or whatever; plus which I got more customers moving to The Island every day, they're moving to Jersey, they're moving upstate. It's tight, Mama, how business is."

"For your brother, too." Sophia sighed. "Even in wholesale now."

"So what else is new? I think I can still manage. Why?"

"Because I been talking to your brother; I been talking to Georgie Nye, does my taxes; I been talking to that lawyer your father went to before he died, Mr. Betzdorf. We're spread very thin, is why."

"I don't follow you. Who's spread thin?"

"Mashie, I can't keep up with both the wholesale and the retail businesses any more. I gotta make a choice here. Neither you nor Joseph's doing good."

Myron looked down at his empty place-setting. Why didn't he see this coming? Which it's the same thing as 1936. He should have bought Joe out when their father died in '40. He—and not Joe—should have owned the building with his mother. Now they were going to sell it and force him to close the business.

"Mama, what am I gonna do? You and Joe sell the building out from under me, I can't go into business with him. There's no room. So you think I should maybe open a brain surgery business or something, I'm good with the knife?"

"Sell is not the first choice."

"Jesus Christ! You wanna raise my rent?" He wished there was something he could put in his mouth to chew. "This is like what the Italians do. I can't afford any more rent, Mama. You know that."

Sophia stood up slowly, holding Myron's gaze. She turned away from him and went into the kitchen. He heard her banging around in there, getting out a pot, filling it with water and setting it on the stove to boil. This wasn't cooking, that much Myron knew. This was anger.

When she came back in, it looked as though she had switched faces, as though she'd opened the freezer and found one that had set into a stony mask. The mouth didn't move.

"You're right," she said. "Sell is better."

■

Vito and Teresa Bellamonte loved to entertain guests for dinner. Their dining room was vast, with a table that opened to accommodate leaf after leaf till the room bulged. The table was covered by a tablecloth that must have taken Teresa a decade to embroider. The Bellamontes would put out an antipasto heavy on meat and cheeses, maybe some conch or mussels, baked clams, then a couple meats from one of Vito's markets, a salad for cleaning the palate. Chianti by the gallon. They'd have cannoli fresh from the bakery he owned and endless cups of coffee. In the living room later, Sambuca with three beans in it.

With his brother Louie, Vito Bellamonte now owned not only every meat and fish market in the neighborhood, but also Myron Adler's chicken market, the bakery, a florist and three produce markets. He'd dreamt about acquiring Myron's place for years—three whole blocks now—and tonight's dinner was to celebrate the realizing of that dream.

When the Adlers walked in at six on the dot, Danny didn't see anyone he knew. It was amazing enough that his father had gotten his mother to be ready on time; to find a face he recognized was asking too much. His father hugged all the strangers and made introductions, but Danny couldn't concentrate on names because the food smells were so overwhelmingly wonderful. He could eat everything he saw! The Bellamontes fussed over him. They stroked Danny's neatly parted and slicked-down hair, pinched his cheek the way his Grandfather Jules would, squeezed his tiny biceps and kept pulling him onto their laps to stuff bits of antipasto into his mouth.

Above the clamor, he heard the doorbell ring and saw his Grandmother Sophia enter. She kissed Myron, removed her coat and held it out for one of the Bellamonte's sons to take away. Her face looked grim, as though Sophia knew ahead of time that red wine would be spilled on the creamy carpet. She kept her hands folded beneath her bosom during the introductions and had only nods from across the room for her grandchildren and daughter-in-law. Danny didn't like the look of things just then, but the hubbub continued and he was distracted again.

No sooner had Sophia settled in an armchair then the doorbell rang again and Danny saw his Uncle Joseph come in. He shook Myron's hand, shook Vito Bellamonte's hand, kissed Teresa Bellamonte's hand, and almost sprinted to his mother's side. He knelt next to her armchair, patted her hand, then stood to survey the room. Catching Danny's eye, he winked and pantomimed the stuffing of an olive in his mouth.

Something strange was going on, Danny understood that, but no one had explained to him what it was. He tried to keep track of his parents and their tempers, but so much was going on that he had trouble sensing them. His mother sat perched on the edge of the sofa, a plate of stuffed mushrooms and asparagus in her lap, her lips alternately flattened to a sort of smile and then puckered as though drawing on a cigarette. She was talking to several Bellamonte women at once. Danny's father was laughing over in a corner, talking to Vito Bellamonte out of the side of his mouth. Danny could see the ash from his father's cigar grow longer and then fall to the carpet, but no one seemed to care. They were all so cheerful, yet they seemed ready to cry. Except his brother Richard, who stood near the table nibbling slices of salami and cantaloupe wrapped in some kind of ham. He just seemed like Richard.

Suddenly someone stormed into the chair beside Danny, pushing him over against the arm and squashing him like a beetle. Danny tried to wriggle out but couldn't. He tried to turn his head to see who it was, but that didn't work either. He hoped he wouldn't throw up.

"Hey, whaddya say?" said John Bellamonte. He was the family's oldest child, a boy of fifteen, and he took up a lot of room for someone so skinny. "I hear you're a baseball fan."

Danny tried to straighten out. His arm was twisted up around his head and his knees were mashed together. It was hard to breathe.

"Yeah," he said into the chair's wing.

"Who you root for?"

"Dodgers." Danny's voice didn't sound right, as though it were echoing around in his head.

"Good for you. I thought maybe you were for the Yankees or something."

"Nah." His foot was starting to tingle. "I like Mickey Mantle, though."

"So you wanna see my collection?"

The only way Danny could move his arm was to put it around John's back. He also freed his leg and let it dangle over John's. No one was coming to rescue him. At least he could breathe now.

"What kind of collection?"

"You'll see."

"Where is it?"

"Upstairs." John sprang out of the chair, releasing Danny to topple over into the space he'd just vacated. "C'mon."

Danny sat up and looked around. No one was paying any attention to him and they all seemed to be all right. He still couldn't figure out what was going on, but no one appeared to be in any immediate danger. And besides, he'd like to see whatever it was that John had up there.

Balls, that's what. John had about a dozen dirty old baseballs on a shelf above his bed. Several of them had torn seams and a few were lined with cracks. They all had writing on them. God, Danny wished Richard was up here to see this. A library of baseballs.

"Here, lookit. I got this one off the bat of Ted Kluszewski back of home plate two years ago, a foul ball almost took my hands off. This one I caught in the left field bleachers, a homer by Shuba, I think it was in '52. This one's Sal Yvars, you ever heard of him?"

Danny couldn't believe his eyes. All he could do was nod his head, without taking his eyes off the balls.

"Right," John said. "Yvars is a *Paesano*, you gotta love the guy, but he didn't hit too many homers and I got one."

"What's this?" Danny pointed to the last ball on the shelf, which looked in danger of falling off.

"I'm a little embarrassed to tell you. This friend of mine, Paulie Quinto, he had two tickets to a Yankees game last year. So he took me along, I mean I'da never gone to the Stadium if it was up to me, I'm with the National League all the way. Anyhow, this is a homer by your boy, Mantle."

Danny held it close and read the writing. 'Home run to right, Mickey Mantle, bottom of the eighth two out, Yankee Stadium, July 1956.'

"How come they look so worn out?"

"Hell, kid, me and my friends play with them, that's why."

"You mean you play baseball with these. In games?"

"Sure. They don't do much good sitting over my bed."

Danny was stunned. If he caught a ball, he'd never touch it. He'd put it on his desk top or on his book case and guard it with his life. Like his mother did with almost everything, he might even wrap the ball in plastic to preserve it.

He handed the ball back, shaking his head in wonder. "This is great."

"Go ahead," John said. "Keep it."

"You mean it?"

Danny looked at him to see whether John was kidding. He held his breath. John smiled at him.

"You bet," he said. Then he put an arm over Danny's shoulders and led him downstairs to the table.

After dinner ended, after drinks and smokes and toasts, after the exchange of small gifts between Teresa Bellamonte and Faye and many good wishes in English, Italian and Yiddish, the Adlers finally left. While they hovered at the door to put on their coats, Danny was in a daze. The Bellamontes had offered him a sip of Sambuca and his parents even let him take it. Vito walked the Adlers to their car and embraced both Faye and Myron at the same time. He patted Danny on the head and shook Richard's hand. Then he held the door open for Faye and smacked the trunk as the Buick pulled away from the curb. Danny fell back against his seat with an enormous smile on his face.

The drive home was silent. Danny couldn't tell if his parents were happy or sad or angry, and normally that would worry him. He'd learned to be vigilant of their moods and adapt his behavior accordingly. Maybe they were just tired. He kept hefting the baseball that John Bellamonte gave him, tossing it up an inch or two and catching it again. Amazing! A ball hit by The Mick, and John had just given it to him like that, for nothing.

Out of the darkness and silence, Richard suddenly snatched the ball in mid-air. Danny had forgotten his brother was even there.

"Hey!" Danny said.

"What's this?"

"It's a baseball that Mickey Mantle hit. John Bellamonte gave it to me. He caught it at Yankee Stadium."

"Dad, did you hear that? Danny stole a baseball from the Bellamontes."

"He what?"

"Danny stole this baseball from John Bellamonte's room." Richard held the ball up so his father could see it illuminated in the rearview mirror by the headlights of cars. "See?"

"Did you take that?" Myron growled.

Danny didn't know what to say. He shook his head because he couldn't find his voice.

"I asked you a question, Mister."

"John gave it to me."

Myron looked quickly into the back seat, then at Faye beside him and ahead at the traffic. Faye remained quiet, smoke wafting round her head, a cigarette jutting from the corner of her mouth.

"Bellamontes don't give nobody nothing," Myron said. "You hadda take it."

"I didn't take it, Dad. I swear."

"Get rid of that thing, Rick. I don't wanna see it, ever."

Richard rolled down his window and tossed the ball toward the gutter. It happened so fast, Danny didn't have time to cry out.

■

"Or short men," Myron said.

"What?" Faye put down her knife and fork. She looked at her husband, but leaned towards Danny and pointed at his plate. He was not eating his peas fast enough.

"I go into any clothing store, I buy a suit which I have to wait a week for the merchandise to be altered. How about a line of suits for short men?"

"I don't understand what you're worried about. You can work for Red the rest of your life."

"I don't wanna work for your brother the rest of my life, all right? Nothing against Red, but I have to think past this here, which I been running my own place since I was 19."

"Mr. Business Man. Maybe you could learn something from my brother if you stick around him awhile. Daniel, eat your peas, they're getting cold."

"Just listen to me." Myron pointed his knife at her. "This is a good idea. Saves money on cloth, for instance. Maybe they can cut an extra pair of pants out of the material, which it gets all used up on pants for a regular size guy. And you probably don't need a tailor because a short guy's gonna have short arms, he can wear the suit as is."

"But I thought you knew, darling. You're going to be selling women's clothes for my brother, not men's. Maybe you should plan to develop a line of clothes for short women."

Richard finally looked up from his plate. He smiled and said, "Yeah. How about you sell short skirts? I'd love to see that."

Myron slowly turned away from Faye and stared at Richard. "What did you say?"

"Nothing."

"You think this is funny, huh?"

Richard froze. He had a spoonful of peas in front of his mouth, but was looking down into his plate and didn't seem to notice them.

"Leave him alone, Myron," Faye said. "It was just a joke."

"A joke?" Myron leaned over and swatted Richard backhand across the face. The peas went flying over his shoulder and hit the wall. Danny watched as a few stuck to the wall, then slipped down. He tried not to laugh. Then he tried not to cry, as the inside of his nose started tingling and his eyes filled with tears.

■

The night before they moved, sleeping amid masses of boxes that crept up his bare walls and blocked the faint starlight that used to come through his window, Danny had a dream. It seemed to last through the entire night.

The living room in their new house was bare in the middle, its oak floor gleaming in a strange light. Furniture was shoved around the room's perimeter—his father's easy chair covered now in a sand-colored fabric that looked soft as a dune, their old sofa redone to match it, a glass coffee table with chrome legs reaching for the ceiling and a rocker in some blonde wood he had never seen before. The thick drapes were tied back to let in a violet sunset glow and sabbath candles flickered in saucers that seemed to float above the window ledges.

Faye stood in one corner of the room, swaying to an inner music. Her hair was feathery and natural, a rich brown color instead of the Champagne Beige she'd had it tinted last month to replace the Golden Apricot. It shone. She softly set the Victrola's needle arm down and turned to smile at Myron through the static, spreading her feathered boa like an angel's wings before flying across the room into his arms. He caught her, holding her above his head a moment where she floated, breathless, before he lowered her to the floor. *Heavenly shades of night are falling, it's twilight time.* Their hands touched and fingers twined, the room suffused with ocean mist from just down the street, they were moving together to the smooth blend of the singers' voices, and Danny could see that love was in their eyes, their separate days were given up to a mellow music, and then they were twirling, *together, at last at twilight time.*

■

The house was white stucco, with a red tile roof that bled down the walls when it rained. There were front and back porches where sand blown north from the beach collected. There was a glass pole near the back porch designed to frustrate woodpeckers. A screened patio overlooked the large grassy yard that spread out from the back door, surrounded on its three other sides by thick hedges. A perfect miniature football field, except that the house's owners didn't want the Adlers to set foot on it.

The owners, Bert and Ev Haas, lived in the Bronx but spent their summers and occasional weekends in a small apartment in the basement of the house. Ev Haas reminded Danny of a slightly younger version of his Grandmother Sophia. Her black hair and eyes, the dark hollows of her cheeks and throat, and her black clothes hadn't yet faded to gray, but her body and face shared the same frozen, downturning cast and he knew that a smile might shatter her. Squeezed into the unfinished part of the basement, among pipes and drains and mysterious mechanical equipment that only Bert Haas could touch, there was a pool table beneath a single naked bulb. Some nights after dinner, Myron would take the boys downstairs for a game. In a corner beneath the window, they found the top of a ping-pong table that could be laid across the pool table when the Adlers got tired of eight-ball or nine-ball pocket.

For the first time since Danny had been born, he and Richard had separate rooms. Richard was eighteen; he said he wasn't moving anywhere if he still had to share a room with his ten year-old brother. Bad enough he had to leave Brooklyn and all his friends, the neighborhood he'd spent his whole life in, bad enough he would have to commute to work every day like his father. A room of his own or so long, folks.

Danny missed his brother's raspy breath in the darkness as he fell asleep. He missed Richard's presence when the nightmares came, his brother's half-blind stare in the morning light, the smell of his clothes in the closet. But he didn't miss the punches that bruised his thighs and shoulders, the savage noogies, the smoking cigarette placed casually on the edge of Danny's desk to annoy him while he played dice baseball. He was learning to be alone through the night.

In the sunken living room, the Adlers had a fancy chair no one sat in sequestered by the fireplace no one lit. It was a crown-topped, button-backed Hitchcock that came from Franklin Delano Roosevelt's summer house at Campobello. Faye had bought the chair at an auction, where the Roosevelts sold personal items to raise money for polio research. She loved to say that she got the chair for a song. It appeared in their house one winter afternoon, shortly after they had moved. Myron sauntered over to it when he got home from work, studied it while fitting a cigar into his brown plastic holder, nodded and never said a word about the chair.

There was a disc stuck low in its back that bore the number 75. Tucked away in a drawer of her chiffonier, Faye had a booklet which proved to any doubters that item #75, desk chair, was from the estate of Franklin Delano Roosevelt. When people came to visit their new home, she would send Danny to fetch the booklet. He never minded. She kept it beside her stash of licorice twists and if company was there, she would never bawl him out for taking one. This represented a huge victory for Danny in The Licorice Wars. Licorice twists, chocolate flavored licorice ropes, Nibs, hard candies. Faye would buy packages of licorice to set out in her various bowls, dishes and jars, always ordering Danny to leave them alone. But he loved licorice and simply could not obey her. His approach was to raid her supplies equally—one from each container, a few from each hiding place—so as not to tip her off. Of course, he was sure she always knew when he'd staged an assault because she probably counted the stores late at night after he'd gone to sleep. Raided licorice cost Danny countless hours of lost television, of afternoons indoors instead of playing ball with his friends, of evenings when no one in the house would talk to him. Faye didn't particularly like licorice herself; chocolate was her passion. And when she bought a kind of licorice that Danny didn't care for, like those raspberry flavored mutations, she'd throw them away and never buy them again. He wondered who the licorice was for. His father was diabetic, Richard was a gum chewer, and Danny never saw a guest take any. He guessed they were not for anyone so much as for the War effort.

When the chair first arrived, its cane seat sagged where the President had sat. Danny imagined him writing at his desk up there at Campobello Island, dressed in a dark suit even though it was August, a cigarette in its holder clamped between his teeth. He would look up from the paper, his jaw jutting cloudward, to seek inspiration by gazing at the gorgeous Bay of Fundy dotted with all those other little islands. This was a place he had come to since he was a child, since he was Danny's age. Danny could see himself there, waiting to swim with Franklin in the cold water. Their faces were drenched because of the summer heat, but he would be done with his work soon.

Danny examined every detail of the chair. Its lavish arms were scarred by ash. The seat front was nicked, he assumed, by Roosevelt's braces. Its black paint was badly faded. From across the room, it seemed twisted slightly to the left, as though looking for the door. Faye couldn't stand it. If the chair was going to be in her living room, the chair was going to look right.

She had it tightened to a timeless silence. She painted it over in deep black, covering the wreaths of golden flowers that had twined up its limbs. She decorated it with stripes instead. A black leather cushion was glued to the chair back. Another was placed on the seat, its tassels dangling to the floor. The tapered legs, turned in a dozen rings, were hidden from the window's light when she placed the chair near the fireplace. Daily, she swept dust from the fireplace floor with a broom intended for ashes.

Danny always imagined that area of the living room as cordoned off, existing behind velvet ropes strung from the piano to the patio door. He came to grasp that the big white house was one in which life was arrayed rather than lived, that unlike Richard he would never try to sit in the Roosevelt chair, and that his mother would retouch a Picasso if its colors didn't go with her living room.

He had fantasies of stripping down the finish on the Roosevelt chair. He would restore the original detail, loosen the chair's tongue until the cane would sing under his weight. It would take skills he didn't have and couldn't imagine acquiring, but that wouldn't stop him from fantasizing. He could feel the bite of the sandpaper. Before long, it would be Danny and Franklin again in the cold waters of the Bay of Fundy. He would sit in the chair and read while being warmed by the first fire ever lit inside his mother's home. He would eat his dinner in the chair: oozy food, purple food. He would drag it out to the backyard or keep it in his room, sitting there like the President waiting for inspiration.

■

Myron still got up before dawn every workday. He drove his new white Buick into Manhattan's garment district instead of the Brooklyn Battery, but again he was the one who unlocked the doors in the morning. He was the one who brought the place he worked in to life daily. He loved puttering around in silence for an hour before his co-workers arrived.

It was possible at that hour for Myron to imagine the walls lined with coops instead of racks from which dresses hung. Their silence took some getting used to; he kept waiting for the dresses to cackle and squawk when he walked in. Deeper into the shop were shelves where skins were stacked—the leathers from which Raskin coats and dresses would be cut—and in one corner there were piles of furs for collars and cuffs. Sometimes a few of the furs would seem to be alive, their soft hairs blowing in a breeze from the windows Myron would open.

Raskin Fabrics occupied two floors of an old building. All of the upper floor and three quarters of the lower was factory space. Getting off the elevator on the lower floor, a retail customer was immediately in the showroom, which then sealed when the elevator doors closed. Mirrored walls and bright lights made the room feel enormous. It was not open to everyone, only to those friends of Red's or his wholesale customers to whom he chose to give special favors. And this was Myron's clientele. When he wasn't waiting on them, or preparing to wait on them, he supervised the cutters and blockers and stitchers on the upper floor.

Red Raskin greeted him in the same way every morning. His brother-in-law hunted through the factory and showroom until he found Myron, put a well-manicured hand to his thick neck and drew Myron close to his chest. The two men hugged quickly, Myron's face pressing against Red's tie, and clapped each other's backs several times.

"Thanks, Mashie. I wanted to have you with me for the last ten years."

"Good to be here."

"So what's today?"

"Today we got that Mrs. Laszio Szabo at one. She's going home to Hungry tomorrow, which she needs a trunkful of new clothes to take along. So this morning me and the boys are pulling together some winter outfits to show her. Then there's your pal Desjardins at three-thirty."

"Well I'm not here when Desjardins comes, you mind? He's bringing his wife, you remember Lola."

"I remember Lola."

And he certainly didn't mind. Lola Desjardins was tall and lean like a tennis player, her smile loose as her walk. He'd seen her a month or so earlier, when Red and Gus Desjardins were talking in Red's office one evening. Lola sashayed off the elevator to drag her husband to dinner and the theater, gracing Myron with a relaxed, lopsided smile when she saw him checking skins in the corner. Yeah, it'd be nice to help her out. Myron didn't even mind Mrs. Szabo at one, whom he thought of as the lost Gabor sister. Selling dresses turned out to be a lot like selling poultry, only you got through two, maybe three customers a day instead of a hundred. But then, a Raskin suit'll cost you a bit more than a pullet for supper. This is just what you need for that party, Mrs. Szabo, and if you pack it away properly you'll still have something left over for next week.

At exactly one o'clock, the shop wall swished open and Mrs. Laszio Szabo marched off the elevator carrying a shopping bag that looked ready to burst. Myron was standing against the mirror directly in her line of view so she wouldn't have to look around for him and be confused by all the smiling images of herself. She would never make a morning appointment because she couldn't possibly be finished with breakfast before noon. In fact, on the phone she'd been slightly irritated to be rushed into a one o'clock, which was still morning to her in all but the most technical of senses. However, since Myron was booked for the remainder of the afternoon and she would be on a ship for Europe the next day, one would have to do. It was still possible to smile.

"Hiya, Mrs. Szabo. Nice day."

"On the Danube, perhaps. In Manhattan it is fit only for penguins today."

"Well, you'll be on that Danube there pretty soon, Mrs. Szabo."

"You may call me Ibolya, Myron darling."

"Right." Myron would sooner try pronouncing *Magyar Koztarsasag*. "You wanna cup coffee, a shot of schnapps or something?"

"What I want is what I told you on the phone I want, and as quickly as possible. A half dozen winter suits, a stole, two hats. Two suits for the trips to Debrecen where my Laszio is from, the remainder for Budapest—day and night—and of course Prague. Laszio cannot expect me to spend a month in Hungary without taking me to Prague too, wouldn't you say, darling?"

"What's in Prague?"

Mrs. Szabo closed her eyes, put her head back, and cackled. A few seconds later, she even squawked. Myron refused to let himself imagine wringing her neck and passing her back to the plucker. He smiled back at her, waiting her out.

"You are a very funny man. I must tell Red how I approve of you. Now fetch me something to try on."

At 3:10, when Myron had hoped she would already be gone, Mrs. Szabo emerged from the dressing room and stood facing him with her hands on her hips. Perhaps it was taking so long because she combed her hair differently for each outfit. Perhaps it was because she had to wear a different pair of shoes for each. He could hear her rummaging through the shopping bag for them. Whatever the reason, he was getting anxious because he wanted to be free when Lola Desjardins arrived.

"So?" Mrs. Szabo glared at Myron as though her indecision were his fault. "In Budapest, they do not wear such colors together."

It all came to him in a flash. You don't reason with them and after two hours you don't be polite. You reach in the coop and do what you have to do.

"That's for Prague, dear."

She recoiled slightly and her eyes opened wide as though he'd smacked her. "Yes. I see." She went into the dressing room and emerged to hang the rest of the outfits one by one over hooks along the wall. "So what do you think for the opera, Myron darling?"

"That one."

She was gone, with a kiss for each cheek, by 3:25. Myron left the showroom for a quick tour of the cutting floor and a shot of Scotch. He liked the feel of leather scraps under his shoes, reminding him of the clots of feathers he was accustomed to. Picking up a few of the boldest new designs, something outrageously bright for winter wear, something layered and soft, something high on the throat, Myron arrayed them among the more conventional styles on hooks around the showroom and leaned back against the wall to wait for Lola Desjardins.

Of course she was late. Myron hated this part of the work, doing nothing but waiting, ignoring his impatience. At his market, when there were no customers he had plenty to do around the place. If he wasn't there in front to greet them, they'd shout his name into the market's echoing maw and he'd shout back *awright, be right there*. Not at Raskin Fabrics, though, not hardly. No shouting, no customers waiting.

It was a combination of his daydreaming and the suddenness with which the wall opened. One moment, Myron was seeing a wall full of coops and smelling the overwhelming odor of blood and chicken shit, the next moment this tall, lithe young woman was standing before him with her toothy grin and her hand thrust out.

"Lola Desjardins. You must be Myron Adler."

He looked up at her, shrugging himself off the wall to take the hand. It was huge, the fingers reaching to his wrist.

"Which it's my pleasure to make your acquaintance."

"I don't exactly know what I'm after, Myron. Can I call you Myron?"

"Sure, Lola." He nodded and pointed behind her. "That's why I've tooken the liberty of selecting a few items for you."

11

The Adler Family Circus

THE WINTER OF the 49-star flag was very difficult for Richard Adler. So was the spring of the St. Lawrence Seaway. It was looking like you could eliminate 1959 altogether and Richard wouldn't complain. No dates, no new friends, no progress at work. His life was his weekends, when he could drive back to the old neighborhood in Brooklyn and visit the people he'd known all his life.

At 19, he had dropped out of New York University and begun working in the children's dress industry. Faye's Uncle Maxie owned the business and gave Richard a job, starting at the bottom as an office boy, a sweeper, a go-fer just as Uncle Maxie himself had started in 1915. Maxie swore to Richard's future if he stuck it out.

"Don't take this job," Faye had told him, "if you're going to quit it like you quit everything else. I don't need you to embarrass me in front of my Uncle Maxie, thank you very much."

"Ma, it's *my* idea."

"So was delivering newspapers in the seventh grade, which lasted one week. So was painting your Aunt Birdie's kitchen when your Uncle Herb had to finish three walls and the ceiling. So was going to NYU."

Richard tore open a fresh pack of Kents and lit one before answering. He had to make her understand. "My future is in the world of dollars and cents, not school books."

"Your future, young man, is in the garbage dump if you walk out on Princess Dresses."

In the year since leaving college, Richard had gained sixty pounds. He was lonely and had nothing to do except drive all the way out to Long Beach after a day's worth of sweeping floors and running errands. He knew no one on the entire island except his contaminated family and he wasn't getting paid enough to live on his own somewhere else. So he was stuck. But he was doing well at Princess Dresses and Uncle Maxie had called Faye to tell her just that. She would have preferred that Richard stay in school, if only because she knew in her heart he would fail her and her Uncle Maxie.

Now at twelve little Danny was the family's only hope for a college degree. All he thought about, though, was being a baseball player. Faye wasn't sure what to do about that. She'd 'misplaced' his baseball card collection during the family's move from Brooklyn to Long Beach. But instead of reading the books she'd bought him, Danny was playing dice baseball games now for hours on end. With all his trades and his notebooks full of statistics, dice baseball ended up taking more of his time than the cards had. She hated the constant clicking sound of dice coming from his bedroom and the murmur of his voice announcing play-by-play. Between that and the clacking pool balls from the basement, she thought Danny was turning into a ruffian just like his father. And just like his father, he was the shortest boy in his class. Sure, he was turning out to be a wonderful little athlete, but what serious person really cares about that anyway? Danny had about as much chance to be a professional baseball player as Faye had. Who would have thought that Faye Raskin, of all people, would end up involved with a family such as this? A family of artists, maybe, scholars and diplomats, a houseful of Nobel Laureates perhaps. No, instead it's the Adler Family Circus.

In August, Richard was in an automobile accident. He fell asleep driving home from the city in the early morning hours. Good thing he wasn't on the bridge when it happened or he'd have drowned.

Richard drove a small, white Plymouth Valiant. He finally had met a woman who did occasional design work for Princess Dresses. After leaving the shop he would drive to Queens, pick her up, then drive back into Manhattan for dinner and a film.

That summer night they saw *Room at the Top*, with Simone Signoret. Debbie loved the film; Richard found it interminable. By the time he left her Queens apartment, it was 2:00. He was tired, relaxed, but felt he could drive home blindfolded since he had made the trip so often.

Though not a coffee drinker, he stopped at an all-night diner near Idlewild Airport for black coffee and two doughnuts. On the car radio, Bobby Darin sang "Mack the Knife." Richard tapped his ring on the steering wheel and sang along while he drove.

At the western edge of town, ten minutes from home, Richard plowed into the back left side of a Chevy stopped for a light and was jolted awake. He jerked the wheel as his car knocked over a fire hydrant, flooring the accelerator in his daze. The Plymouth smashed into the wall of Rothman's Deli. Only the raised cellar door, which stuck out a few feet from the wall and slowed the impact, saved him. He was hurled through the windshield and landed on his back on the sidewalk. The gearshift lever stuck out the side of his knee like a branch.

He got up, wandered toward the corner with blood pouring from cuts in his scalp. "I fell asleep. I fell asleep."

"Shut up, buddy. Just stand still and shut up." Two men had come to him from a tavern. " Or maybe you should sit down. An ambulance is on its way."

"I fell asleep."

"Will you shut up?"

The police came to the Adlers' home at 4:00 to tell them about the accident. From his bedroom at the end of the hall, Danny could hear his parents' hushed voices. Their urgency told him this might be worth getting up for.

As he walked down the hall, Danny met his father coming back from the doorway, his plaid flannel robe flapping open. He told Danny to get back to bed, then went into his bedroom to get dressed. Danny stood outside the room.

"What is it?"

"The police. Your brother's had an accident. We're going to the hospital."

"How is he? What happened?"

"Go to bed."

"Oh God, oh God," Faye moaned through clenched teeth. "Why won't they tell us what his condition is?"

"He's not dead. That they would have told us."

"Will you hurry?" Faye had put on a house coat and slippers and was ready to leave.

"Just a minute." Myron was knotting his tie carefully, looking in the mirror. He combed his hair and brushed his teeth.

"You're crazy, do you know that? Richard is lying in I-don't-know-what-kind-of-condition, and Mr. Myron Adler the clothier is dressing up."

"Control yourself for once, willya, which we'll be there in fifteen minutes."

At the hospital, Myron went quickly into the emergency room to see his son. Moments later, he strode out to speak with the nurses and various personnel. Faye stood beside the treatment room door, her back against the wall, eyes shut tightly.

Slowly, she edged her head around the jamb and peeked in at Richard. He waved to her.

"Hello, ma. I thought that was you. Come in, I'm all right." Richard lay on the table, cleaned and stitched. "Just some cuts on my head, they look bad but they're ok. It's my leg that's bad. Want to see?" He began lifting the bottom of the sheet.

"NO!" She held up her right hand, palm toward him. "I don't have to see anything. It's enough to see you're alive."

"Sorry."

"What happened?" It came out more of a moan than a question. Myron returned to the room before Richard could answer.

"We can see the car in a few days," he said. "The officer said he doesn't know how you got out alive."

"I don't remember anything."

"That's right. And don't say anything to anyone about it, big-mouth. No speeches about falling asleep at the wheel, no stories about the long night with your sweetheart. Which it's all a blank, right?

Richard came home from the hospital two weeks later. Faye plumped him up on four pillows, said, "Don't worry, you're home now," and left the room.

He settled back in bed, wondering if Debbie would really come to the house to see him, if she would climb into bed with him as she did at the hospital. Maybe he could play some games with Danny when he got home from school—*Careers* or the quick version of *Monopoly*.

There was a movement at his door. He turned to see Sugar Adams, a tray of juice and toast in her hand, smiling at him with her hip cocked against the jamb. She'd agreed to come out from Brooklyn three times a week to care for him.

"Sugar!"

"Richie, I swear, some people will do most anything to get out of work."

Sugar was the only person in the world he'd let call him Richie anymore. Seeing her face again made him forget the pain in his leg.

"How'd she talk you into coming out here?"

"Hush your mouth. Now drink this juice and don't spill any of it."

"How can I hush my mouth and drink juice at the same time, Sugar?"

"Neveryoumind."

Richard was not simple to care for. He didn't like to read, didn't want to watch daytime TV and certainly wasn't about to draw, which his mother kept suggesting. Maybe a jigsaw puzzle once in a while. The highlight of his week was *The Many Loves of Dobie Gillis*. He was by and large extremely grumpy, playing game after game of solitaire and occasionally convincing Sugar to play blackjack or poker.

In the evening, he liked to watch *The Millionaire* or *77 Sunset Strip*. A Yankee game would be on radio or TV. They had no chance to beat the White Sox this year, but the Dodgers were threatening to be back in the World Series again for the first time since '56. It sounded so strange: the Los Angeles Dodgers.

Less than six weeks after Richard was out of bed and back to work, Danny nearly drowned in a canal that was cut from the bay into the island's northern side. He'd ridden his bike to a playground by the bay, his basketball under one arm, and tried to pass between a stop sign and the curb at the canal's edge without dismounting. The bike didn't fit. The next thing Danny knew he was in the water, his bike sinking from sight, his basketball floating toward the bay, and his sodden wool jacket dragging him under.

He'd fallen about fifteen feet before hitting the surface face-first. There didn't seem to be any way to climb back up the slick wooden planks of the canal's side and he wasn't sure he could swim to the far end. But he felt strangely calm, as though being in real danger were familiar, nothing to panic about.

No one had seen him fall. No one was peering down into the water to find him.

"Help!"

It wasn't a very emphatic scream. He knew he was too far from the basketball court to be heard. Besides, it made him self-conscious to yell for help and he didn't want to risk getting any more canal water in his mouth.

Danny dog-paddled to the canal wall and held on to a post. He thought it would be smart to get rid of his jacket, but he was cold and anyway, his parents would kill him if he lost it. Oh God, they'd probably kill him for losing his bike and ball anyway, but he was too tired to work the jacket off. Looking toward the bay, he noticed a boat tied to the wall. Moving with one hand against the wood, he told himself there had to be a way down from the street to the boat, even if he couldn't see it from where he was.

Only after he'd spotted the rungs nailed to the canal wall did Danny begin to cry. By the time he walked home, he was shivering, dizzy, and terribly sleepy. His mother wasn't there and Sugar Adams wasn't coming to the house anymore, so the only thing he could think of doing was to call his father at work. That frightened him more than being in the water had, but he didn't know what else to do. He'd never called his father at work before, though the phone number posted on the side of the refrigerator had always greeted him after school.

Myron was strangely calm when Danny explained what had happened. He spoke in a voice Danny barely recognized as his father's, telling him he'd be right home, telling him to take a hot shower and dress warmly afterwards but not to go to sleep, to wait for him, he'd be right home. And he was. His father got home from Manhattan so fast Danny thought he must have fallen asleep even though he'd tried hard not to. Myron got home even before Faye, who was at the beauty salon.

Danny had a mild concussion, borderline hypothermia, no permanent damage. For weeks, though, he kept hearing his father's voice, which got mixed up with the gentle movement of the water in his dreams.

By December, the Adlers seemed healthy again. They planned to celebrate the holidays at home and invited the Aragons, the Sussmans and the Sabbeths out from Brooklyn for a party. As a joke, Myron bought both sons first-aid kits and had them gift wrapped for Christmas.

Monday, December 14, was warm for that part of the year. At 6:30, Myron left home as usual for the drive to work. Richard left at 7:00, to drive along the same route Myron had driven a half-hour earlier. It was the approved plan for daily travel, Myron and Richard having acknowledged their inability to function together that early in the morning.

When he passed the wreck and glimpsed the man lying on the right shoulder of the road covered in blood, Richard felt certain for a moment that it was his father's car, his father's body on the ground. A white Buick with red trim. A man that short. Richard checked his mirror after speeding by the scene, but traffic blocked his view. Besides, he didn't really get a good look at the man because of the emergency personnel around him.

This time the police did not come to the home. They called Faye in mid-morning.

"Hello," an unfamiliar voice said. "To whom am I speaking?"

"Who is this?"

"This is the police. Is this Faye Adler?"

"Yes. Oh my God."

"Mrs. Myron Adler? Of 144 Coolidge Avenue? Is this the right party?"

"Yes Yes Yes. What is it? What's happened?"

"Mrs. Adler, your husband has been involved in a traffic accident. He has been taken to Queens General Hospital. We think you should come there as soon as possible."

Faye recalled Myron's words four months before. *He's not dead. That they would have told us.*

Queens General was about halfway between home and Manhattan where Myron worked. Faye had enrolled in a driving school after they moved from Brooklyn and, after failing three exams, had finally gotten her license two months ago. She'd never driven near Queens General on her own. She picked up the phone to call Myron for directions. Realizing the mistake she was making, Faye began to cry. Then she dialed her Uncle Maxie's number and got Richard on the phone.

"Ma?"

"Oh my God," she said.

"What now?"

"Your father's been in an accident."

"You're kidding." Richard remembered the wreck he passed on the way to work. "Is he hurt?"

"He's in Queens General."

"How is he?"

"I don't know. I don't know how to get there. Tell me how to get to him, Richard."

Richard gave his mother detailed instructions on the route. "Turn at the Shell station, just past that diner we ate at."

"They make terrible brisket."

"Right. I mean left. Turn left there." Richard remembered the time Faye ended up in Oyster Bay, on Long Island's north shore, while trying to visit her mother on Manhattan's upper west side. He'd better be careful so she didn't get even more confused than she already was. He took a deep breath and made her repeat the directions back to him. "Don't worry if the signs say Long Island, Ma. Just follow what I told you."

"You get hold of Danny, all right? Call him at school or something, I just can't do it. I want to go to Myron. Your father."

"I'll take care of it. See you at the hospital later. Please, be careful."

The first thing Myron said to her, when he emerged from anesthesia, was, "Tell my barber I won't make it this afternoon. I had a two o'clock."

Both legs had been shattered from thigh to shin and his pelvis was fractured. Ribs and collarbones were cracked, a shoulder was dislocated, his spleen and kidneys bruised. For the seventh time in his life, Myron's nose had been broken.

Faye knew she had to take care of Myron herself, despite the care provided by the hospital. He would soon make demands for special food, special service. He was diabetic and on a diet to which he adhered faithfully, though he wouldn't return to his doctor for check-ups. "He gave me advice and I follow it. Why should I keep paying him for more of the same?"

He'd become a finicky eater. Faye got in touch with Sugar Adams and convinced her to come out from Brooklyn again. Every day, Faye brought meals that Sugar had prepared. Meat loaves, flanken, chicken fricassees, sausages, things that could be transported and heated in the hospital facilities.

"They'll serve him that protein bread he likes for breakfast," she told her friend Irma, "provided I bring it to them. He likes soft-boiled eggs, too, but the best I can do is the hard-boiled I bring every few days with the bread. And fresh fruit, don't ask, Myron Adler has to have fresh fruit every day."

A month after the accident, Danny accompanied Faye and Richard to

Queens General for the first time. Fearing contagion, the hospital forbade visits from children, but would allow Danny this one brief call—a kind of inspection, really—because of the seriousness of the case. Myron had been placed in a ward with two dozen patients. He could not be moved to another hospital closer to home. When his legs healed sufficiently, they might be able to bring him to Long Beach, but there was no telling how long that would take.

He was in traction with pins through his heels and thighs and tubes in his nose. Danny tried not to stare at the scabs all over his father's face, neck and chest, or to stand back because he smelled spoiled.

"We'll play catch before long," Myron said to Danny in a gasping whisper, "don't you worry."

Danny couldn't speak. Listening to that strange voice, trying hard to focus on Myron's cloudy eyes, he realized that he did not know his father as well as he thought. The man strung to this bed was the same man Danny used to pounce on in the bed in Brooklyn, the same man who bounded up the stairs every evening in Long Beach to wash himself for dinner and eat in near silence, listening to his wife chatter about the things his children had done wrong that day. But it seemed to Danny that he'd never met the guy before. Myron had always been so active and physical, so menacing. Danny thought injuries like these, to his father's legs, must cripple such a man's spirit as well as body. He was deeply impressed. He was also terrified. His father's pain, the uncertainty of their future—which he hadn't grasped until he saw his father's true condition—the loss of his presence, all welled up around him until Danny felt as trapped as Myron. What would happen now? How would the family get by?

"I miss you," Danny managed to say.

Myron tried to turn his head far enough to look into Danny's eyes. He groaned, letting his head sink back to the pillows, then pointed an unsteady hand at Richard and waved his fingers. It was a code Richard understood. He led Danny over to the other side of the bed. Richard put his hands under Danny's shoulders and hoisted him so Myron could see Danny clearly. No one spoke. Myron gazed at Danny as though memorizing every feature, then shifted his eyes to study Richard. It seemed as though the entire ward had come to a stop. A tremor passed through Myron's face. Then he closed his eyes and fell asleep.

At the elevator on the way out, Richard pressed the Down button, turned toward Faye and Danny, and fainted. He hit the floor hard. Neither his mother nor his brother could react quickly enough to catch him as he fell.

"His head," Faye cried. "Oh God, no!" She put her hands to her face and watched as Danny bent over his brother.

"Rick? Are you hurt?"

Richard sat up, shaking his head. He scooted back so that he could rest against the wall for a moment, shut his eyes and tried to figure out what had happened. Then he looked at his brother and mother, reached out for Danny's extended hand and stood up.

"Sorry, folks." He steadied himself against the closed elevator door. "I don't know what came over me."

"Should we get a doctor?" Faye asked.

"I don't need a doctor. I'm fine. People faint all the time, it's no big deal."

"I didn't faint," Danny said.

Richard glowered at him. "That's because you're too young to give blood." He held his arm out so Danny could see the bandage in the crook of his elbow.

"Well, I would have if they'd let me."

"And you're also too young to understand anything that's going on. So just shut up and let's get out of here."

In the car while they were driving home, Danny asked again how Richard felt.

"Leave me alone. It's nothing."

"But maybe you should see a doctor."

"What do you know?"

"Will you two stop bickering?" Faye said from the back seat. "Your father prone on his back in a hospital, each of you almost dead already once this year, and me having to take care of a family full of casualties. Have some concern for *me*."

Richard and Danny, chastised, stopped their arguing. Without mentioning it, both knew they would soon pass the spot where Myron's accident had occurred. It would be on their left, between the Paragon Oil and Mister Pants billboards.

"There it is," said Danny softly. Faye was looking out her window in the opposite direction, daydreaming, seeing the Sherwood Diner and getting hungry for an omelet.

"At a diner, you can get anything you want," she said.

She thought how long it had been since she had gone out for the luxurious kind of dining she enjoyed so much. And how long it would be before she would be likely to go again. Maybe the boys would enjoy a New Year's Day dinner at La Serenata or Lennie's.

"If he just moved up another fifty feet," Danny said, "he could have pulled off the road into that little spot there. He'd have been far enough off the shoulder so the guy's car wouldn't have hit him." He hadn't, though, and the other car had jumped the curb and pinned Myron against the trunk as he was about to open it to remove the spare tire.

"I drove right past it," Richard said. "I'm glad I did. If I stopped, I probably would have killed the guy who hit him."

"Did you see the pictures?" Danny asked.

"I've never seen anything so gruesome. He's got his hands raised up like he's trying to push everything away. I wonder if he was still conscious."

"And his clothes. They're in a box up in the attic. Have you seen them?"

"I put them there," Richard whispered.

"What are you two talking about up there?" Faye shifted uncomfortably. With Richard's car wrecked in August, and now the Buick wrecked, they'd had to buy a used Ford. It was too small for Faye's taste and rode roughly.

"Nothing," Richard said. "Just about the Knicks and Celtics. We're thinking of going to a game at the Garden next month."

"No you weren't. You were talking about the accident. I know it happened back there. I don't care if you talk about it. You don't have to worry about my feelings."

The next day, Faye began to go public with her trials. She pulled into a gas station and, while the attendant bent to put air in her rear tires, she leaned out to speak to him. Holding onto the half opened door, she told him she was seeing some hard times.

"My husband was in a terrible accident, you know. The other man's fault of course. I've never seen such suffering. And me? I go every day to Queens General Hospital to be with him. What else can I do? Did you ever?"

She told Irma about irony. "Every day I have to drive right past where the accident took place. Sometimes I swear I can see my Myron's blood on the pavement."

"You should look the other way, Faye."

"I can't. That's all. And those kids. I tell you I'm scared to death one of them will get hurt again. What could I do then? With my luck, he'd be in some hospital in New York City or Far Rockaway, and I'd have to be in three places every day. This would kill me."

"Just thank God you've got your children. And some very good friends, too. Don't forget that."

Faye spoke to her brother about money. "The insurance doesn't cover enough of it, Red. I don't know what I'm going to do."

"Don't worry. You'll get Myron's check every week, just like if he was working. I'll deal with the doctors and the physical therapist when he needs one. You just worry about Rick and Danny."

Red called a physical therapist, who visited Myron and spoke to his doctors. They agreed to order a hospital bed, a set of parallel bars, and other exercise equipment for the home. They would be delivered in four months, or later if he wasn't ready to get out of the hospital by then.

"He'll have to learn to walk all over again," Faye told the boys. "It'll be just like with a baby. It'll be painful to watch him and you know your father, he isn't very strong that way. I don't know if he can make it."

On New Year's Eve, Danny, Richard, and Faye went out for the evening. Faye turned down invitations to parties and Richard canceled the date he made months before. The boys dressed up, insisted that Faye buy and wear a new dress.

They went to La Serenata for dinner. It was Myron's favorite local restaurant and they talked about him with the owner, Vince. Vince suggested baked clams and shrimp marinara as appetizers and veal, steak and chicken entrees. They left themselves in his hands. They drank wine which Vince provided on the house, even giving Danny a glass.

Diary of Anne Frank was playing at the Atlantic and *Ben-Hur* was still at the Beach. They left the choice to Faye.

"Let's see Anne Frank. I want to cry."

Getting home past midnight, they sat in the sunken living room and talked quietly for an hour. It was the first time, Faye pointed out, that they had sat down to talk with each other in so long. Since before the accident, even.

Danny was anxious to get to sleep. Richard was certain he wouldn't be able to get any sleep. They sat in silence for several minutes, looking at the spotless fireplace.

"Let's drink a toast," Faye said.

"That might help," Richard said. He went to the bar and got a bottle of brandy and three cordial glasses.

"Your father always wanted to buy some of those big snifters for his brandy. I never did. You know why? They wouldn't fit in the bar and I didn't want them cluttering up my kitchen cabinets."

"That's all right," Danny said. "I think these little glasses are cute. I like to hold them."

"Let's drink to 1960," Faye said. The artificial cheeriness in her voice disappeared as she added, "it surely can't be worse than 1959."

"I'll drink to that, Ma," Richard said.

Myron mended slowly. The doctors praised his spirit, his strong heart and remarkable body. But by June, it was clear that his left leg would have to be rebroken and reset if he were ever to walk again.

It would take months before he was ready for that surgery, though. They told Faye she could have her husband moved nearer home in May. On Friday the 13th, exactly six months from the day of the accident, Myron was wheeled into an ambulance outside Queens General Hospital and driven to Long Beach Hospital. Richard rode in the ambulance with him and Faye followed in the car. He was installed in a room on the hospital's first floor, overlooking the bay. The surgery was set for mid-July.

Danny had seen his father only once in the last six months. Now that Myron was so close to home, being prohibited from visiting was harder for Danny. One evening in late May, Danny rode his bicycle over to the hospital, accompanied by his friend Jay. They tried every door around the sides and back of the hospital to see if there was one they could sneak through and make their way to Myron's room. No luck. They explored the back side of the building, along the bay, but found nothing helpful. Danny sat at the water's edge looking out toward the marsh across the bay, thinking he was at least sharing the view his father had.

Jay was a year older than Danny and nearly a foot taller. When he thought of the idea, he let out a whoop and yanked Danny's Dodger cap down over his eyes, almost knocking him into the water. They found two tree stumps in the mud at the bay's verge that were roughly the same size and lugged them under the window of Myron's room. They placed them so that Jay could stand with one foot on each stump, legs comfortably spread. Then Jay squatted and Danny climbed onto his shoulders, using the hospital wall for balance until he was standing upright. They sidled the few inches over to the stumps. Jay carefully put a foot on each stump and, with Danny clutching the wall, raised them both up. Danny's head was now fully over the window ledge and he could see into his father's room. He rapped on the window, but his father didn't turn his head from the television perched high the opposite wall. Danny rapped harder, keeping his elbows on the ledge for balance. Myron's head turned slowly and Danny began to wobble on Jay's shoulders in excitement. He steadied himself. When Myron saw his son's face smiling at him through the hospital window, backlit by the first hints of sunset, his laughter was so loud both Danny and Jay could hear him as clearly as if they were sitting with him in the room.

They visited that way several evenings a week. Myron persuaded the nurses to leave his window open so he could talk to Danny. They kept up on the pennant race, on Danny's day camp activities, and whatever Danny was reading. The night before his father's surgery, Danny laid a yellow rose, which he'd learned was the state flower of New York and which he'd just bought at the flower shop, on Myron's window sill before blowing him a kiss goodnight.

Myron was home in time for Danny's Bar Mitzvah in the fall. The bedroom looked more like a gymnasium, with its parallel bars, weights and apparatus attached to the hospital bed they'd rented. Myron's old bed was pushed against the wall by the door; Danny would sometimes come into the room in the middle of the night, his sleep disturbed by dreams, and lie down in the extra bed.

Myron was able to spend a few hours each day in a wheelchair and had begun talking about going back to work. By year's end, with a built-up shoe to compensate for the difference in length between his legs, he could walk across the room using canes.

1961 was a year of great hope, of John F. Kennedy's inauguration, the Geneva Conference resuming, Atlas Computers, and manned space flight. The United Nations General Assembly condemned apartheid. In 1961, base-

ball added new teams in the American League and expanded the season to
162 games; Roger Maris broke Babe Ruth's record for home runs in a season.
These events would have upset Myron deeply, for he opposed changing the
game he loved, but 1961 was the year in which Myron died of a myocardial in-
farction while exercising on the parallel bars in his bedroom.

12

Evening Services

DANNY WAS SITTING at the kitchen table eating Rice Krinkles mixed with green grapes when his Uncle Joseph walked into the room. It was a week after Myron had died. All the mirrors in the house were still covered, there were still hard little benches in the living room for the mourners to sit on, the refrigerator was stuffed with strange food, and Danny could find nowhere in the house to be alone.

Uncle Joseph was wearing Myron's flannel bathrobe and a pair of Myron's slippers, which shuffled familiarly over the linoleum. For an instant Danny thought his father had returned; this whole last week of evening prayers and sitting *shiva* in his memory had been a dream. But of course that was impossible. Danny's father would never be seen with his face covered in such a stubbly white hash of whiskers, or with his dingy fringe of hair in such disarray.

Danny wondered why Uncle Joseph had never gotten married. All the other aunts and uncles had, and all of them had children, so that Danny had a dozen cousins scattered through the five boroughs of New York City. His father used to say that Uncle Joseph never married because he never found anyone to compare with Grandma Sophia. Danny's mother said it was because Uncle Joseph never met anyone to compare with himself. Maybe it was simpler than both of them thought. Maybe it was because Uncle Joseph looked like this in the morning.

Uncle Joseph's head jerked once in Danny's direction, as though he'd sneezed. During this week, with Uncle Joseph living in the house, Danny had come to understand that the sneeze meant Hello. He nodded back.

"Good morning, Uncle Joseph."

"*Gut morgen, boychik. Vos macht ir?.*"

"I'm fine."

Joseph turned the burner on under the kettle, then sat across from Danny to wait for his water to boil. As soon as he'd settled, emitting the deep sigh that Danny had come to expect, Uncle Herb shambled into the room. His darker stubble and longer hair made him seem more sinister than his brother, but even though his eyes were half-closed Uncle Herb's face was creased with a morning smile.

"Don't say anything," he told Danny, putting up one hand like a traffic cop. "Not a single syllable. It's much too early."

Uncle Herb took the kettle off the burner, added more water, and replaced it on the stove. He came over to the table, joints clicking the way Myron's always had, and sat to Danny's left. Without speaking, Uncle Joseph got up to retrace his brother's steps and moved the kettle onto the flame from the unlit burner where Herb had put it. Then he turned to face the table, raising his eyebrows.

"Nu?" he said. "It's time we talked to him, Herbie."

Uncle Herb nodded. "Danny, it's time we talked to you."

The cereal was at its soggiest now, just the way Danny loved it, but he put his spoon down and looked across at his uncles. He wiped a dribble of milk from his chin, then absently fiddled with the torn black ribbon on his tee shirt that symbolized the grief in his heart.

"Two more days and we go home, Danny, the week of mourning, the *shiva* is over," Uncle Joseph said. "You understand what I'm saying?"

"Thursday night," Danny said.

"All right. So you also understand what happens after that, what you have to do for your father?"

Danny shook his head. This was news to him. "For my father?"

"Well, for all of us, Danny," Uncle Herb said. His voice was much softer than Uncle Joseph's. "For your aunts and uncles, your grandmother. For your mother and your brother too, since Richard refuses."

"You're a man now, Danny. You've been *Bar Mitzvahed*. You have a prayer shawl of your own that your grandmother brought home from Israel for you."

Danny felt the burning in his nose that presaged crying. He swallowed hard. "I put the prayer shawl in Dad's coffin, Uncle Joseph. You asked me to put something important in there with him."

His uncle closed his eyes and bobbed his head. "I see. Nevertheless, you got responsibilities as a Jewish man."

"This is something only you can do," Uncle Herb added. "Everyone's going to count on you."

Danny looked from one uncle to the other, trying to decide if this was a joke they'd cooked up, or some test of his smarts, maybe a misguided attempt to ease his grief. But they were serious, he could tell that easily enough. They were looking at Danny with their round Adlerian faces and enormous eyes wide open, with not even the glimmer of humor to be found in them.

Uncle Joseph continued, saying, "You must go to the synagogue every night, for the sundown services and the evening services, and you must say *Kaddish* for your father just like we've been doing all week. It's up to you now, Danny."

"I thought Richard had to do that."

"Your brother is 22 years old, he doesn't listen to anybody anymore. Nu? He's got a life of his own and he told us No."

"Just like that, No." Uncle Herb scratched at his stubble. "He's not gonna do it."

"So what do I have to do?"

"Like your Uncle Joseph said. You go to the synagogue every night at sunset. We'll take you there tomorrow night and show you everything. Rabbi Horowitz will introduce you to the other mourners the first time, and he'll keep track of you through the year. You go, you say the *Kaddish* for your father at the right times for eleven months, and then you come home for dinner. That's all there is to it."

"Every night?"

"Yes every night. It's only eleven months," Uncle Joseph said, rising to get the whistling kettle. "You're fourteen years old, *boychik*, what else do you have to do that's so important?"

■

Danny liked the way sundown set the synagogue's stained-glass burning bush ablaze. It was an enormous window set into the back wall, a memorial circle within the otherwise plain pale brick. On sunny days, he always tried to look back at the exact moment the bush caught fire.

There had to be a dozen colors of glass in the window. Three shades of blue alone, incredibly vivid reds and orange, ballpark green grass. His favorite pane was the clear one, though, barely noticeable at the heart of the flame. This, he thought, must be God. Or maybe it's the voice of God made visible, something like that. He could have spent the whole ninety minutes each evening looking at the window, but never allowed himself more than a few quick peeks.

The men at the synagogue on weeknights were all old. They wrapped their heads and shoulders in ancient prayer shawls, disappearing into them like turtles, and mumbled their mourning prayers while rocking back and forth. Even though he knew every word, Danny couldn't understand a thing they said.

These men, Rabbi Horowitz told him, were praying for all the dead from the holocaust. Most of them had lost so many relatives to the Nazis that they felt their obligation to mourn would never be over. Danny watched them and felt confused. On the one hand, his loss seemed somehow less than theirs. He was grief-specific, present to mourn for his father within the community, and then to stop coming as soon as his year was up. On the other hand, his loss seemed greater because it was narrower and more sharply focused than theirs. All Danny knew for sure was that he didn't like being in the same room with them, though he was grateful ten or more always showed up—a *minyan*—so that the services could proceed.

The old men would check to make sure Danny was there before they began the services, but no one spoke to him. No one came over to put an arm around him and ask how he was doing. No one explained why 365 nights worth of prayers were necessary or what would happen if he failed to show up some night. Would his father's soul be lost? Would Danny's own soul be lost? Perhaps his father would not be allowed to rest, but would wander somewhere up there with the Hindus, Muslims, Catholics and other Jews who hadn't been properly escorted to the Hereafter, or wherever dead people ended up.

He remembered Cantor Schmallenstein once telling the Hebrew school class that there *was* a hereafter, but the Torah never really described it. Lot of good that did. Rabbi Horowitz would sit in his office with the door ajar before services began, but Danny didn't feel he could go in to ask about things he was probably taught and had forgotten. For all his years in Hebrew school and *Bar Mitzvah* training in this building, the Rabbi's office was the place you got sent to when you did something wrong. He didn't feel like barging in to ask for clarification now; a young Jew did his duty and didn't ask why. If Danny knew anything, he knew that.

In February, there was a blizzard. Not as bad as the blizzard of 1958, which Danny remembered because it came on a weekend and he didn't get to miss any school. But bad enough to bring the whole island to a stop. Power lines were down on Park Street, traffic barely moved, most of the shops stayed closed. At about 4:30 he got his bicycle out of the garage and rode the six blocks to the synagogue through the snow. Now that the wind was gone and there were only flurries, it was peaceful to be outside. He loved seeing the way his tires cut through the snow. It was nearly up to his pedals and he could reach it with his toes on each downstroke.

When Danny arrived and locked his bicycle beside the building, he found the synagogue's doors were locked. He didn't realize that was even possible. He thought they would always be open, there would always be someone around—Rabbi Horowitz, Cantor Schmallenstein, maybe just Olaf the janitor or Mr. Baron, the President of the Men's Club—someone to make sure you could get inside. He walked around to the back. All the doors were locked.

The day had never gotten very bright, but Danny could tell it was now close to sunset. He stood at the top of the stairs, moving back and forth before the front doors, trying to keep himself warm. Only a few cars were passing along Park Street and none of them were turning his way. Danny didn't want to think about what it would mean if ten men couldn't make it. If they weren't able to hold services, he couldn't say an official *Kaddish*, could he? Then what? He decided to wait a few more minutes.

Danny heard the tire's chains before he saw the Rabbi's car, which approached from the direction of the beach. Flurries and wind-blown snow were visible in the headlights. The car stopped. The window rolled down and Rabbi Horowitz, leaning across the seat, was waving at him.

"Is that you, Danny?"

Danny came down the stairs and approached the car. He bent to look in through the window. The steering wheel had knocked Rabbi Horowitz's hat back on his balding head, revealing a yarmulke underneath. Good, Danny found himself thinking, at least he's keeping warm.

"No one's here, Rabbi Horowitz."

"I know. Sometimes this happens, there's nothing we can do. Please get in the car, Danny, you'll catch your death of cold."

This was an amazing development. Danny couldn't imagine sitting in the Rabbi's own car, being on the same front seat with him, chatting while the heater blasted them both. But he couldn't imagine refusing the command, either.

"I'm kind of wet, Rabbi."

"Get in, please." The Rabbi sat back up. "I've got plastic seat covers."

With the engine running, and exhaust mingling with snow in the headlights, Danny sat rigid beside Rabbi Horowitz trying not to look at him. There was a strong cinnamon odor that made Danny's mouth water and behind it a fainter fruity scent of pipe tobacco. He wondered if the Rabbi ever listened to the radio. Hey, Rabbi Horowitz, you like Dion and the Belmonts?

"How long have you been standing out there, Danny?"

"Oh, just a few minutes. I was afraid I was late."

"Do you want me to drive you home?"

"I brought my bike, Rabbi." Danny looked out the window and saw his bicycle, covered now with a layer of snow. "But what about services? I need to say *Kaddish*."

"Not tonight, Danny. We're going to have to skip it tonight."

Danny expected to hear those words, but they went through him like the day's blizzard wind. "But what happens?"

"What do you mean?"

"If I can't say the prayer for my father, what's going to happen?"

"Nothing's going to happen, Danny."

"Nothing?"

The Rabbi turned his face away from Danny for a moment, looking up through the windshield, his eyes shifting as though he'd just glimpsed a passing angel. He let his head fall back against the top of his seat.

"I see. Danny, God will understand about tonight, don't you think? He knows you came to the synagogue, that you intended to pray and sing to Him tonight, celebrating the joy of life despite your loss. He saw you ride through the snow and He knows what is in your heart. It will be all right."

"But I thought I had to say the prayers. I have to do it every night for the whole year."

The Rabbi nodded, turning to put a hand on Danny's shoulder. "So. We will say the *Kaddish* together, Danny. You and me, this one time. God will hear us and be happy."

Danny finally turned to look at the Rabbi. He watched the man's eyes, vast behind his tortoise shell glasses, slowly close. A smile spread the thin lips. Danny straightened in the seat, looking forward into the blustering night. As the Rabbi's voice raised itself in song, Danny joined him, softly at first, but then with greater power as he felt the Rabbi's hand leave his shoulder.

■

One evening in April, Karen Bloom was waiting for Danny when he left the synagogue. It was warm enough that Karen's jacket was unzipped and she wore no hat. She sat astride Danny's bicycle, leaning a shoulder against the wall, reading A *Tale of Two Cities* by street and window light. Her black hair, usually gathered in a pony tail, was loose and frizzed at her shoulders.

"Your mother told me where you were," Karen said as Danny approached. "She said you come here every night."

He stopped about five feet from her. Beside loose hair, Karen had on lipstick and eyeliner, and a snug pair of green corduroy pants. Danny realized she was dressed up.

"Just till November," he said.

"So when do you do your homework?"

"Sometimes I can get it done after baseball practice. Otherwise, I do it after dinner."

Karen smiled, her braces glinting in the criss-crossing lights. "Is that why you never call me?"

Danny looked down. He noticed that his tires needed air. "I call you sometimes."

"Oh, about once a week, if I'm lucky." Karen got off his bike and walked over to him. "You didn't tell me anything about this."

His fender was crooked. One handlebar grip was missing. "I didn't?"

She shook her head, but she was smiling. "We've been going together for three months as of tonight, Danny. Did you know that? It's sort of our anniversary, and it's so nice out. Would you like to go to the beach for a while? I brought my bike." She pointed behind him to the streetlight, where she'd rested it. "We could ride up there and then take a walk."

"I've got to get home for dinner. My mother gets really mad if I'm late."

"You didn't eat yet? God, you must be hungry. We could just take a short walk, ok, to celebrate? I've got some peanut butter crackers in my purse you could have."

"Ok, I can probably get away with a half hour. I'll tell her services started late because they had trouble getting a *minyan*. That's happened before."

It took them less than ten minutes to get to the beach and chain their bicycles to the handrail of the boardwalk. Karen led Danny across the soft sand to the nearest jetty. When they were perched on the rocks—far enough out to feel surrounded by surf, but close enough to the shore to stay dry—she gave him her package of crackers and leaned back to look at the sky. It was much colder by the water. Karen's jacket was zipped and her hair was tucked up under a winter hat that she'd pulled out of a jacket pocket.

"The book's pretty good," Karen said. "But the way it's written is so weird. 'It was the best of times, it was the worst of times, it was the age of wisdom, it was the age of foolishness.' Sometimes I wish he'd just get on with the story. Are you ready for the test?"

Danny nodded. Actually, he thought the story was terrific. Two guys as alike as brothers on the outside, yet so different inside. He liked that. But what really got Danny was the idea of loving somebody so much that you'd trade your life just to make her happy. That was the kind of love he was interested in. Danny admired Sydney Carton for what he did, switching places with Charles Darnay, and he thought it would be good to play in the same infield as Darnay, especially if the game was close.

A wave broke higher up on the jetty and the spray hit them. They backed up a little closer to shore. Karen settled on the same rock with Danny, so he had no choice but to lean against her. She put an arm around him and shivered. They sat quietly for a few minutes watching the breakers.

"I've really got to get home," he said.

Karen held him in place. "There's something I want to ask you first."

Danny was getting cold. The wind had picked up along with the tide and they were getting sprayed again in their new perch. Karen turned toward him and looked into his eyes as though thinking the tears there were from sadness instead of wind.

"Does it make you miss him more, going to services every night?"

He shook his head. "Do you ever go to the synagogue?" he asked.

"On the high holidays," Karen said. "And we have a Seder every year at home."

"I don't know, going to services every night is weird. I don't have to think about what I'm doing anymore. I say the prayers by heart, do what I'm supposed to do, and then leave. Everybody does the same thing the same way every night. I think I could sing "Runaround Sue" and nobody'd notice. Not even me."

"Do you think of your father at all?"

"It's like I don't have time to."

Karen was silent for a moment. Then she pressed against Danny and kissed him. "That wasn't what I wanted to ask you, really."

A pair of gulls circled overhead, bugling wildly. To Danny, their music seemed like the center of prayer.

"Then what is?" he asked.

Karen put her face against his neck. Her voice was mixed with the sound of waves. "Why don't you touch me, Danny?"

He tried to look down at her, but the top of her head was stopping him.

"Here," she said, moving his hand to her breast. "When we kiss."

Danny didn't breathe. Karen put her hand over his and squeezed it.

"I didn't think you'd let me," he said.

"But I wanted you to." Danny could feel her breath against his throat, making him suddenly colder than the wind. "Didn't you know that?"

He kissed her and felt that he would never be able to stop shaking. He was getting warm now, feeling the rocks press into the soft part of his lower back, and trying to remember what she'd just said.

"I thought you'd get mad at me."

"Only for hiding from me," Karen said.

■

Danny looked around while the old men were chanting and thought all the sun's power was focused on the one clear pane at the center of the burning bush. None of the colors surrounding that pane seemed alive, as though sunset light were compressed tonight into one intense beam. It struck the floor between aisles. Danny shuffled out of his row and moved back to stand beside the light. Engrossed in their prayers, no one paid any attention to him, not even Rabbi Horowitz, who was facing the congregation but had his eyes closed.

Almost immediately, it was time to sit. The prayers continued but Danny was no longer pretending to follow them. He would know when it was time to rise for the *Kaddish,* as he knew when it was time to inhale and exhale, so he felt it was all right for him to daydream.

Sitting beside the light, watching it begin to fade as the sun continued setting, Danny felt overwhelmed by a sense of loss. He turned sideways in his seat, wanting to reach out and hold the light still. It was beyond him to keep his arms in place. Reaching into the aisle, he suddenly remembered reaching out to his father. They were standing across from one another, at opposite ends of the parallel bars in his father's bedroom, and all the world seemed shrunken to the width of those two horizontal bars which supported Myron in his efforts to walk again. Slowly, concentration gouging deep creases in his face, Myron lurched toward Danny along the track the bars made. He kept his eyes on Danny's and Danny couldn't look away, didn't know what to do. He felt like backing away, backing all the way out of the room, but understood that he must not move. If he moved, his father would lose his grip and crash to the floor. He reached out. Sweat popped off his father's face with each jerky step. Then Myron was right in front of him, his ragged breath pouring over Danny, his eyes boring into his son's.

"Get my chair, Danny."

■

They were sitting in the living room. Richard was in Myron's easy chair with a box of butterscotch cremes open on the hassock. Danny was opposite him on the couch with a geometry book spread on his lap and a notebook face down on top of it. Faye stood with one hand on the back of the Roosevelt chair, the other holding a cigarette to her mouth.

"I don't want to hear it," Richard said. He leaned forward to get another piece of candy and point at Danny. "You either find time to help her with the chores around here or you turn in your spikes."

"I'm not quitting baseball. Period, end of discussion." Danny turned his notebook face up. "Now if you two will excuse me, I've got homework to do."

"You see what I mean?" Faye said. "That's how he talks to me."

Richard chewed the candy, his eyes on Danny, and swallowed loudly. Then he picked up another and threw it across the room. It smacked Danny in the forehead. He jerked back, knocking the book off his lap.

"I'm talking to you, Pee Wee," Richard said. "Now pay attention."

"Jesus Christ, Rick. What the hell is this?" Danny was trying to control his anger. He picked up the book. Richard, grinning, was obviously trying to provoke a fight and enjoying himself enormously. "You're not my father."

It was awfully hard to tell who was on whose side anymore. Just a week ago, Faye had come into Richard's room on Sunday afternoon, while he was watching a ball game, and started berating him about coming home so late after his date the night before. Danny couldn't hear what Richard said to her, but she stormed across the room and screamed back that he wasn't giving her anywhere near enough rent money for her to put up with such things. Danny came to the doorway to see what was going on just as his mother took a swing at Richard's face. Richard, standing near the desk where his television sat, caught her wrist and pulled Faye toward him. Then he pushed her away so hard she lost her balance and, with the force of Richard's shove behind her, sailed backwards onto his bed. There was utter silence for a moment before Faye shrieked, struggling to get off the soft mattress where she was still bouncing in place, and then burst into tears. Danny would never forget the sight of his mother flying through the air.

"Watch your mouth," Richard said, sitting back in the easy chair. "I'm warning you."

"Why don't you watch your own mouth," Danny said. "That should be easy since it's always full."

"That's enough, now," Faye said. "He's got to go to the synagogue in a couple minutes."

"I thought you wanted me to talk to him," Richard said. "I came home early just for this."

"Enough already, I said. I got plenty to worry about without the two of you at each other's throats."

Danny slammed his book shut around the notebook and stood. "I've got a test tomorrow, ok? I'm going into my room to study."

He started to stalk across the room. Richard got up from the chair so quickly that Danny didn't have time to react. His brother grabbed Danny's shoulder, spun him around and knocked the books from his hands. Richard crowded him back against the fireplace, towering over him, using his extra hundred pounds to hold Danny still. But suddenly Danny was neither still nor under control. He slid away from Richard as he'd slid away from tacklers during the football season and erupted into motion, eyes wide, a sound more like a roar than words coming from the depths of his throat.

Danny was much too quick for Richard. The first two punches knocked his brother back into the easy chair as much from their surprise as from their force. Richard's glasses had flown off and shattered against the fireplace brick. He tried to get out of the chair, but Danny shoved him down again, flung the box of candy in his face, then picked the hassock up over his head when he finally heard Faye's hysterical cries. He stopped. Richard, utterly blind without his glasses, had his hands up in front of him to ward off whatever might come next.

Danny couldn't master his breathing. He set the hassock down. As he turned away from both his brother and mother, he thought *the sum of the squares of the lengths of the sides of a right triangle is equal to the square of the length of the hypotenuse.*

PART
III

1962-1974

13

To Tell the Truth

FAYE KNEW WHERE Europe was relative to New York, and she could place the Caribbean. These were locales she'd been to personally, very nice areas to go. But she was a little ragged when it came to American geography, to Denver or Chicago or Texas, places nobody really went. Faye knew they were out there to the left, of course, but she couldn't exactly say what was near what. That first month at the agency, geography became a slight problem—correctable, but awkward nevertheless—when she booked two clients from New York to Dallas via Quebec. Since the owner of the agency was an old friend from the apartment building in Brooklyn, geography didn't cost Faye her job. As to Mexico or Peru, for heaven's sake, she figured it was her business to convince clients not to go to such dirty, dangerous places anyway, so why worry about where they were, and since there was nothing worth seeing once you got beyond Hawaii, why concern yourself about the Pacific at all? As a gesture of contrition, however, she bought a map of the world. It was too big to hang on the wall of her cubicle or spread on her desktop, so she left it rolled in a crevice beside her filing cabinet.

Night after night, Faye brought an array of bright, exotic travel brochures home from the office to study. She also brought guidebooks too dense with text to bother over, airline and cruise manuals that a person would need a magnifying glass to read—forget about those—along with fare comparisons and currency handbooks that she never even bothered to bring in from the car. Sometimes she brought little souvenirs like swizzle sticks or coasters emblazoned with hotel insignia. She would spread her brochures on the dining room table and invite Danny to pore over them with her. In six months, Faye would qualify for free or reduced-price trips herself, including accommodations at all the best hotels and sometimes meals. There were plans to make. By then, her Myron, may he rest in peace, would have been dead two years. It was time she got out and met someone, no? A woman of 53, still young yet, one child grown and out of the house, the other only a couple years from going to college. She was a catch, but a catch had to be out there swimming in order to be caught.

"I keep looking for brochures on this place I once heard of, Carmina Burana," she told Danny. "I think it's somewhere west of Portugal. But there's nothing in the files at the office. I don't want to ask anybody about it because then they'd try to go instead of me. It's such a marvelous country, wonderful food and the weather is perfect year round."

Who would have thought Faye Adler would end up a travel agent? One early afternoon, just over a year after Myron had died, Faye was sitting in the dining room enjoying her breakfast when the phone rang. She considered not answering it. Most of her Brooklyn friends had stopped coming out to visit her, those that had relocated to various towns on Long Island were too busy with their new lives to keep in touch, and she hardly knew anyone in Long Beach. So who could it be that she was interested in talking to? Still, Richard was at work, Danny was in school, and it was possible that the call had to do with one of them. She wouldn't be at all surprised if something dreadful happened, it was about time again.

"Faye, this is Abe Wolfe from Lenox Road. Been a long time."

"Yes, Abie, a long time." She wished she hadn't answered the phone. Who needed to hear about Abe Wolfe's wonderful wife, the beautiful Eleanor Langevin from Canarsie who once modeled for Lucky Strikes, or his wonderful children Galen the cello prodigy and Ruthie the runner-up in Miss Brooklyn of 1961, or his wonderful business that made him such a rich man he couldn't visit his old friends? "My Myron's been gone fourteen and a half months already, may he rest in peace. So tell me, how are Ellie and the kids?"

"Great. I got nothing but *naches* from the whole family."

Faye remembered Abe's doleful, round face, his jowly laughter and tiny fingers. He had archipelagoes of scarlet pigment scattered over his face and neck, vivid patches that seemed to have flamed up from some caldera hidden deep in his chest. It was nearly impossible to look at him for more than forty seconds without having to glance aside for a rest. She also remembered Abe's gorgeous tenor voice. They had performed together in a production of *Guys and Dolls* put on by the synagogue that all their Brooklyn neighbors went to. How mortified her Myron had been when Faye sang "Take Back Your Mink" and began a mock striptease, flinging her gloves into the seventh row.

"So tell me, Abie, you done any theater lately?"

"Nah, nah. Though Ellie and I did see "The Night of the Iguana" on Broadway. We just got there at a bad time, the curtain was up. But seriously, Faye, I tell you I'm just too busy to do anything these days. That's why I'm calling."

"You're calling because you're too busy to call?"

"Nah, nah, I'm calling because I need help. Why don't you come work for me?"

Faye almost dropped the phone. She hadn't worked for a living since mid-1937 and was trained to do nothing except paint mannequins. But it was clear she couldn't sit home for the rest of her life, living off her late husband's on-going monthly paychecks, God bless her brother Red for sending it.

"Doing what, Abie, cleaning floors?"

"Doing what, she asks. Booking trips, darling, bringing in clients, making cold calls."

"What do I know from booking trips?"

"So I'll teach you. To do this work, you don't have to be an atom scientist. C'mon, Faye, do it for me, I need agents."

"Abe, look."

"No, you look: you're an outgoing woman, flamboyant and you got a lot of cultural pretensions. I used to love hearing you talk. This is everything a travel agent needs to be, except so what if you don't know the ins and outs of the business yet. You'll learn everything you need in two weeks, guaranteed."

"Well, I *have* been to Brussels and Paris."

"There you go."

Faye started working at the agency three weeks later. She found that she didn't at all mind going in to an office three days a week. However, getting up at 7:30 was another matter, something even further from her experience than having a job. At such an hour, she required an arsenal of wake-up weaponry. Danny was ordered to shake her before he ate his breakfast and shake her again before he left for school. He was not to leave the house until she was standing on her feet. Though it wasn't technically his fault that Faye would always lay back down when he shut the front door, she threatened to throw his television set into the ocean if she was ever late again. She purchased a wind-up alarm clock with a bell that rang loud enough to shatter the sleep of the dead, and an electric alarm clock that simply wouldn't stop buzzing till she turned it off, and a clock-radio that she set to play the loudest, most offensive music she could find.

The other two days a week, Faye could work at home, speaking on the phone all day without getting dressed, as she would have anyway. She re-established contact with many friends lost after the move from Brooklyn, or lost after Myron's accident and all those years of practically being chained to hospital beds beside him, or lost after Myron's death. She even found the courage to call people she hadn't spoken to since she had married Myron a quarter century ago, including some of the men she had gone out with then and whom she had now learned were single again.

One such call had led to Faye's first date since her husband's death. Dashing little Peter Porcelain, who could forget a name like that? Peter had been a young chemist when Faye knew him. Later he'd been involved in the development of frozen tv dinners and of course had made an enormous fortune.

Faye phoned him on a Tuesday, the morning after she saw him appear as an impostor on *To Tell the Truth*. It practically gave her the shock of her life. She had been sitting in the dining room, not paying much attention to the blaring television, poring instead over travel brochures—tour packages of Spain and Morocco, very romantic stuff—when she heard a voice that sounded vaguely familiar. Faye looked up from a photograph of downtown Tangier to see Peter Porcelain himself standing there, his hair as frizzy as it was in 1935, though faded and quite a bit further back on the bulging forehead, his nose as narrow and curvy, his eyes still miles too far apart. Would you look at that!

"My name is B.C. Bain," Peter said.

"The hell it is," Faye shrieked. She leaned over the dining room table to turn up the sound. "Danny, come in here this instant and look at what's on tv."

Danny said something she couldn't make out. He was probably on the phone, or doing his homework, or standing in front of his mirror to practice his batting style. *He'd better not break another mirror or he'll feel me practice my batting style on his head.*

"Get in here," she shouted.

Bud Collyer began to read the affidavit. "I, B.C. Bain, landed a 415-pound striped marlin at Cape Brett, New Zealand. This was my second record-breaking catch of the year, since I had already caught a 153-pound amberjack off Cat Island in the Bahamas."

The camera panned along the three contestants all claiming to be B.C. Bain. They looked solemnly out at the nation, even Peter, who looked like he did when Faye had told him not to call her anymore. Then the camera moved to show Kitty Carlisle leaning over to whisper something in Orson Bean's ear. *Probably she sees right through Peter and knows just from looking at him that he can't be some fisherman named Bain.*

Danny appeared in the doorway. He slouched against the jamb, a paperback novel shut around his index finger to mark its place, looking exhausted. Faye beckoned to him with her finger. "I know Number Three personally," she confided. "He used to be my boyfriend."

Danny rolled his eyes and started to back out of the room. "That's nice. I've got to finish reading this and write a book report tonight."

"Tsssst, it's true," she hissed. "Now stay put and shut up so I can hear this."

Bud Collyer droned on. "You might conclude from this that I am an inveterate fisherman, but nothing could be further from the truth. Until this year, I had never been fishing before in my life. A pharmacist by training, I am the owner of two small drug stores in Columbus, Ohio, and have always been so subject to seasickness that I could not even enjoy taking a bath in my tub. Don't ask me for the secret of my success, panelists, because there is none other than sheer, blind luck."

There was applause. Faye watched Peter sit primly in his chair, just as he used to sit at her parents' dinner table when he came to call for her. He was always willing to make small-talk with Jules and Ava, to discuss the state of affairs in Europe or the nuances of the gold market, never in a rush to leave.

Faye's parents had liked him immediately and thought he would be a good match for her. A chemist, Jules Raskin would say to his daughter when she got home later. You always need science, unlike a fox coat or a Packard. Although, he would add, what kind of name is Porcelain anyway?

Peggy Cass started right in on Peter. She could hardly keep a straight face.

"Number Three, how in heavens name did you lift a 415-pound fish out of the water. You'll excuse me, but you don't look like you could lift a smoked whitefish."

Faye had to hand it to him, Peter was calm and cool. He smiled at Peggy Cass as though she'd just forgotten that the atomic number of Boron was five.

"It isn't a matter of strength, Miss Cass. It's a matter of having the right equipment and then letting the equipment work for you until the fish gets tired. Two crewmen helped lift the marlin into the boat at the end."

How did he have the nerve! It was right then, when she saw what a splendid charlatan Peter was, that she realized she should call him at home and let him know she was a single woman again. Somehow she knew, even before he confessed as much to Bud Collyer at the end of the round, that Peter was still single. Yes, call him and see if perhaps he has any travel plans in mind.

"Which way do a striped marlin's stripes run, Number Three?" Orson Bean asked.

"Vertically," Peter said without hesitating. For good measure, he added, "along the sides."

He bamboozled them, even Tom Poston who looked like he might have gone fishing once or twice in his life and should certainly have known Peter was an impostor. Especially when he said he used chum for bait. That didn't sound right, even to Faye. What kind of worm was a chum anyway? All four panelists voted for Peter, despite Faye's cries of disbelief.

"Will the real B.C. Bain please stand up!" said Bud Collyer.

Peter actually leaned forward as though to push himself up out of the chair. He looked to his right, down the row of fellow contestants, then relaxed back in his chair with a huge grin. Oh, he was a lot bolder and cleverer than he used to be. Maybe he'd like to talk about a nice cruise down to Puerto Rico and the Virgin Islands, catch himself another applejack, hah hah. Or how about a two-week tour of Czechoslovakia, where Faye suddenly remembered his parents were from. Didn't she have something here on Czechoslovakia and Poland? Bratislava on his father's side, Prague on his mother's, that's right, it was all coming back to her now. Of course, the name wasn't Porcelain until you took away a few of the "c's" and "z's."

"He sure fooled them," Danny said. Faye had forgotten he was there. "Guy's cool."

When Faye called Peter the next morning, the line was busy for almost two hours. Big star, everybody he knows is probably calling to congratulate him. She kept trying and just before noon heard his tired voice.

"Well, well, Mr. Porcelain," Faye said. "Or should I say Mr. Bain the famous fisherman?"

"So who is this? Trudy?"

Faye lowered her voice nearly an octave and said, "Why, Peter darling, I thought you'd never forget me. When we went to the Russian Tea Room, I spilled not one but two samovars of tea in your lap. Hmmm? You once tried teaching me how to play tennis and I once tried teaching you to sing 'Begin the Beguine.' As I recall, I proved hopelessly clumsy and you proved hopelessly flat."

There was a long silence that she was tempted twice to break. Finally, Peter said, "Faye? You have to be kidding. Faye Raskin?"

"Hello, Peter."

They decided to meet for dinner at Ruby Foo's on Friday night. All she had allowed him to know was that she was a widow and that she was in travel. No sense pushing him too fast. After all, he probably had dozens of calls from people offering ways to spend his money. That was certainly not what Faye Raskin was after. Or not all she was after.

He was there waiting for her, at a table for two near the center of Ruby Foo's vast dining room, when Faye arrived. Just like the old days, having a man wait for her smack dab in the middle of a suitably expensive, suitably chic restaurant. Peter stood as she approached, pulling out her chair, adjusting it after she'd sat. Faye was absolutely thrilled. Not so much to be with Peter Porcelain, Mr. Frozen String Beans himself, but to be consorting again. Wasn't that Pearl Bailey sitting over there by the wall?

"You haven't changed at all," Peter said, pouring her a cup of steaming tea.

"And you have already demonstrated in front of millions of people what a fine liar you are."

"It's good to see you, Faye."

"Darling, who's Trudy?"

After won ton soup packed with shredded pork and greens, perfectly crisp egg rolls, and an order of spare ribs large enough to constitute a full meal, they shared his favorite moo goo gai pan and her favorite lobster Cantonese. If he was still not an adventurous eater, at least he had an appetite and wasn't cheap.

An hour later, sitting back for the final round of tea and talk, it was just as Faye had thought: Peter never married. He had lived at home with his mother until the woman suddenly died of heart failure in 1960, on the very same day that Peter's dear friend W.F. Libby won the Nobel Prize for using radioactive Carbon 14 to date archeological findings. This was a day of such confused joy and sorrow that Peter never got over it. He lived alone now in an apartment in mid-town Manhattan and, as he put it, piddled in his lab a few days a week.

Faye kept waiting for a chance for the conversation to segue into travel, but apparently Mr. Porcelain never went anywhere these days. Finally, when he summoned the waiter for a bill, Faye decided to charge ahead without the benefit of neat transition.

"So, Peter, have you thought at all about traveling soon?"

"Is this an invitation?"

Well, that didn't work. She allowed her enormous eyes to close slowly and a smile to ripple across her lips.

"Only in the sense that I would be glad to make arrangements for you. As I may have mentioned, that is my profession now."

He glanced at the check and surprised Faye by simply throwing down a few bills. He didn't study it, didn't redo the math or ponder an appropriate tip. All right, he's a scientist, he probably computed the whole thing while they were ordering. But she was impressed; how cavalier!

"Shall we go for a brief stroll?" he asked as they were putting on their coats in the lobby. "Or would you rather we go back to my place for a bit?"

"It's winter."

"Of course. Then let's just go to my place, it's not far. I'll bring you back here to your car afterwards."

"Afterwards?" She took a little extra time buttoning her coat. "What I meant, Peter, was simply that it's a good time for travel. Someplace warm, perhaps."

"Yes. You can tell me all about it when we get there."

He wasn't grasping what she was saying. Perhaps her delivery was a little too subtle. They stood just outside the door while pedestrians detoured around them. Faye raised the collar of her coat and tried to remember where she'd parked.

"Are you making a pass at me?" she asked.

Peter's eyes flickered as though stuck in mid-blink. He took a step back.

"Not yet, Faye. I thought I'd wait till we were indoors, what with the weather and all."

"But you'd have to wait till hell freezes over, Peter."

"Oh, do you book passage there too?" He thrust his hands into his pockets and his lower lip jutted out as though something in the pocket had released a hidden spring there. Faye realized that, despite the passage of time, Peter Porcelain down deep remained the little boy she'd had no intention of marrying when they knew each other half a lifetime ago. Perhaps that's why he had changed so little over the years. "Same old Faye Raskin, I see," he added.

"So what did you think, I might have turned into Jacqueline Kennedy?"

■

The small plane banked and Danny realized they were going to crash. He tried not to look, but through his window's spattered disk the blue waters of the Caribbean were approaching fast. Maybe that's why they spelled it with two "b's," because the water was so extra-blue.

What a place to die. Here he was, a fifteen-year old virgin on a spring holiday with his mother, his leather wallet now permanently etched by the outline of the only condom he'd ever owned, and he was going to drown in a place called the Virgin Passage.

When he'd agreed to travel with Faye, the plan had been to take a twelve day trip to Saint Tropez, this very exotic spot in France that she'd heard about where they could go for practically free, and where everybody between the ages of fifteen and a hundred fifteen would find someone to fall in love with. Danny's friend Larry, who was knowledgeable in these matters, said that on the beaches of Saint Tropez the women wore no bikini tops.

But Faye had gotten things confused. Instead of Saint Tropez they were going to Saint Thomas, this little island in the West Indies where Larry said the best things were how good the bay rum was and how cheaply you could buy cologne. Big deal. Danny didn't like rum, and on his dresser there was still a vat full of cologne because he didn't have many occasions to wear it.

Just before leaving on the trip, Danny had taken the train into Manhattan to have dinner with his brother. Richard, now a wise twenty three-year old salesman of hospital supplies, lived in the East Village and took Danny to dinner at Mario's, his favorite Italian restaurant. They marched together through the kitchen, where the staff greeted Richard like a long-lost relative from Napoli, and into an ornate dining room. As soon as they were seated, Richard solemnly reached across the table and, in plain view of anyone who might be looking, handed Danny a condom.

"I sure hope you're gonna need this, kiddo," Richard said.

Danny had to restrain himself from asking if, by parting with it, Richard was giving up on using it himself. Richard had gained another twenty pounds and was past two fifty already. Danny was worried about him. He rolled the package around in his hand underneath the table, surprised to realize that there was only a single rubber inside, and asked how many times you used one. This set Richard off even worse than Danny would have by asking about his weight.

The plane was leveling, but Danny could tell the descent was continuing. No one else seemed to realize how close they were to the end. The plane's shadow ran just ahead on the water like a playful dolphin, and it was clear that there was no hope. Nothing was visible but the purest blue. This had to be what his mother—her eyes now shut beside him and her hand clawing into his forearm as it had since they took off from Puerto Rico twenty minutes ago —called ultramarine when she was fiddling with her paints at the dining room table. He would miss that, oddly enough. Miss seeing his mother mixing colors on her old palette with the television blaring across the table from her, mixing colors but never painting with them, then spending hours cleaning up after herself. How could he miss such things when all he wanted in life was to leave home and live on his own, counting the months till he graduated from high school and could go away to school? It must be the shock of his impending death. What he would miss, he realized, was the ongoing possibility that his childhood would straighten out, the hope that he'd wake up one morning with parents—or for the last two years a mother, at least—around whom he would not have to exercise continual vigilance and caution. Around whom he was safe. The ultramarine waters came steadily closer while Danny watched as though hypnotized. When the plane actually touched down on the runway at the sea's edge, he was confused because there was no sign of a splash. Seconds later, realizing they had landed, all he could do was lay his head against the seat back in front of him and sigh.

Puerto Rico had been a bust for both of them. About the best thing Danny had done was convince a taxi driver to show him the shack where the great rightfielder Roberto Clemente had been born. Of course, when he got back to the hotel in San Juan and told his friend the concierge about the cab ride, the man had shaken his head sadly.

"He take you for a ride, all right, Daniel."

"What do you mean?"

"No one in Puerto Rico knows where this house is. Clemente, he come from a very poor part of the country. Everything gone before he become a big star."

"But I took a picture."

"Si, Daniel. Maybe it was the right place after all."

Every night for a week, Danny and Faye would dress up for dinner, admiring each other's outfits and giving each other encouragement. Then they would go down to the dining room separately, eat at separate tables, and pretend not to know one another until the next morning. Once, coming back from a solitary walk around the grounds near midnight, Danny saw his mother dancing in the bar with a man. Tall and wide, with long white hair flowing down to his shoulders, the man seemed to move in four directions at once with a few spins thrown in for good luck. Faye had her head against the man's shoulder, her gaze going in the opposite direction from his, and she looked dizzy. Danny imagined that she was talking, which explained why the man was nodding—unless he had Parkinson's Disease, like Uncle Herb—and that both of them were happy.

Seeing them made Danny feel mixed up and restless. What next, he'd stumble in on her kissing somebody, or necking on the living room sofa? Would she want to talk to him about her dates, what the guys smelled like and discussed in their cars, what they were after? Danny was having enough trouble getting somewhere with his own dates.

He left the bar area and headed for the lobby, passing through it with his head down, trying to avoid stepping on the stars scattered through the carpet. San Juan should have been more fun than it was turning out to be. He was allowed to gamble—though it would have helped if he had some money or liked the idea of risking it on a bet—and he could get a drink easily enough. On the advice of the concierge, he'd sampled a gin rickey, which he liked, then a rye and ginger ale, which he thought he could get used to. He toured the rain forest in a dented van with no doors, admiring the huge bananas and lush plants but glad to get back to the air conditioned hotel. He practiced his diving in the swimming pool until he could do clean swans and half-gainers. But he had no luck meeting girls, which was the point of this extravaganza as far as Danny was concerned. Once, he'd approached a girl who was huddled on a chair in the lobby, smiling at her as he crossed the space between them, and as soon as he stopped in front of her she darted around him like a half-back, fleeing to the elevator. He was ready to leave Puerto Rico three days before the scheduled departure.

Deplaned in Saint Thomas, they took a cab to the harbor area. They were staying in a hotel run by two women his mother told him were lovers. Danny wished she hadn't told him that, because now all he could think about were the two women in bed together. It had been driving him berserk since she mentioned the fact as they were packing to leave San Juan.

Faye thought this secret made The Ginger Thomas perhaps the most sophisticated, avant-garde hotel available in the Western Lights, or wherever the hell they were. It was probably going to be the place she met a man who would sweep her off her feet. Good luck, Danny thought, the guy better be a power lifter.

She was delighted to meet Gloria Duvivier, the co-owner of The Ginger Thomas, who accepted Faye's business card and led them silently to their rooms. She seemed annoyed at their arrival. As she strode down the hall, head barely moving, haunches rolling within her thin white slacks, Danny thought the woman was stunning. Not at all what he was expecting. A sleek woman, with piercing blue eyes framed by shaggy salt-and-pepper hair, she reminded him in some strange and exciting way of a wild Siberian Husky. He was glad he wore a tight tee shirt and shorts, though he wasn't sure this woman would even notice his compact physical charms.

Delighted or not, Faye couldn't resist complaining when she saw their rooms. Danny could see it coming in the way she folded her arms and refused to touch anything.

"Miss Duvivier, is this the best you can do for us? I mean, end of the hall, no view, and these teeny little beds. I'm from an important New York agency, you know, and we send a lot of clients to San Tomaz."

Danny wanted to evaporate.

"Mrs. Adler, this is peak season, everything's been booked for a year in advance. I was fortunate to find two rooms for you anywhere, let alone on the same floor."

Faye pursed her lips as though considering this explanation. Then she nodded and bade Gloria a good day. When she turned back to Danny, she was beaming. Over his mother's shoulder, Danny was astounded to see Gloria wink at him before she left.

"Now, of course, they'll give us the best of everything," Faye confided. "To stay on my good side. I hope you learned something, Daniel. Go unpack, I must rest for a few hours."

Danny unpacked quickly and headed for the street. But he only got as far as the hotel's veranda, where he found Gloria sitting like a queen in her white wicker throne. He shifted instantly from dash to saunter, then stopped as though the veranda had been his true destination all along. Beside Gloria on a matching throne was a very dark woman, a Crucian from Saint Croix who was at least as tall as Gloria and, Danny thought, even more beautiful.

"This is Edna Clair, Mr. Adler," Gloria said. "Or E-clair, don't you see."

"Now stop that, Gloria," the woman murmured.

Danny couldn't help himself. He burst out in laughter, then turned away to hide his embarrassment by looking at the indented coastline and bustling harbor of Charlotte Amalie.

"I believe he gets it, don't you?"

"My friends around here call me Ed," Eclair said. Her voice sure was creamy. "Now tell me how old you are, Daniel. May I call you Daniel?"

"Danny." He risked looking at them. "I'm sixteen. About."

"I wondered," Eclair said.

"He's very sturdy for sixteen, wouldn't you say?" Gloria reached over and put her hand behind Eclair's neck, flexing gently. Eclair's eyes closed slowly and as they opened Danny could only see their whites for a moment before the deep brown irises came down into view. He tried to look away.

"Tell me, Danny," she said, "do you lift weights?"

He nodded, conscious of his arms now folded over each other, his biceps bulging nicely. "For football. I'm kinda small, otherwise."

This made both of them put their heads back and laugh. It was a charming music to hear, but he hadn't thought he was being particularly funny. Did they think he was a pygmy or something?

"Pay no attention to us girls," Gloria said. "You're a sweet young man and it's a little treat for us to tease you."

Both women looked at him frankly, warm smiles on their faces. This was as confusing as it was amazing. Gloria and Ed might be the most beautiful women he'd ever seen. It filled him with excitement to think they were actually lovers, to sit before them on the steps while they flirted with him and with each other, knowing that later they would be doing the most intimate things together and that both parties would have female bodies. Things he was desperate to do to just one female body. He smiled at them to show he wasn't offended by their laughter, then looked off to the ridge of hills that traversed the island and refused to imagine them naked together this morning in the sticky heat, their tongues everywhere, pleasure so thick in the room that it radiated through the open windows.

"We're glad you came along with your mother," Eclair said. "What do you hope to do while you're here in Saint Thomas?"

He opened his mouth, but no words came out. He ran a hand through his hair, which he'd spent ten minutes brushing into submission before coming downstairs and now, damn it, had mussed.

"My mother goes on these free trips," he said. "These travel agent inspections, or whatever they are. She's hoping to meet somebody, you know?"

"A man," Gloria said.

"My father died about two years ago."

Danny could see a look pass over both women's faces as they glanced from him to each other and back.

"I wondered," Eclair said.

"So she wants to meet men," Danny said. "Especially men who aren't like my father. Diplomats and violinists and professors and barons, those kind."

"What was your father like, Danny?"

"He was a butcher."

"But what was he like?" Gloria said again.

Danny was silent for a while. Good question, Miss Duvivier. My father was huge, even though he was short, and too solid to dent though he had two shattered legs and only one eye. I found it once, blue as the Caribbean, in a drawer beside his bed. He kept it in a suede box and I opened it thinking I was going to find a ring. My father wore Old Spice, was almost bald, got a haircut once a week. He beat me and my brother, but then again so did my mother, and now I think it was because he couldn't let himself beat her. My father was a man that everybody who didn't live with loved. I miss him so much.

"People say he looked just like me," Danny said.

"Do you know something, Danny?" Gloria said. "You never told us what you hope to do while you're here."

"I don't know," Danny said.

"Yes you do," she whispered, putting her arm around Eclair's shoulders. "You just mustn't want to so badly, or you'll frighten her away."

■

The next day, Faye had appointments to visit various hotels and restaurants, meet the owners and gather information to better serve her clients. Having accompanied her on a similar excursion in Puerto Rico, Danny was allowed to go wherever he wanted. They would meet on the veranda of The Ginger Thomas before dinner.

Danny explored the harbor and duty-free shops, walked into the ridge of hills above town, swam in the hotel pool. Toward afternoon, a steel band set up their instruments near the shallow end and soon the area was filled with guests. Danny liked the strange sound and joyful movement of the musicians. Waiters brought colorful drinks with umbrellas sticking out of them, balancing a half dozen on their trays and dancing through the crowd. Several girls about his own age and wearing skimpy bikinis were dancing together in a space they'd cleared among chaise longues. At a table near the bar, he saw Gloria and Eclair sipping drinks, surrounded, smiling. Although they wore sunglasses, Danny was certain they were watching him across the pool where he sat on a deck chair pretending to read *The Return of the Native*, which he had to write a report about when he got back to school.

When the song ended, two of the girls grabbed hands and dashed across the patio to dive into the water. They were the two Danny thought were the prettiest. One, especially, the shorter one, with thick auburn hair and freckles all over her face and shoulders. Just as he was thinking *don't run on the wet tiles* he saw her slip. It happened so fast, she didn't have time to scream before the back of her head hit the concrete rim of the pool and she disappeared into the water. No one seemed to have seen it happen. The girl's friend surfaced halfway across the pool, facing away, and immediately began to stroke toward the far end.

Danny jumped up, kicking out of his sneakers, yanking off his watch. He sprinted toward the pool and dove deep toward the sector he thought the girl might be in. After a few powerful strokes, he saw her lying face up near the bottom right where the floor began its steep slope into deep water. She was no more than a foot away from the side; you'd have to be looking right into the pool and standing at its edge to see her. When he reached her, Danny was nearly out of breath. He grabbed for her arm but missed, knocking her head back, then reached down again and got hold of her under the arms. He used the pool floor to push off and was up into the air faster than he'd thought was possible.

Gloria and Eclair had seen him race into the pool and, by the time he broke the surface, had gotten enough people to the right place to help lift the girl from Danny's arms. He flopped backwards into the water and floated till he could catch his breath. He didn't want to get out. He didn't want to see what was happening inside the ring of people working on the girl. She would be all right, that much was clear from where he lay. He closed his eyes for a moment. When he opened them, Eclair's face was visible from where she stood at the end of the diving board looking down at him. The setting sun was almost precisely behind her head, blotted out for the moment but surrounding her in light. Their eyes met. When she smiled at him, Danny thought: *Sunburst.* He rolled over and swam toward the ladder at the side of the pool.

14

Lululand

IT SEEMED AS though every radio station in Connecticut and Massachusetts was playing Lulu. If Richard heard "To Sir, With Love" one more time, he was going to yank the damn radio out of the dashboard. He punched one of the buttons, got the last chorus of "Daydream Believer," which might be even worse, and sure enough they hit him with Lulu again.

He flicked the on/off knob. Fine and dandy. He could drive the last few miles in silence. Maybe there'll be better music come 1968. Cutting to the right, flooring it, Richard passed a DeSoto that was doing no better than forty-five in the passing lane. Why don't they confine all cars ten years or older to the two-lane highways so a salesman can get where he has to go on time? Richard was jumpy and impatient, the old Wednesday slump. He turned up the heat, then reached over to the glove compartment and unwrapped a Three Musketeers bar. He checked his watch and began to think about his eleven o'clock, Dr. Harry Tufts.

Probably the whole thing, all of life, was predetermined. For example, here's a doctor named Harry Tufts and over the years his practice gets confined more and more to helping men with baldness problems. Excuse me, with alopecia, and Harry Tufts spends his life trying to help them keep hairy

tufts on their shiny domes. Richard could sell him all kinds of creams and sus-
pensions, hair-replacement products, stuff to inject right into his patients'
bald places. The doctor was a very nice guy, had heard absolutely every joke
about his name and still could laugh with you, could look at you without dart-
ing his eyes up to your hair. This was going to be an easy call. Richard could
move enough product to pay for his entire week's travels.

The prospect made him so happy he turned the radio back on. "Ode to
Billie Joe." Hey, gotta love that rockin' beat. You know something, Bobbie
Gentry, I don't give a shit what you and Billie Joe McAllister threw off the
damn Tallahatchee Bridge, all right? Bam, change the station. "The Rain, the
Park, & Other Things." Bam. *Listen while I play my green tambourine.* No
thank you. He turned it back off.

By the end of 1967, when he was twenty-eight, Richard had progressed
from selling hospital supplies through selling pharmaceutical supplies to selling the actual pharmaceuticals. Kept most of his clients as he changed fields.
He was at ease around hospitals and physicians, a natural salesman, always
kept them laughing, and he loved driving his Pontiac LeMans along the New
England thruways at exotic speeds singing along with the radio. Except, of
course, when they played this new shit about drugs—not pharmaceuticals,
but drugs—or when they played Lulu. His brother Danny, the college boy,
probably loved the stuff. "Incense and Peppermints," that was another one.
What kind of name for a rock n' roll group was Strawberry Alarm Clock anyway? Give Richard doo-wop, give him The Drifters or The Coasters or The
Platters, and pass The Serving Dishes. What was wrong with Chuck Berry
and Little Richard, or even Gene Pitney for Christ's sake? You could tell the
world was going to hell in a handbasket simply by listening to what was happening to rock n' roll.

Just then, slowing down to pass through Norwich on his way to Worcester,
Richard had a brilliant idea. A flash. It came so forcefully, he thought for an
instant that he'd been rear-ended by that Impala he'd noticed roaring up behind him. Richard whacked the steering wheel, snapped his fingers, and
jabbed the radio back on. Hey, they're even playing a real song this time!
You're just too good to be true, can't take my eyes offa you. You tell 'em, pal.
See? This was how genius really worked, you didn't need to be reading Shake-
speare and Neetch to be smart.

It was going to be the idea of a lifetime, what they call a breakthrough, Richard could see that right away. Never mind this synthetic DNA stuff he'd been hearing rumors about, or heart transplants which were never going to be a winner from a pharmaceutical standpoint. Too bad he was about five years late for those beta-blockers; man, he could've made a fortune with pronethalol. Forget it, now he was on to something real. But he'd have to get hold of the right partner. What he needed was someone in textile designs.

I love you baby, and if it's quite all right I need you baby.

Of course! Thank you, Mr. Frankie Valli. All Richard needed was Zola, girl of his dreams, all two hundred pounds of her. They were quite a pair, Richard and Zola; the Kansas City Chiefs could've used them on the defensive line against Green Bay in the Super Bowl. She sat around their apartment day and night sewing, doing her embroidery work, designing muumuus and skirts and shifts. He couldn't tell one from the other, it was just a pile of garments to him, but now he saw that Zola and her *schmattes* were perfect. My partner's sitting right at home watching soap operas, thimbles on the end of every finger. She could whip this product out in ten minutes each. How hard could it be?

Because you go into the hospital, you go into the doctor's office for tests, what's the first thing they make you do? Right, take off your clothes, put on a gown, let the whole place see your naked back and ass because the damn things don't close up on you. Privacy gowns, that's what this world needs. The market would be enormous. Gowns that actually covered your body decently, but still allowed the doctor access to whatever he needed to see. People don't like to put a gown on over their heads because it messes up their hair. Fine and dandy, so it has to slip on like a coat, but not button up so the doctor can get his hands on you, and it's got to be adjustable so they don't have to stock a bunch of sizes. Easy enough, you just need something to hold it in place on the side, a series of snaps maybe, or this new stuff, Velcro, that Zola's been using instead. He could work the details out later.

Call them Adler Medical Gowns. Which brought Richard to a whole other area of thought, a topic that he'd been considering for years now. His name.

This was serious enough that he turned the radio back off. Silence is golden. Richard figured every kid went through a phase when he was sure he was adopted because he couldn't possibly be his parents' child. Not these people! But Richard knew he was his parents' child. He'd acquired enough features from each of them—his mother's nose, his father's mouth and voice, their combined tendency toward obesity—to explode the adoption theory. And he was certainly the product of their upbringing, the yelling and the beatings and the constant put-downs. Which was the whole point in a nutshell. Now that his father was dead, there was nothing whatsoever to control his mother. The woman simply did not know how to love. It was not his fault, it just was so. Richard couldn't stand talking to his mother any more and hadn't called or seen her since February of 1966, which made him feel somehow freed of his past. When the phone rang, he made Zola answer it to be sure he didn't accidentally speak to his mother. And what about brother Danny? Used to be a great little kid, Richard remembered that period fondly, the early fifties. But every year since the kid turned about ten he had only gotten worse. A smart mouth, flashy little athlete, always with the diets and the workouts, a book in his face whenever he was at home, no time for anything and anybody, too busy to empty the garbage. Everything Danny did seemed to be a way of saying Richard wasn't as good, wasn't as smart, wasn't worth as much. Plus now he's in college, has every opportunity in the world before him, you ask him a question and he quotes stuff back at you that rhymes, or he says 'One never knows how one will feel in advance,' like he's off floating outside himself or something. Meanwhile here's Richard driving into Worcester, Mass, with a snowstorm racing right behind him, trying to think about medical gowns that don't show your ass to the world.

That did it. For years Richard had wanted to change his name and now he was going to do it. Period, end of discussion. He turned the radio back on, *You say goodbye and I say hello*. It was true, he was no more an Adler than he was a McCartney or a Lennon. When the name came to him, it came in a flash even brighter than the flash accompanying the idea of privacy gowns. When you're on, you're on, son. He would turn the letters of Adler inside out, pop in an extra "e," and become Richard Leader.

Leader Medical Gowns. Go With the Leader!

■

In a motel outside Natick, Richard stripped down to his boxer shorts and sat on the queen size bed. He propped himself against the wall on pillows, and spent the evening sketching Leader Medical Gowns. The room was littered with balled-up paper from two hours worth of false starts and mistakes. He was certainly no designer, but he had confidence in Zola and knew if he could give her the general idea she'd take it from there.

When he checked the clock, Richard was astonished. Nine-thirty, he hadn't eaten and hadn't called Zola, who was definitely not going to appreciate that. If he wanted to get her rolling on the Leader Medical Gowns project, he certainly shouldn't start by pissing her off. He'd give her a call, then go somewhere for a quick bite, come back and do a few more sketches before turning in.

"Hey, babe."

"Your mother called."

"You know, you could say like 'hello, how are you' first. Cheer me up a little, I'm on the road. Get around to Faye after a couple minutes of small talk."

"She's away. Rome, I think she said."

"I don't need to hear this. She called from overseas to tell us she made a pass at the Pope, right, and he wants to marry her."

"It's about Danny."

"Jesus Christ. So what did The Scholar do, win a spelling bee?"

"Richard, your brother is in the hospital."

"What's wrong with him?"

"They don't know. He's been sick for a couple of months and finally went to a doctor. They put him right in for tests."

"Good. He's very good at tests, I'm sure he'll be all right."

"He might have leukemia, Richard."

Richard took a deep breath. He lifted up his sketches, tucked the phone under his chin and sorted through them without really seeing anything.

"Or the poor baby might have overworked himself and be tired, huh? Or he might have a math test he wants to get out of. I'm sure it's nothing."

"Well, your mother was nearly hysterical."

"Doesn't mean anything. She gets hysterical when she burns toast. Is she coming home to see him?"

"She said she can't possibly leave the tour now. She hasn't even seen the Uffizi yet."

"So Danny should wait a month before he dies?"

"She was worried. Anyway, Danny's in Saint Joseph's Hospital. That's one of yours, right? You know people there."

"Look, Zola, let's talk about something I'm interested in, ok? This call's costing me money."

"Richard."

"I had this wonderful idea, Zo. This one's *it*. I'm gonna make some serious money on this."

"Like your scheme for alcohol-free whiskey?"

"Just listen to me, for Christ's sake," Richard kept his voice steady, but he flung a pillow across the room, where it knocked over the ice bucket. "You sound just like my mother."

"What was that noise?"

"What noise?"

"Sounded like someone was breaking into your room."

"Medical gowns, Zola. I want to talk to you about medical gowns that don't let your tush hang out."

After the call, Richard felt ravenous. When he finally got her attention, Zola had understood what he was after and liked his idea. She'd do a few mock-ups right away and have them ready when he got home next week. She'd be a great partner. Who knows, it might even be time to marry her, though Zola Leader was a bit much to say.

He got dressed. The motel clerk had told him about a good seafood place a couple blocks away that served dinner till eleven. Richard drove there, the Pasture & Strand, and ordered a Dewars on the rocks while he waited for his dinner.

Leukemia.

Danny probably got a cold or something, let it go too long and now it spread. Richard had heard about guys letting themselves get sick enough to keep them out of the draft, he wouldn't put that past his brother, though sometimes it backfired and they never recovered. How ironic. Or maybe Danny had one of those nervous breakdowns, what with all the pressure of taking a couple classes every day. Now everybody's supposed to drop what they're doing and run to the poor boy's side.

Richard tried to recall the last time he and Danny had fun together. Maybe it was the summer after their father died, Danny was fourteen, fifteen. Richard had gotten hooked up with a softball team in a New York City men's league. They were sponsored by a Greenwich Village place he knew called Café Bizarre and he'd talked the manager into letting his baby brother play. Danny was a good infielder, quick, with a nice arm, and he became the regular shortstop. But he hit about .160. Of course Danny blamed it on him, complaining that Richard was always yelling instructions and commenting after each pitch so finally Danny couldn't hit the ball past the pitcher. Kid never could take instruction. But he caught everything they hit onto his side of the field and he was Richard Adler's brother so they let him play.

The waitress brought Richard his salad, drenched with French dressing just the way he ordered it. Good sign. He felt confident about the steak and lobster combo he had coming, rice instead of zucchini thank you very much.

The Café Bizarre team was some unit. Richard remembered their snazzy uniforms, black shirts with white letters and numbers and trim, black pants with a thick white stripe down each leg, black socks with white markings, black spikes with white laces, black caps with a white B and white button on top. Outfielders would move back when Richard dug in to hit, he came up looking like a thunderstorm. He either belted a tremendous shot over everybody's head for a home run or he was out. No singles, for sure no doubles or triples since he weighed a good two sixty and how fast did you expect him to run. He started calling himself The Big Bazoo from Café Bizarre. Soon every time he came to bat, the guys would start chanting BIG BAZOO, BIG BAZOO. Sure it was a good time, but now that Richard thought about it, the good time was *despite* Danny, not because of him.

He tore into the loaf of bread and sopped up his leftover dressing. Should have ordered an appetizer, probably clams on the half shell, because he was too hungry tonight. He'd waited too long before heading out to dinner.

One of the last places Richard and Danny had gone together was a summer carnival. It had been set up for a week or two in Oceanside, a town just across the bridge from Long Beach. They got into a big argument over the name of the town.

"Dumb name for a town," Danny said between licks of his ice cream.

"No dumber than any other."

"That's where you're wrong." Richard hated it when Danny took this tone with him. Maybe he ought to push the ice cream up the young man's nose. "How can this be Oceanside," Danny continued, "when we live right beside the ocean, and we're Long Beach, and Oceanside is ten miles away from the side of any ocean? Answer that one."

Always had a mouth on him. "OK, wise guy," Richard said. "Maybe this whole area used to be one big town, including both Oceanside and Long Beach. The whole thing was called Oceanside since at the time it was beside the ocean. Now let's drop it."

Danny was still blabbing when they reached the ski-ball stalls. He couldn't stop talking about it until Richard challenged him to pitching balls at milk bottles. Later, he challenged Danny to a strength test, the kind where you swing a sledge hammer and try to make a weight ring the bell. Danny, too busy arguing about Oceanside, didn't hear where he was supposed to hit, though, and on his first swing there was just the sound of his grunting and the hammer hitting the base of the contraption. Nothing moved. Richard laughed so hard, Danny nearly swung the hammer at his gut.

Another one that had nothing to do with Danny being a joy to know. Hell, how far back did Richard have to go to find a good memory? The entree arrived, along with a glass of Pinot Noir. Richard held the glass up to the light. Nice. The last thing he'd seen that was this color was a bag of blood back at Worcester General. He bent over the plate and inhaled deeply before digging in.

One evening—their father was alive and the family still lived in their Brooklyn apartment—Richard was doing a rare evening's homework when Faye asked him to empty the trash. Danny, who must have been eight at the time, was playing with baseball cards, not exactly working out the formula for relativity or anything. He'd never taken trash to the incinerator by himself. Richard asked him to do it as a favor, but Danny said he was too busy with his cards. Richard countered that homework was more important and soon they were yelling at one another. He jumped up, ran over to where Danny was squatting with his cards, grabbed one—it was a Ferris Fain, son of a bitch, Richard could still remember that—and tore it in half. He threw it at Danny, stared for a few seconds with his jaws working, and sat back down.

Danny ran into the kitchen, grabbed a butter knife from the drawer, dashed back and threw it at Richard. Eight years old, he throws a knife at his older brother over a Ferris Fain card! It missed by six feet and landed behind the radiator. Of course, Richard's parents didn't believe him. Not their precious little Danny. Richard had to fish the knife out with a coat hanger to get them to believe him. This is what his childhood was like, so if he wants to forget about it and everybody connected to it, why can't they all just leave him alone?

He finished his dinner and wine, surprised to be full. He'd started the entree convinced he'd have to order another one, maybe some lamb chops medium rare, but now he wasn't sure he even wanted the chocolate cheesecake. What the hell, it was too early to go back to the room. He ordered a slice, with coffee.

A few months before Richard moved out of the Adler house for good, this was Long Beach now, he woke up one morning with a shaft through his back as though sunlight knifing through the gap in the curtains had pierced his body. His kidneys were on fire. Richard moaned and struggled to get out of bed. Looking down the hall as he staggered toward the kitchen, Richard saw that Danny had put his head under the pillow and was holding it tight over his ears to block out the sounds. Thanks for all your help, little brother. Richard looked up the number for the hospital emergency room and managed to dial, but collapsed before anyone could answer. Danny heard him and the phone crash onto the floor. Finally he went into the kitchen to find Richard lying there, moaning. Danny picked up the phone. A woman was saying HELLO, HELLO, so he said very carefully that his brother just fell down and looked like he was hurt and gave their address.

Kidney stones, Richard remembered. He dug into the cheesecake. Kidney stones, I'm writhing around on the linoleum and the image that keeps flashing before me is the pillow over my brother's ears. And everybody said he was a hero for helping me out.

■

The weather had turned even colder. Richard loved cold weather, heat could really cripple a big guy, but a whole day below zero was uncalled for. It wasn't even Thanksgiving yet. There was snow everywhere and never mind an arctic wind, this wind was from Jupiter. With all those nuclear weapons tests going on—even China had them now—and more nuclear submarines float-ing around out there than dolphins, it was no wonder the weather was falling apart.

Richard parked in the new above-ground lot across the street from Saint Joseph's. He'd planned to stop at the hospital anyway, either on the way up or the way down, so it wasn't a special trip or anything. Archibald Dinwiddie, call me Arch, the hospital's administrator, was a nice enough guy for a blue blood. Richard had known him since the hospital supplies days, a good five years now. Started out to be a doctor, dropped out of med school and went to some fancy business school. At least he was honest about wanting to make money out of the health profession. Dinwiddie had invited Richard to his house for dinner once and they'd stayed up till midnight talking about whether Jews believed in the soul. How the hell was Richard supposed to know? He faked it pretty well, though, talking about the spark of life and his poor dead father. Dinwiddie didn't eat meat and as a result, taking him out to dinner was very tricky unless he was willing to make a meal out of the salad bar. Richard also knew a couple of St. Joe's doctors fairly well; he'd taken one of them, that vascular guy named Mossi, to a Red Sox game this summer. Sox were in the pennant race, Yastrzemski was going after the triple crown, and Mossi thought Richard was a miracle worker for getting such good seats. He got together with some of his fellow docs and ordered enough stuff from Richard to make it all worthwhile, too. So he should be able to find out about Danny, sell some product at the same time, there was nothing lost in stopping there. He locked the door and flipped the keys from hand to hand as he walked toward the elevator.

In the administrator's office, Richard had to wait fifteen minutes because the weekly staff meeting ran overtime. Hazards of the profession, he tried not to let it bother him. That way the customer felt a little guilty and might buy something extra to make up for it. Richard accepted a cup of coffee and flipped through the magazines, news and health crap, no sports, no pinups. He'd have to talk to the man about this selection. Underneath them all, Richard found an alumni bulletin from Colgate University. Must be Dinwid-die's *alma mater*. Wouldn't you know it!

Richard had forgotten all about Colgate. Three years ago, it must have been, he'd driven Danny upstate to visit the Colgate campus in Hamilton.

Had to be twenty-seven below zero; Richard had hung a Three Musketeers bar out of the car, the flap of its wrapper pinched in place by the shut window, and in two miles had himself a frozen treat. They stayed in this rickety old hotel off the town square, with cranky radiators and windows that shivered in the cold. They walked down the street to a movie theater after dinner, unable to stay warm despite two layers of winter clothes, and watched *Sex and the Single Girl* together. Danny thought they were doing something incredibly risque and was as nervous as if Richard had taken him to visit a prostitute. Then they froze their asses off walking back to the hotel afterwards. Never even spoke about the campus tour, or the goofy Dean they'd met with for two hours. Just before he turned out the light, Richard had asked what Danny thought about going to Colgate and they both burst into wild laughter. Next morning they drove to Cooperstown and toured the Baseball Hall of Fame. Richard had been there once before, when he was selling pharmaceutical supplies and upstate New York was his territory. But Danny hadn't. He was awestruck. Richard could see Danny struggling to hold back tears as he stood in front of the exhibits.

It was sweet, sure, but forget about it. A momentary lapse. It was the last Richard had seen of that Danny. Hell, it was the only glimpse he'd had of the kid he used to love since when? Since their father died, probably.

"Mr. Dinwiddie will see you now," the secretary said. Richard was so lost in thought he hadn't noticed the meeting breaking up or its members filing out past him. Not a good sign, Mr. Leader.

"I want to thank you for the Mets cap you sent my son," Dinwiddie said after getting through the handshake, backslap and greeting. "He was thrilled; he didn't have one."

"Here, I brought him a Washington Senators cap this time." Richard reached across the desk and handed it to Dinwiddie. "Figure if I bring him only the lousy teams, he won't already have them in his collection."

Dinwiddie smiled. "I want you to know I really appreciate your kindness, Rich. So what brings you to St. Joe's today? Got a cure for cancer to sell my doctors? An anti-inflammatory that won't mess with the stomach? I could use some good news."

"Sorry, Arch, routine stuff today." Richard sat back and paused, as though he had no agenda for the meeting and was in no hurry. Just making the rounds. "I'll be seeing a few of your docs, thought I'd touch base with you first."

"So this is a courtesy call?" Dinwiddie wadded up a memo and launched a hookshot into the wastebasket against the wall. "That's two. You have nothing new to sell?"

"Hey, fall is a slow season in the business, you know that. Everybody's focused on their odds for a Nobel Prize, patients are actually going to be sick because of the cool weather, nobody's got time for anything but restocking. That's why we don't introduce products in winter."

"All right, what's going on? Are you sick?"

"I'm fine and dandy."

"You want to see a doctor? You got the clap, want to lose some weight, something bothering you at home?"

"I never noticed this before. All you do is ask questions. Is that something they teach you in business school?"

"What are you doing here?"

"Like I said, just touching base before I head over to the office building. But while I've got your attention, you could maybe give me some information about a patient. He came in a couple days ago for tests."

Dinwiddie's brows, his shoulders, fingertips, voice—everything shot skyward. "A patient?"

Richard nodded. "While I'm here."

"You know I can't do that, for Christ's sake."

"See, I got you to make a statement." Richard hadn't planned to do this. He was ready to leave, but couldn't get himself up out of the chair. "Arch, it's my brother."

"What's your brother? He's at St. Joe's? Why didn't you call me?"

"It's nothing. I just thought, since I was coming by, you know, I'd ask how he was doing."

Dinwiddie looked at Richard as though for the first time, his eyes narrowed, boring in on him. Richard felt trapped.

"I'll be right back," Dinwiddie said. He stepped out to talk with his secretary, then left the office. Richard swiveled in his chair so he could see the photos on Dinwiddie's wall, the lovely Mrs. Dinwiddie and cute little Archibald III, a framed diploma from Wharton. Richard never heard of them, did they have a football team? He wondered if he should mention to Dinwiddie his idea about a new kind of gown, see what his reaction was. A business whiz, a guy in the hospital field. Richard was trying to decide between solid pale blue and earthy beige with brown stripes when Dinwiddie returned. He had a file in his hands, which he flipped open as he sat behind his desk with a sigh. He went through it quickly.

"Daniel has been here four days and the nurse can't recall a single visitor. Says here the father's dead, where's your mother?"

"Rome, I think."

"Italy?"

"No telling, with her. She could be in upstate New York by mistake. Could be in Georgia, wherever there's a Rome."

"What does she do?"

"She's a travel agent."

Dinwiddie looked up at him. He seemed upset. "I know you're a funny guy, Rich, but this is serious. Kid's been here alone, he's probably pretty upset."

"Not if you let him read. You let him read, he's probably in ecstasy."

"He's probably not. His spleen and liver are swollen, part of his face is paralyzed, something they call Bell's palsy, he's anemic, has headaches, chest pain. And he's completely exhausted, sleeps fourteen, fifteen hours a day."

"Yeah, well, we all get tired." Which Richard certainly was now. Pushing too hard. He'd have to take it easy the rest of this week, find some relaxation while he was on the road.

"What's with you? Your brother's very sick."

"So what's it called, what he has?"

"Infectious mononucleosis. It's a blood disease, they think it's viral in nature. Involves the white blood cells. We'll be discharging him tomorrow."

"Not leukemia?"

"No. Sometimes it presents similarly upon examination, and like I said it involves the white blood cells. But blood tests are conclusive. Daniel's got mono."

"Which means he's not going to die, right?"

"Of course he isn't. Six, eight weeks of bed rest and he'll be back to normal. Does he have somebody to take care of him?"

"How do I know?" Richard stood. "Besides, it doesn't sound like he needs much taking care of. Wish I could just sleep for a couple months."

"That's it?"

"What's it?"

"Wish I could sleep for a couple months? Something very strange is going on here, if you don't mind my saying so. You mean since he's not going to die so he doesn't need your help?"

Richard smiled. "Speaking of help, I appreciate yours, Arch. But I'd better let you get back to work, right? I've taken up enough of your time already."

Dinwiddie waved a hand and looked back down at the file. "Don't worry about it. He's in 409, you want to see him?"

Richard reached across the desk to shake Dinwiddie's hand. "Nah, not now. If there's time, I'll drop in later, after I've seen Mossi and Hosticka and what's his name, Bloch. I've got to do a little business. The kid's going to be fine and dandy, he doesn't need me."

They stared at each other for a moment. Dinwiddie didn't reach for Richard's hand right away, just held his eyes.

"Anything else I can do for you?" he asked.

"Yeah," Richard said. "You can let me have a gown, one of those deals that lets your ass dangle out the back. My fiance collects them."

■

Along Highway 24 between Brockton and Taunton, the music fell apart altogether. Richard lost his Boston station right in the middle of a non-stop Everly Brothers half hour, and the suburbs put him back in Lululand. Bam, shut the thing off. He could sing Everly Brothers songs to himself for the last twenty miles or so. Didn't sound the same without that perfect harmony, of course, but Richard actually preferred the solo sound anyway. He loved it when the one brother sang by himself in his trembly voice, like he was scared to go it alone, *You don't realize what you do to me.* When you stopped to think about it, The Everly Brothers were just freaks of nature. High tenors, third of a note difference between them, voices that fit together perfectly, probably through some kind of chemical quirk that a scientist could explain. Molecules, that was their secret if the truth were known. They could just as easily have turned out to be Siamese twins sharing a common hip joint, a pair of sisters with three eyes or The Everly Humpbacks. *Bye bye love, bye bye happiness.* Hell, maybe it was better to listen to Lulu.

Richard had two quick stops to make in Taunton, a clinic and a hospital. Then he could check into a motel he liked near the edge of town, give Zola a call, and maybe find some company over at that bar near the river. He'd be in great shape for Providence in the morning.

When he called, Zola answered on the first ring, as though she were just sitting there waiting to hear from him. Richard hoped she might be hard at work on Leader Medical Gowns by now, so it would take a while to pry herself up out of the living room chair she worked in and get to the phone.

"Did you see Danny? How is he?"

"He's fine, I talked to some doctors at St. Joe. What he's got, they call it the Kissing Disease, if you can believe that. Danny? I said to the doctor, you've got to be kidding. Unless he can get it from kissing himself."

"How did he look?"

Since he's not going to die so he doesn't need your help?

Hey Arch, did I say I'd help him if he was going to die? The kid doesn't need my help. Why, Danny Adler could probably bring himself back to life, if it came to that.

"He was asleep when I got there." The lie came easily enough. Hell, it might even have been true, Richard just didn't stop to verify it. "I didn't want to disturb him. They said he needs to sleep for two months."

"Did you leave him something so he knows you were there? Some magazines or flowers maybe?"

"Sure, a couple football magazines." Richard stretched and yawned, signalling to Zola that this part of the conversation was at an end. "Nothing to worry about, babe. Tell me what you did today on the gowns, I'm really counting on you."

Richard left the room as though chased. He hadn't bothered to unpack his sketches or lay out his clothes. Time to cut loose.

He had forgotten how far out of town the bar was. Richard drove halfway to Dighton before finding Clancy's, a red shack back among some trees and off to the left, not the right as he remembered. He'd crossed the river a half dozen or more times and was ready to turn around, figuring he'd dreamed the place last time. He heard it before he saw it.

Richard snuggled into a booth on the side, where he could see the bar and also follow the dart games. Bright purple and pink neon pulsating from the juke box bathed his table as he studied the menu. He found the garish light soothing, though normally it would be enough to drive him nuts. Somebody liked Sam Cooke. Could be worse.

By the time Richard finished his first bucket of steamed clams, he'd been joined by a thin red-haired woman who appeared out of nowhere. He was watching the door as well as the bar; no one like her had come in. She hadn't emerged from the bathroom behind him either, nor from the backroom where there were pool and shuffleboard tables. Some things it didn't pay to think about. He ordered a second bucket.

She was there, a glass of something pale that was probably watery whiskey in her left hand. She might be nineteen, she might be thirty, it depended on how you looked at her. Then as quickly as she'd arrived the woman slid back out of the booth to play some Aretha Franklin and Diana Ross, gliding over the floor with a kind of lanky lope, and returned to sit across from him swaying through the shoulders and smiling sleepily.

"I don't dance," Richard said.

"And my name is Sharon."

"Are you hungry, Sharon? Thirsty? Can I get you anything?"

For reasons Richard couldn't explain, her gesture of refusal seemed to melt something in him. Sharon's head ticked once left, once right, then centered on him again and he found her overwhelmingly sweet, like a child who wanted nothing in return for her affection. It was easy to give her a smile. He dipped a chunk of bread into the clam broth and lifted it to his mouth, dribbling some liquid down his chin while he chewed and laughed.

"Richard," he finally said. "Richard Leader."

He talked for two hours, stopping only once to go to the bathroom. He was an inventor and entrepreneur, an orphan from the slums of Brooklyn who had been all over the world and especially loved the South Seas. He'd begun his wanderings after his baby brother died of leukemia. Nah, there was no one special person in his life right now, but that was exactly what he was looking for. Sharon seemed to get smaller and younger as she sat there. She agreed with him about everything, hippies had ruined rock n' roll, no one outside New England knew how to serve clams properly, the gowns doctors made you wear sucked, and heavy men could be wonderful lovers.

"So you want to come with me, see my sketches?"

"I'd love to, Richard."

It was amazing how simple the whole thing was. Someone like Sharon, no expectations, no demands, she brings out the best in a guy and because of that she gets the best out of him.

Just outside the door, she slipped an arm through his and brought him to a stop. It felt wonderful to have such a slender wisp of a girl clinging to him, so light and free.

"Where's your car?" he asked.

"I don't have one."

"How will we get you home?"

"Oh Richard, I think you'll give me cab fare, you know? Fifty ought to do."

"Fifty? Jesus, Sharon, where do you live, Vermont?"

She chuckled and drew Richard close. It was still a lovely night. There was no point in losing that now.

15

Domestic Spaces

AFTER SEVEN YEARS of travel—after all of Italy except the islands, and half of Spain, after England and Denmark twice each, after countless cruises and package tours, Barbados and Jamaica, after almost dying from a virus during the High Holy Days in Monaco of all places, and a full month when she never got warm in Holland, after more than a hundred fifty thousand miles in search of a suitable man—Faye finally met her second husband downstairs in the basement of her apartment building. It was New Year's Eve, the turn of the decade, and she had almost given up hope.

After all, 1969 was probably the worst year since her Myron, may he rest in peace, had died. This was the year of secret bombings in Cambodia, My Lai, race riots in Kuala Lumpur. One awful event after another, though they didn't directly affect Faye's business because nobody was traveling to the Orient nowadays anyway. But in 1969 alone sixty-five airplanes were hijacked, which was terrible for her European travel clientele. And with the protests and marches and shootings, with violence everywhere, Woodstock and Washington, Hurricane Camille, with Charles Manson and the Chicago Eight, exactly where were you supposed to book somebody domestically?

Yet it was more than turmoil and more than money. It was more than feeling trapped at home. By 1969, her parents could no longer manage by themselves in the Central Park West apartment they'd shared since Faye was a little girl. Her brother came up with the idea of moving the Raskins to a nursing home in Long Beach, across the street from The Camelot, Faye's apartment building. She could look in on them every day. Good in theory, Red meant well, but with Faye's busy schedule and her father's increasing senility, not so good in practice. In April, the old man had begun to stalk the nursing home hallways, opening doors at four in the morning calling *Ava* in his sleep. Jules had given up bathing himself in May; by June, he'd taken to watching cartoons and reading the newspaper over and over all morning instead of taking walks along the boardwalk. Ava still got dressed everyday, put on her jewels, her fox stole in the cool weather, but she was growing irritated because, as she said, everyone around her was disturbed. Then on the same July day that Neil Armstrong walked on the moon, Ava Raskin had a massive stroke. She was rushed to Long Beach Hospital near midnight; Faye could hear the ambulance wail from her bedroom as it bore her mother away, swore that she knew what happened before the phone call came. Ava died before dawn. No one told Jules, her husband of sixty-six years, thinking to spare him the grief they felt he could no longer manage or comprehend. Two days later, as he sat peacefully scanning the newspaper with a cool morning breeze off the ocean rustling its pages, he found Ava's face smiling up at him from the obituaries. After that, he no longer recognized Faye on her daily visits, insisting that she was his wife's sister and she should go find Ava immediately. In December, Jules too went into the hospital. Faye visited him there, the waters of the bay visible from his window and leaching gray from a sky that seemed to come down to meet it. A commuter train only two shades darker than the water and sky clanked across the trestle, passing a marina where pleasure boats rocked in their winter resting places. While Faye stared outside, Jules opened his eyes, for the first time in months said something lucid to her—*nice pearls*—and died.

She was now officially alone. Both of her children were off on their own. One of them, the big one, refusing to talk to her since early 1966; she would never understand what made him do it. Faye would call and always the girlfriend would answer. She would write to him and: nothing. Once, a miracle, he actually picked up the phone on a Saturday afternoon. She had called during a football game and he wasn't thinking right. *I don't want to do this*, he said over and over like a mantra. Do what? *Hear your voice, talk to you, acknowledge that you exist.* Can you imagine! *You never knew how to love.* She'd been the best mother she knew how to be. A child doesn't talk like this to a mother, doesn't just up and abandon her. And the other son, the one on whom she had pinned her hopes, now he lives all the way across the country, he put the whole continent between them. Studying to build big beautiful houses for rich families to live in. Domestic spaces he calls them, maybe someday he'd design a domestic space for his mother. Both of her parents dead, no husband in sight. Was it any wonder Faye was dreading the nineteen seventies?

The Camelot Apartment Association organized one party every year. On New Year's Eve they turned the recreation room into a banquet hall and catered a dinner-dance at thirty dollars a head with music piped in from the local radio station. Faye didn't have that kind of money to throw around, even if they'd had live music.

Nevertheless, New Year's Eve was New Year's Eve. When she mentioned the party to Peter Porcelain, whom she had continued to see off-and-on through the years of her widowhood, he was slow to grasp the point. She knew she should never handle such delicate matters over the phone. Peter needed to see her eyes in order to grasp the subtleties of what she was saying.

"You're right," he'd said. "Sounds like a dreadful way to spend the evening. I'll speak to you next week."

"On the other hand," she came back quickly, "it's probably better than sitting home alone watching Guy Lombardo."

"How?"

"How what, Peter?"

"How is a party with radio music piped into the subterranean basement of the Camelot Apartments better than sitting home alone watching Guy Lombardo?"

"Why when you've seen as much of the world as I have, darling, you realize there are certain times one should not be alone, *a tout prix.* Wouldn't you agree?"

He was silent for a moment. "Oh, I get it," he sighed. "It's not that you don't want to go and it's not that you don't want to go alone. It's that you don't want to pay."

Reliable Peter had called for Faye at seven-thirty. He was dressed in a dark suit on the border of navy and charcoal with very hushed pinstripes, a gorgeous lilac silk shirt open at the throat and an ascot that accented everything perfectly, even his socks. Mr. Porcelain the Famous Chemist, Founding Father of Frozen Dinners, was a sharp man, there was no denying that. Too bad he'd spent so many years taking care of his mother. It had spoiled him for commitment.

They had been seated at a table for ten, smack in the middle of the rec room. They had to wait forever for their food, which gave Peter plenty to grumble about as ten o'clock approached and he flatly refused to wear his party hat. Their backs were right next to the crowded little dance floor, and they were directly in line with the speakers from which big band music blared. The whole space was smoky and overlit, draped with cheap blue and pink crepe paper to suggest festivity, and ventilated by one small window high up the far wall. It let in a few meager vapors of fresh air that hung suspended like icy daggers throughout the room. Placed next to Faye was a widower whose sister lived in the Camelot Apartments. The poor man had just lost his wife six months ago. His name was Irving Elkus and he never once asked her to call him Irv.

So it was that in the final hours of 1969 Faye had been despairing of life and love, but by the first hours of 1970 she was filled with anticipation. Atwitter, she said later. It occurred to her that Faye Elkus wouldn't be any worse of a name than Faye Adler.

Irving Elkus was a retired civil servant. Faye would admit that she'd fallen a long way from the diplomats, violinists, professors and barons she'd planned for. For example, there had been a man who sold magazines and newspapers out of a kiosk on a lower Manhattan streetcorner. The person who brought them together was no longer Faye's friend. There had been a man who dispatched trains in the wee hours of the morning, a former baker who now delivered bread to supermarkets in a truck that he owned but who had a mildly redeeming passion for opera, there had been a janitor, and there had even been another butcher. Irving Elkus the civil servant was a supervisor; he had a pension plan and health insurance, and he was terribly handsome. All right, he'd need a little help with the hair style and haberdashery, a change of eyeglasses, and he had a small speech impediment concerning "l" and "r," nothing she couldn't work with. One look, and Faye was convinced. By the time the radio was playing "Auld Lang Syne," Peter Porcelain was driving himself home to his mid-town apartment and Faye was telling Irving Elkus he should certainly think about visiting Paris in the springtime.

■

"Irving, turn left here," Faye said.

"I can't."

"Why not? I told you to turn left."

"This isn't Lenox Road yet."

"I think I would know the street where I lived for twenty years. Now turn."

"There's a delivery truck double parked there, I couldn't get through even if this was the right block."

"Irving Elkus, may I remind you this is not Rachel Elkus sitting next to you, may she rest in peace. This is Faye Adler you're talking to. Just do what I tell you."

"Yes, dear."

He jerked the wheel sharply left and sped across the oncoming traffic, though he had to run over the curb to complete the maneuver. Faye gasped. She readjusted her hair, and sat there shaking her head as they waited behind the delivery truck. No way around it, her body declared, the man was a fool. She took a deep drag on her cigarette.

"Go around him, darling," she said.

"There's no room."

"Of course there's room, don't be ridiculous."

When she talked this way, squawking like a chicken, Irving thought she could have been the most brilliant actress in the world if she'd only had the chance. He'd never seen anything like her. It was just a role she played, The Harridan; he knew it wasn't really her. A little game, that was all, a touch of drama to spice things up. Underneath, she was just a little girl who wanted to be loved. Still, he wished she hadn't mentioned Rachel.

Irving inched the car left, to the street side of the truck, trying to gauge how much space there was between it and the cars parked against the curb. Maybe if they'd taken his Rambler instead of Faye's Fury they could have gotten by. Not with this boat. But she wouldn't be caught dead riding around her old neighborhood in his beat-up, corroded jalopy that was a refugee from the mid-fifties. Suppose someone she knew saw her?

Of course, it was Irving's old neighborhood too, which was the whole point of this trip. They were going to show each other where they'd lived their previous lives, where their respective families had grown up. They were going to point out the grocer, the Chinese laundry, the drug store they'd both used, places where they probably had stood in line next to one another without knowing someday they would fall in love like this.

Irving couldn't make it past the truck. He glanced at Faye, but her head was back against the seat and her eyes were closed as if she could no longer bear to witness his efforts. He put the car into reverse and positioned them behind the truck's open rear doors.

"Delivering bread there to the little market," he said. "How long can it take? We'll just wait, all right?"

"Look," Faye said, pointing to the market. "Chinese, can you believe it? In this neighborhood."

"I think they're Korean."

"Don't contradict me."

"The name over the door, dear. Soon Yun Rho. That's a Korean name."

"Oh? And exactly how many countries have you been in, Mr. World Traveler?"

"I'm just saying . . . oh, there he is. We'll be out of here in a minute."

The driver climbed into the rear of his truck and shut the doors. Through the rear windows, they saw him rattling around in there, but the truck still didn't move.

"Go out and tell him he's holding us up. Tell him to move at once."

Irving smiled. He reached over and patted Faye's hand. "You look beautiful today, dear. Did I tell you that yet?"

"No, Irving Elkus, you did not." She turned her face toward him and actually batted her eyelashes. Probably that little twitch at the corner of her lips was a smile. "And I hope you never forget again."

He enjoyed making Faye happy, serving her, treating her like a princess if that was what she wanted. Irving was convinced he could help bring out her joyful side, which he was sure was her truer side, even if it was sometimes difficult to find.

Someone pulled up behind the Fury and began honking. The owners of the market came to the door, shook their heads and retreated.

"Are you warm enough?" Irving asked.

"Warm? I'm hot! Do you know why I'm hot? Because I have to sit here for three hours behind a bread truck when we should be in front of my old apartment. Because you won't go out and tell that absurd little driver to move at once. This whole situation is entirely your fault. Now do something about it before I do."

He patted her hand again, then put the car into park, fixed the emergency brake and opened his door. "Lock the doors, dear. I wouldn't want anything to happen to you."

With the horn still honking behind him, Irving knocked on the truck's back doors. Nothing. He knocked harder. "Excuse me," he said.

The doors flew open and a florid man glared down at Irving, hands on hips and feet spread wide. He seemed to have grown in the few minutes he'd been inside the truck, as though rising like dough in its warmth.

"Whaddya want, buddy?"

"Sir, you're blocking the street. We can't get by."

"Tough shit."

"We've been sitting here patiently. But it's really been quite a while and my fiancee is uncomfortable."

The man squatted down so that his knees were almost at Irving's eye level. He looked briefly over Irving's shoulder, then back down at him.

"In the car, that's your fiancee? Gonna bust the windshield, she doesn't stop smacking it. Who's she mad at, you or me?"

Irving turned around to comfort Faye, gesturing with his hands as though spreading a benediction. In the glare off the windshield, he couldn't see her face. Then he couldn't see anything. The truck driver had planted a foot between Irving's shoulders and shoved him into the hood of Faye's Fury. Irving's glasses went flying as he slammed into the car and then rolled onto the street.

"Asshole!" yelled the driver.

The truck's doors shut. In a moment, it was gone. Faye was screaming inside the car and struggling to get herself out. The car that had been honking behind theirs squealed past and disappeared down the street. Faye looked around to see if someone would come over to help, but the whole block seemed abandoned.

Irving got to his hands and knees, looking up into the doorway of the market. Without his glasses he couldn't see the proprietor staring back at him. The man disappeared a moment, then returned with a rag which he gave to Irving before retreating into his store.

Finally, Faye stood beside Irving and handed him his glasses. She took the rag from him and threw it on the sidewalk, then reached into her purse for a small packet of kleenex. She opened it and withdrew one.

"That rag is filthy," she said. "Here, you can clean up with this."

Irving stood, one hand on the Fury's hood for balance, and dabbed at his face. There was a little blood from his nose, some swelling of his upper lip, but he didn't think anything was broken. Even the glasses were intact. "I'm all right, it's nothing."

Faye took a deep breath. "Look at your pants," she said. "Brush them off before you get back in the car."

■

Faye had to set three different alarm clocks. She also persuaded her friend Irma to call at six in the morning and let the phone ring until she answered it. Irma, however, had been through this routine often enough. When Faye finally picked up the phone, after fifteen minutes of ringing, Irma hung up before she had to hear her friend's voice.

Faye went to the bathroom, then without even making a cup of coffee she dialed the number for Daniel's apartment in Seattle, where he was a graduate student. She could never get the time difference straight. Of course he was home, it was three-thirty in the morning.

"Who died?" he asked when he heard his mother's voice.

"I've been trying to reach you every night for a week, Daniel."

His answer was a long musical yawn, then the word "Finals."

"I thought maybe you were with someone, you know?"

"Mmmm hmm." She would get nothing from him on that topic. Lately, Faye was trying to find out if Daniel perhaps preferred the company of males, which would be all right with her, after all she'd spent years in the theater. He had a simple answer: *I'm just busy.* When and if he married, then Faye would get to meet her, not before.

"So what do you hear from your brother?"

"Did you really call me in the middle of the night to ask what I've heard from Richard? *Danny, for years we had nothing in common except our last names and we were better off forgetting about the heritage that went with it. That's why I changed mine. I have nothing else to say to you.* I haven't spoken to him in at least a year, maybe a year and a half. I keep telling you that. He won't return my calls either."

"God in Heaven!" Faye reached for a kleenex and blew her nose, which jerked Daniel upright in his Seattle bed. "Why is this happening, Danny? Why does a child turn away from his family like this?"

"We've been through this already, Mother. The last time we spoke, Richard told me that it was too painful for him to be connected with either of us. We're part of his past that he needs to, I think the word was jettison. Apparently his doctor agreed that if it made him miserable he didn't need to do it. *Richard, we have to stay in touch or they will have won.* He's now Richard Leader of Whippany, New Jersey, and as of a year or so ago his latest scheme was Leader Hospital Packs—everything a person might need for a two week confinement, in one handy piece of soft luggage. Comes in rose or ecru. Now you know as much as I do."

"I know nothing. I know a child should not bring such unhappiness to its mother. I know that what went on in our family was no different from what went on in every family in our apartment building. Probably every family in Brooklyn. I know that Richard is sick and needs my help. But this is not what I called you about, darling."

"Where are you? I forgot to ask."

"Home. Where should I be? The travel business is very poor right now. Sometimes your mother has to eat stew for dinner twice a week, like a peasant. Don't ask. Now the reason I'm calling is to share some wonderful news with you. Irving and I are getting married."

"Irving? Which one is Irving, the envelope salesman? No that's Freddy. The guy from Pittsburgh who wholesales bolts? Hold on, that's Geoffrey with a G. Wait a minute, Irving's the fellow with the flower shop in Queens, right? The guy with the Vandyke."

"You know perfectly well who Irving is, young man. The wedding is March twenty-eighth. I want you to be here with me."

"Mother, I don't know if I can do that. I've got classes to take, classes to teach. I'm also working a few evenings a week doing drawings for an architectural firm."

"That's very nice, you're such a busy boy you can't come to your own mother's wedding? It's a whole month away, you've got plenty of time to work everything out."

"Plus I don't know if I can afford a ticket." Daniel had to resist the impulse to laugh. The excuses sounded pretty flimsy, all right. He hadn't been home in nearly two years.

"Nonsense. I'm paying for the ticket, I'll pay for a motel as well, and I'll handle all the arrangements."

"That's what worries me the most. Wait a minute, let me check my calendar." Daniel put down the phone and climbed over the body sprawled beside him. Margaret Chang reached a hand up and caressed him as he passed. Daniel would love to see the expression on his mother's face when she got a look at Margaret's. Faye might actually be speechless. For a moment, anyway. *Well, dear, she certainly is exotic.* It would be fun to bring Margaret to the wedding. He climbed back over her and picked up the phone. "All right, mother, that week looks like it could be doable. But I'll have to talk to some people first before we finalize anything."

"I'll make tentative reservations. Don't worry about a thing."

"Mother?"

"What is it."

"Don't book me through Guadalajara this time."

"I never did such a thing."

■

Margaret Chang was holding onto Daniel and calling his name. She had heard his screams. She would not let them get at him anymore. The door was closing and Margaret was pulling Daniel up out of the dark shaft by his shoulders. It was amazing how powerful she was. All that dancing in the mornings and her weekly tai chi.

"Daniel," she was whispering in his ear, "it's all right. I'm here."

"What?" *Where am I?* "What is it?"

"Are you awake?"

Daniel's heart was pounding and he could not catch his breath. His blankets were tossed aside, doubled over onto Margaret, but he was drenched in sweat despite the room's chill.

"Jesus," he said, turning toward her. "I haven't had one of those in a year."

Margaret put the covers back on Daniel and draped her leg over his. She thrust herself closer still, warming him all along his body. "It's all right."

"Sorry. I probably woke you, huh?"

"Doesn't matter. Daniel, I never heard a sound like that before in my life. It was like a ghost was in the room." She caressed his neck and cheek. "You were sort of moaning, thrashing all around going *ooooooo wooooooo*. It was so ghoulish."

"So I've been told. All I know is that in my dream, I was screaming *help*. Quite clearly."

The doctors had told Daniel night terrors came from a different sleep stage than dreams. They were hallucinations, not nightmares; the state of fear and agitation they left you in was so intense because the distorted images were so vivid, absolutely real. Night terrors were more common in children, but Daniel had had them all his life. Until last year.

It wasn't difficult to figure out. When Daniel moved west, the night terrors stopped. That abruptly, as though they couldn't make it past the Rockies. Then in the middle of the night he gets a call from his mother, agrees to go home, and before dawn he awakens with another night terror. Always some form of relentless chase, always he slows down till he is finally reduced to clawing along the street on his hands and knees trying to escape, always an open door to be trapped behind. Sometimes the hallucinations might be set on city streets, other times in the desert or on a mountain side, often in the apartment he recognized from Brooklyn, but no matter where they were set there was always the immobilizing door and the stalkers coming toward him.

"Woooooooo. Oooooo whoooooooo," Margaret said. "Like that."

Margaret Chang was an architecture student too. She drew boldly and brilliantly, holding the pencil between her middle and index fingers, lower lip clamped firmly between her teeth, and was considered the most gifted student in their class. She'd won a full fellowship and had two job offers in Los Angeles waiting for her when she graduated. Lustrous black hair hung in a braid to her waist or sometimes swung free, blowing into her mouth when she walked outdoors. She wore thick glasses to class and to work, their enormous frames teetering on the tiny bridge of her nose and hiding her high cheekbones. But she wore contact lenses to play and appeared so different with her face exposed that it was like seeing her naked. She liked to look at Daniel over her shoulder, hair concealing part of her face, and he realized that artful concealment was at the heart of her drawing as well. Margaret had a gift for detail; her designs addressed simple human needs and she loved to solve problems of the competing demands for privacy and intimacy, for comfort and style. It was Margaret who led Daniel away from his absorption in corporate and institutional spaces, making him realize why he had come to architecture: to design homes, to imagine spaces in which family life could thrive.

He knew who she was before they actually met. Margaret was standing on the front porch of Professor Randall Wheaton's home near the university, looking off toward Mt. Rainier while the other new architecture students clustered around hors d'oeuvres in the living room. Daniel was late because he'd wanted to unpack his books. He saw her as he rounded the corner and thought she must be Margaret Chang, the only Asian woman among the dozen students listed on the roster he'd picked up at the office. She was small, Daniel's size, had the same wide shoulders and stocky build, and was as lean from her dancing as he was from his running.

"What I want to know, Margaret," he had said, coming up beside her on the porch, "is how we're supposed to learn anything about architecture from a person who would live in a house like this."

She turned slowly toward him, her eyes moving frankly over his face and finding something in it that she welcomed. "Exactly," she said.

Within a week, they were lovers. There were times Daniel didn't recognize his own voice when he talked to her, as though she had located something so hidden in him that Daniel had forgotten it was there. Their pasts were at once similar and contrary, mirror images of the way a childhood could be. Margaret was raised in Vancouver, British Columbia, where her father had owned a meat market in Chinatown. Chickens and ducks hung by hooks in the steamy window, their skin seared, grease dripping onto trays. She remembered her father sharpening his knives in the back room, light gleaming from the blades as they moved against his stone. He would sing Chinese songs to her while he quartered a hog or sliced beef for the spit, and she never minded the gore. James Chang was always gentle with her, his voice soft and intimate, his touch tender. Margaret said he would seldom use his palms to caress his children because they had been too steeped in blood for them ever to be clean enough. Instead, he would stroke their faces with the backs of his hands and gather them into his lap with his forearms. No one beat Margaret, no one hollered or called her names, no one threatened. Her parents were strict, especially as she reached adolescence, but they were accessible, they were fair, and the door to her home was always safe to walk through.

Until the night terrors began, Margaret hadn't believed Daniel when he spoke of his childhood. The descriptions were too fantastic for her to accept, too alien. They seemed more like stories than memories. Then his demons entered their bed and she heard the pure sound of his dreams.

She rolled onto her back, bringing Daniel along with her, and wrapped herself around him. His breathing settled. Often when their bodies joined, they would utter the same words in the same instant: *this is where I belong.*

"Know what we'll do?" she breathed into his ear. "We'll design a special door for your dreamself. We'll come up with a door that will open and close only at your command. A door that loves you as I do. All right?"

Margaret felt him nod, the point of his chin pressing against her collarbone. From their first times together, she loved to feel how well they fit, bodies and souls.

■

Irving Elkus was nervous. Not that Daniel blamed him, but it was amusing to see a sixty-five year old man jittery at the altar. Meanwhile, Faye was down the hall in the bathroom again, her third trip since the Rabbi had entered the room. People smiled—Faye's brother Red and his wife Sasha, Abe Wolfe who owned the travel agency where Faye worked, Irma Arndt of course, who had been maid-of-honor at Faye's first wedding, and even big old Si Sabbath, Myron's best friend whom Faye hadn't seen since she accidentally booked his trip to Budapest with a stop in Istanbul and he'd caught some sort of parasite during the layover—each of them knowing Faye was just being Faye.

Daniel sat there squirming. He couldn't take his eyes off Irving, who had a manic grin etched now onto his face. Daniel would swear the man's teeth had dried out; they no longer gleamed in the bright light. There was a film of per-spiration on his neck, though, which did gleam.

Faye reappeared at the chapel door, curtsied, and took her place beside Irv-ing. She wore a bright pink dress decorated with dozens of small bows, and a matching pink hat and shoes, reminding Daniel of a star magnolia in bloom. Rabbi Horowitz, now totally bald but otherwise unchanged from the year Daniel spent with him in mourning for his father, turned to face the couple and begin the *kidushin*. He looked for and found Daniel, nodded, then searched the room further as though trying to convince himself that what he'd been told was true: Richard was not there.

After the Rabbi chanted the seven blessings and read a portion of the mar-riage contract, Irving stomped on the glass wrapped in linen, then kissed his bride. Now that she was officially Faye Elkus, her first act was to reach up and straighten Irving's tie.

A table had been set up with wine and light snacks to tide people over until the reception, which would be held later at The Sands Beach Club. Daniel embraced his mother, then poured himself a glass of sweet wine and retreated to a corner of the room. In a few minutes, Rabbi Horowitz came to stand with him. They shook hands.

"Can I ask you a question?" Daniel said after they'd each taken a compan-ionable sip of wine.

"Certainly. By the way, it's wonderful to see you here again."

"Thank you, it's nice to be here. Tell me, what's the point of breaking a glass at the end of a wedding?"

"There are many interpretations of that, Daniel. Some say it reminds the wedding party of the destruction of the Temple, others that it symbolizes the transience of happiness. Some say it is to ensure that the union last until the pieces come back together again. Why do you ask?"

"I was just wondering. When I heard the glass shatter, I thought it must be to scare off the demons."

Rabbi Horowitz nodded. "Evil spirits, you mean?"

"No, demons. They're different things."

Daniel drove Irving and Faye to The Sands in Faye's Fury. She sat in front beside Daniel; Irving sat in back and seemed to nod off as they drove the five miles across Long Beach. When he finished parking, Daniel got out and headed into the club, assuming his mother and Irving were following. He held the door for them, but when no one walked through he turned around and found Faye still sitting in the car. Irving's head was barely visible behind her, where he'd slipped down in slumber against the door.

Daniel walked back and could hear his mother before he got close enough to open the door. She was shouting back at Irving, though she remained facing forward, the sound of her voice bouncing off the windshield and re-bounding over her husband like a sneaker wave.

"Wake up, you doddering fool, and open the door for me this instant. I've never been so embarrassed in my life!"

Irving jerked upright. He opened his door, leaped out and opened hers so quickly that Daniel was amazed at his ability to go from sleep to full action without any transition. Then, arm in arm, both smiling, Faye and Irving strode past Daniel into the club.

Before many of the guests had arrived, Daniel pulled Irving aside and led him to the bar. Faye was in the bathroom, straightening herself up after the ride. "Let me buy you a drink," Daniel said.

"I'd better just have Seltzer, Daniel. It's going to be a long night."

"You're going to have a lot of long nights, Irving. They shouldn't stop you from having a belt. Seven and Seven, isn't it?"

"Ok." Irving turned to the bartender. "But light on the whiskey, please."

"I hope you'll forgive me, but I've got to ask you this." Daniel said. "How can you let her talk to you like that?"

"Like what?"

"Out there in the car. Like she was Knute Rockne and you'd just fumbled on the goal line."

"Oh, that. She doesn't mean anything by it. That's just your mother's way, she's really very sweet."

16

Another Round

MYRON JAMES ADLER could not find his father. MJ had checked thoroughly, all the best hiding places. He'd been through the basement, looking behind the furnace and in the dusty old coal bin, even peering into the dark hole down there underneath the mud room and calling *I see you,* just in case. But his father wasn't anywhere. MJ opened the closets upstairs, examined behind the sofa and drapes in the living room, in the pantry back of the big bag of dog food, underneath his parents' bed. He even went to The Door That Is Always Closed, though of course he didn't consider opening it. The Door That Is Always Closed was in the ceiling of his parents' den, above where they kept their drafting tables and sliding stools, their benches and The Great Wall of Sketches. They had told MJ that in every home where children lived there was supposed to be such a door and that it must always remain locked. Only when a child was old enough to face the future alone could The Door That Is Always Closed be opened. On that day there would be a special ceremony conducted by the parents, dressed in robes that were the color of summer skies. The child would stand upon his parents' shoulders and finally reach for the string that opened the door. Afterwards there would be wild celebration and drinking of a clear colored sweet wine that would constitute the child's first official taste of the future. Needless to say, MJ did not think his father would actually be hiding up there. But he was so hard to find today. It was almost—but not quite—time to wonder if his father had vanished altogether, like Uncle Warren Feng Xu. His mother had told him about this man who went for a walk one day along the harbor and Poof, was gone forever. People actually saw it happen. One moment Uncle Warren Feng Xu was walking beside the railroad tracks near the water, searching for the rare Giant Technicolor Seahorse, and the next moment in a puff of vapor he simply disappeared. No sign of him ever again. Knowing that such things could happen made playing hide-and-seek with his father more exciting because MJ could never be sure he'd really find him.

MJ stood in the middle of his own bedroom, distracted by thoughts. There was a cobweb where the ceiling and wall met; maybe that's what happened to his father, maybe he got captured by a spider and dragged away. No, that wouldn't happen; his father lifted weights in the basement so he'd be strong enough to protect everyone, even himself. MJ wished his mother was home because she always gave him ideas about where else to look. But she was at work downtown, drawing houses. MJ loved to draw houses too, like both of his parents, to sit on a stool at a table that slanted and lean both elbows on it. He especially liked building the houses with his parents afterwards, using little wooden sticks on a slab they'd lay on the living room floor.

"MJ."

MJ spun around. Where had that voice come from? It was his father's, he knew that, although the voice was floating on the air like a leaf and didn't sound exactly like his father.

"MJ."

The voice was muffled. Maybe his father was inside the wall? It sounded as much like his father as those stick houses they built were like this house they lived in. But the voice meant that his father couldn't be far away. He hadn't vanished.

"Where are you, Dad?"

"Right here."

When Daniel popped up in the middle of MJ's bed, not five feet from where he stood, MJ shrieked. His father had been right there, lying under his very own blankets, and MJ hadn't even noticed! He ran to the bed and dove on top of it. Daniel held MJ close, laughing, kissing all over his son's face. Then he lugged MJ into the kitchen where they would begin chopping vegetables for dinner.

■

The night MJ was born, Daniel had first called Margaret's parents from a pay phone in the hospital. James and May were overjoyed. The Changs got on both extensions and spoke at once, an unprecedented display, their voices quavery, occasionally lapsing into Chinese and apologizing for it in an instant. May promised to be down to help them the day after tomorrow. She would bring three chickens and a duck, pounds of Margaret's favorite kumquats, and anything else they thought they might need. Did the baby have a large voice? Was he feeding? Did Daniel want a remedy to help him with sleep once the baby came home? Daniel promised to call again tomorrow morning, and then whenever he got Margaret home.

It was beginning to sink in. Daniel Adler was a father. A door opened down the hall and a doctor marched through, fresh from surgery. There was blood on his gown, a few splotches on his shoulders and forearms. Suddenly Daniel saw his own father approaching, apron caked with chicken blood, limp carcasses dangling from each hand, face a blank mask. Myron stopped across the room from Daniel. He held out his now empty arms—for an embrace? to receive his grandson?—but began to fade as Daniel approached, though not before his face softened into a broad smile.

"Yes?" the doctor said, turning to look at Daniel. "Can I help you?"

"No, I'm sorry. It's been a long day."

"You're not kidding."

Daniel stood there in his sea green, vee-neck scrub suit and the paper booties that skated across the floor. A matching cap covered his hair, except for one clump that squeezed itself out of the front and fell over the creases in his forehead. He could still feel MJ's eight pounds twelve ounces in his arms. How did two such small parents combine to produce so much baby? All head, of course, and Daniel found himself vowing for the thousandth time tonight that his son's head would never be filled with the kind of dreams and terrors that his own head held.

It was time to call Faye. Midnight in New York, she'd be up playing Scrabble with Irving for a penny a point while Johnny Carson blathered in the background. The phone rang once.

"Hello."

"Hi, Irving, it's Daniel."

"So late? Oh, you must have news for us. What is . . ."

"Give me that." Faye grabbed the phone away from Irving. "I told you not to waste his money, he didn't call to talk to you. Danny? Did the baby come? Tell me what I have, a grandson or a granddaughter."

"It's a boy, Mother, eight pounds twelve. Myron James Adler."

"Oh my God, you named the baby after your father?"

"Of course."

Faye sighed. "And where does the James come from?"

"Margaret's father. Coincidentally, the 'J' was in Uncle Joseph's name too."

"I thought maybe you'd named him after my father Jules."

"That too."

"So tell me, who does he look like, the mother or the father?"

"The nurse said he looks like both of us. I think he's got my mouth and chin, my stubby fingers. But he's got Margaret's deep color and lots of long black hair. And her nose."

"All baby's have little noses, Danny." She sounded cross, as though Danny were holding something back.

"He's fine. A real howler."

"*Nu*. What about the eyes?"

"What *about* the eyes? They're closed, mostly."

"Yours or Margaret's?"

"It's too soon to tell."

"Well, Danny, they can do wonderful things now with plastic surgery."

"Plastic surgery?"

"On those folds, you know? So he'll look normal."

■

Faye was anxious to see her grandson. Daniel and Margaret sent her pictures every few months, inviting her to visit whenever she wanted. By the spring of 1973, when MJ was walking and stringing together a few words, he still only knew the Elkuses as images in Polaroid snapshots and voices on the telephone. But Faye would not fly to Seattle.

"You should come here, Danny. A child should see where his roots are."

"Mother, it's almost impossible for us to get away from the practice together, and MJ is still pretty young for such a trip. Come to Seattle, you'll love the city. You'll get to meet the Changs and be with MJ. Any time."

"I don't fly anymore, it's too difficult. And besides, I'm afraid. You know I was on a plane once that almost crashed. It had to circle Kennedy for two hours before they could get the wheels down or whatever. Mechanical difficulties, they kept telling us. I prayed. I said 'Get me out of this, and I'll never fly again.'"

"Then take a train."

"What, you want maybe I should walk?"

When they finally did come, it was by car, a trip they made in seven days. Faye called every night from whatever motel they were staying in, keeping Daniel abreast of their progress. *He's an old man, Daniel. Four hundred miles is a big day for my Irving, I don't think we'll ever get there.* But they did. Faye struggled up the stairs, not waiting while Irving gathered up their luggage. She hugged Daniel and Margaret, then looked around for her grandson. A moment later, when Irving walked into the house, he looked as though he'd aged twenty years.

"Grampa," MJ said proudly, appearing from behind the kitchen door.

Irving patted the child's head and said, "Two thousand nine hundred twelve miles." Then he sank into their living room recliner, cranked up the foot rest and fell asleep.

"He goes to Irving before me?" Faye said. "Rotten kid."

■

Daniel wanted to see Richard again. He wanted Richard to meet Margaret and MJ, wanted to talk about their childhood now that he was a parent, but he knew he'd have to do it right. He couldn't call, Richard had made that clear. He could write, but the likelihood of Richard writing back was minuscule and it felt to Daniel like whistling in a windstorm.

As far as Daniel could estimate, there was one shred of hope. What might prod Richard into responding was the idea that Daniel wanted to get in touch again for selfish reasons. For memories, for guidance or wisdom. But he would have to be careful. He couldn't appear to be gloating about his beautiful and glamorous wife, or to be lording parenthood over his brother, who remained unmarried and childless. Maybe he should just fly across the country and show up at his brother's door. *Hello, Richard. Remember me?*

Playing catch in the park with MJ, Daniel came up with the perfect approach. He would try something they'd stopped doing in 1962. Daniel would write down his pennant predictions for the coming baseball season, guessing which teams would be in the World Series and which would win. He'd bet $5 that his picks were better. Might even throw in predictions for the order in which every team would finish. Challenge and payoff might get through where direct appeal had failed.

There were 24 teams now instead of the 20 there used to be when they made their last predictions, and there were two divisions in each league, and playoffs to determine who got into the World Series, and Daniel had never heard of half the players, and dozens were sons of players he remembered from his childhood. But he would do it. No call, no letter, just the predictions with $5 folded into them. He didn't know if it would work, but it felt hopeful to Daniel.

He remembered the last time they'd exchanged baseball predictions, a dozen years ago now. It was a Saturday in March, a couple weeks after John Glenn had orbited the Earth, and Daniel had the feeling that anything was possible. He could be whatever he wanted, probably a painter when his baseball career was over. He was still attending evening services for his father, not imagining that he would never again set foot in a synagogue after the year had ended. He still believed that there was a course to follow, rules to observe that would soften the heart of flame he saw in the Temple's stained-glass burning bush.

Richard had chosen the batting range in Oceanside as the site where they would make their predictions. They entered adjacent cages, put in their quarters, and faced the pitching machines in silence. Every pitch seemed to explode off Richard's bat and catch in the netting above him, he was in a great groove. After each swing he'd call out *That's a home run* as the ball dropped from the nets to the ground in front of him. Danny kept stroking line drives all over the range, leaping from the right side to the left side after ten pitches to scatter hits everywhere.

Their games could not be more different, Richard all power, Danny grace. It occurred to Danny that both were needed for true success, that he and his brother could be ideal teammates. It was just a feeling he had and the feeling made him smile. But then he realized—and the realization made him lose concentration so that he swung and missed the next pitch—that it would never happen. They couldn't play together.

The pitch he'd missed had been the last pitch. Danny put his bat back and walked out of the cage. In a moment, Richard joined him, sweating heavily, beaming.

"Saw you whiff there, boy. What happened?"

"Just tired, I guess."

"Tired? A fifteen year old kid?" He sat down, took out a notebook and pencil. "Ok, what's it going to be?"

"Yanks and Dodgers," Danny said. "No question about it. Dodgers win the Series in six games."

"I don't think so, little brother." Richard leaned back against the mesh of the batting cage. "I see the Tigers and Giants. The Yankees are through."

"Five bucks says you're wrong."

"Where are you going to get five bucks? I'll want the money as soon as you lose."

"You never know. I think this is my year, Yanks and Dodgers like in the old days."

They shook hands and stood. "Listen to you," Richard said. "The old days, like you're some kind of geezer."

Danny smiled. "Care to make it ten bucks?"

"Wise guy." Richard pointed at the cages. "Come on, you want to go another round?"